PRAISE
SLEEPLESS IN STRINGYBARK BAY

'I loved everything about Stringybark Bay, from the vibrant community of characters to the idyllic setting. I didn't want to leave! What a charming and irresistible novel.' —Joanna Nell

'A charming novel . . . you're in for a lot of intrigue as well as heart-warming fun. This is a real treat.' —*Better Reading*

'This is perfect, cosy reading blending natural Australian bush and river-to-coast life . . . ponders the frailty of ageing, relationships and the commitment of friends when the seasons of life call for a bit more compassion.' —Mrs Blackwell's Village Bookshop

'Set in a beautiful location with a fantastic storyline, this book is the go-to read for summer, exploring the fragility of life, and relationships across a broad expanse of time. A wonderful novel that will keep you enthralled right up to the very end.' —*The Chronicle*

'If you have a sunny Sunday to spare, I highly recommend *Sleepless in Stringybark Bay* as a companion to it.' —NZ Booklovers

'At the heart of this endearing story is a close-knit community that is genuine, wholehearted and takes pride in taking care of its own.' —The Burgeoning Bookshelf

'Susan Duncan is a storyteller par excellence. The mystery and its investigation are a mental exercise for the reader and the rest is an experience of life, an invitation to live in this small community and to understand its worth.' —*Living Arts Canberra*

'Filled with a cast of vibrant and quirky characters, *Sleepless in Stringybark Bay* is also about belonging and communities. A perfect holiday read!' —*The Other Terrain Journal*

Susan Duncan took up a cadetship on the Melbourne *Sun* that led to a 25-year career spanning radio, newspapers and magazines. She quit journalism after her brother and husband died within three days of each other and eventually wrote the bestselling memoir *Salvation Creek*. Later branching into fiction, she wrote about good communities creating a sense of belonging and leading to contentment.

Susan now divides her time between boats on Pittwater and raising cattle at Wherrol Flat with her second husband, Bob, writing occasionally for *The Australian Women's Weekly*.

ALSO BY SUSAN DUNCAN

FINDING JOY
IN
OYSTER BAY

SUSAN DUNCAN

FINDING JOY IN OYSTER BAY

ALLEN&UNWIN
SYDNEY·MELBOURNE·AUCKLAND·LONDON

First published in 2024

Allen & Unwin
Cammeraygal Country
83 Alexander Street
Crows Nest NSW 2065
Australia
Phone: (61 2) 8425 0100
Email: info@allenandunwin.com
Web: www.allenandunwin.com

Allen & Unwin acknowledges the Traditional Owners of the Country on which we live and work. We pay our respects to all Aboriginal and Torres Strait Islander Elders, past and present.

 A catalogue record for this book is available from the National Library of Australia

ISBN 978 1 76147 154 4

Set in 12.75/20 pt Adobe Garamond Pro by Bookhouse, Sydney
Printed and bound in Australia by the Opus Group

10 9 8 7 6 5 4 3 2 1

The paper in this book is FSC® certified. FSC® promotes environmentally responsible, socially beneficial and economically viable management of the world's forests.

For Bob, as always

CHAPTER ONE

SAM SCULLY WOKE IN A panic and threw back the sheet. He strode across the short distance to his daughter's crib and laid a finger on the downy softness of her cheek, listening for the rise and fall of her breath. He exhaled with relief.

I've had a nightmare, he thought, his pulse steadying again. Not an uncommon syndrome among first-time parents, or so he'd been warned. He straightened the baby's blanket and sat on the edge of the spare bed in the nursery, where he'd slept each night since offering to take on the midnight and four a.m. bottle-feeding shifts. He rested his arms on his knees and dropped his head in his hands, still uneasy.

A man who earned his living at the mercy of the sea, he knew to trust his instincts, so he rose quietly and padded down the hallway of Kate's house, avoiding the squeaky floorboard he'd discovered when he and Kate, his ex—the mother of his child—still shared the same bed. Very carefully, he nudged open Kate's door.

He sensed stillness. 'Kate?' he whispered. No answer, so he repeated her name, loudly now. He fumbled for the light switch. Stood at the foot of a bed that had been stripped bare and was unoccupied. Quickly, he checked the kitchen, the veranda. Spun around, groping to make sense of Kate's absence. A note, he thought, there must be a note. He slapped his cheeks to bring himself back to his senses and checked his phone.

Four a.m. The witching hour, Kate had told him back in the days when they'd thought they might have a future together. '"The very witching time of night"? From *Hamlet*,' she'd said, adding '*Shakespeare*' in an emphatic tone that was tart with condescension. Sam had asked if she knew what a grown knee meant in boat building, hoping she'd get the point: one person's measure of intelligence did not necessarily indicate another person's ignorance. Later, he'd looked up the meaning of witching hour and found a very murky history about devils, witches and full moons, all pre-dating Shakespeare, but he'd kept his mouth shut. The woman he'd chosen to love above all others, for reasons he'd never be able to explain, could rip out his heart merely by pulling her lips into a thin straight line and turning her head slightly away, her dark hair half falling over her face to conceal her disapproval.

4.01 a.m. No message.

Sam returned to the nursery, took another moment to look in on his peacefully sleeping daughter and then went back to the kitchen to make a cup of tea. Kate had done a runner. He was sure of it. She had a history of disappearing without the common sense or good manners to explain where she was going. After her mother, Emily, died, Kate vanished for a day or two. Soon after, without saying a word, she made a secret trip to England to chase down the truth of her mother's deathbed revelation that she had a half-brother. At the time, he'd excused her behaviour as the result of grief and shock. It was the lack of communication, though, that left everyone confused and rushing to fill in holes. The question was: how long would she be gone this time? He filled the kettle, turned it on. Reached for the coffee. Instant. He needed a bigger hit than a cuppa, and anyway, Kate's posh range of tea required too much finesse to brew in this hour of witches.

While the kettle hummed, he stepped outside and leaned on the veranda rails, trying to think through options. Smelled the briny tang of Oyster Bay at low tide, the rich fecundity of the mangroves on the far shore, and heard the swallowing sound of sea nudging sandbanks. Feeling cold in the early morning air, he rubbed his hands on his bare arms and went back inside. The first month of autumn, but if he'd read the signs right, winter would come early.

He found the only decently large mug in the back of a cupboard, where Kate must have shoved it after they'd gone their separate ways and before he'd returned to help care for their child. He spooned in a serious amount of coffee granules and two sugars. Poured on boiling water and closed his eyes to inhale the aroma. Not bad for instant, he thought, but it would never replace the real deal. He added milk and returned to the open air where he did his best thinking. On the far side of the bay, the rough tops of the escarpment, rising and dipping, were dark cut-outs against the night sky. A shadowy grey gloom blanketed the smooth water. In a couple of hours, the sun would strike the peak of the waterfall and in less time than an impatient sigh, the bay would catch fire, the sea pulse.

Sam thought about his situation. He was a single dad for the foreseeable future, with a six-month-old baby to care for. He was also a barge man who earned his living hauling cargo in the bays and waterways of Cook's Basin, a quirky little offshore community where the only roads were waterways and if you didn't have a boat, it was a long swim to get home. The job wasn't an ideal fit for taking on child care as well, but he would make it work. Claire would be a barge baby. A kid who would learn to read the weather long before learning the ABC. A kid who would know how to spread her feet for balance when a stink boat passed at top speed, creating a head-high wake. A kid who would see the love in his eyes, sense the tenderness in his calloused seaman's hands, understand she was cherished beyond all reason and that he, her father, would do everything in his power to keep her safe: lay down his life for her, if necessary.

He felt overwhelming sadness for Kate, a woman so splintered, fractured, emotionally damaged that she'd abandoned her baby and fled. Yet, God almighty, who wasn't flawed? In Cook's Basin, it was seen as a badge of honour, a sign of creative individuality, a trait handled with forgiveness (if necessary) and understanding (also known as patience), when required. He straightened up. Did he mean flawed (in a deeply human way) or emotionally unstable? He slumped. How could he know the truth? Kate embraced secrecy like a religion. If she ever felt she'd exposed a corner of her mind, she'd rush to use politeness and concern as a diversion. On the rare occasions he felt he was making headway in their communications and he felt confident enough to suggest talking through a problem or issue, he'd find himself isolated on the other side of a solid brick wall without even a window. Leaving Claire, though, was a decision—had he been forced to make it—that would have haunted him for life. Might have even killed him. He drained his coffee. Told himself not to think himself into a bottomless pit, and whistling quietly, went inside to prepare Claire's food. A barge baby. It had a good, solid ring to it.

He tested the warmth of the milk on his wrist and went down the hallway without worrying about the squeaky floorboard. Claire was wide awake in her crib, kicking her legs, waving her arms then stuffing a fist in her mouth, gumming her knuckles. He lifted her high and caught the whiff of a dirty nappy.

'It's just you and I kid, or is it you and me? Your mother isn't here to lay down the law right now, so let's stick with whatever feels right.' Soon, with her tummy full of milk again, Claire failed to fight off sleep, and he laid her back in the crib and tiptoed out to the veranda. He should let Kate know that he was more than fine about taking full responsibility for the baby for as long as she wanted him to, that she should be untroubled by her decision to take some time for herself. It would have been preferable if she'd told him her plans, but he'd keep that little nugget of reproach to himself. He punched in her number. Inside the house, a phone rang. He followed the sound to Kate's bedroom, dragged a phone from under the pillow and was gripped with fear.

He tried to remember what they'd talked about last night, whether she'd thrown him hints she wasn't coping and he'd failed to hear them, but came up blank. It had been a night like any other. He'd arrived after dinner, looked in on his sleeping child, and spent a few minutes discussing Claire's progress. Was it her first smile or wind? Was the rash on her bottom minor, or did it require treatment during the night? Should she have an extra blanket now the weather had turned, or would it be better to switch on the heating? All of it so basic and ordinary, he couldn't—for the life of him—find a clue to suggest what this latest disappearance was about. So he did what he always did in a crisis that involved Kate: he called Ettie Brookbank. Ettie, his closest friend and joint owner with Kate of the Briny Café, was a woman of infinite kindness and generosity, who also vehemently defended Kate against even the slightest hint of local criticism.

'Kate's done a runner,' he said, jumping in before Ettie had time to say hello. 'There's no note and she's left behind her phone, which is usually glued to the back pocket of her jeans. I'm trying not to worry, Ettie, but new mums don't suddenly take off, do they?'

He caught a confused mumble and the rustle of bedding, then Ettie whispered, 'Give me a minute.' Sam heard her footsteps, the quiet closing of a door.

'Marcus is asleep. I'm on the deck. God, it's chilly. Hold on while I get a dressing gown.' He heard her put the phone on the table where he and Kate had dined so splendidly so often but all too rarely in harmony. In a minute, she was back. 'Start from the beginning and don't leave out anything.'

Sam filled her in with a rising lump in his throat. When he had nothing more to say, silence stretched between them. 'Ettie?' Sam said.

'Kate will be in touch when she's ready, and remember, she's a survivor. She's made a choice to go off-grid for reasons only she knows. What matters now is Claire. What time is it?'

Sam checked his watch. 'Almost five.'

'Meet me at the café later. We'll get sorted.'

Sam couldn't drop the topic so quickly. 'There's something skew-whiff in her, Ettie. She hides it well behind a mask that most of the locals call snobbery or aloofness but you and I, we know it goes deeper than that.' He waited for Ettie to make a comment. When she remained silent, he added, 'Do you reckon having Claire has tipped her over some kind of edge or something?'

He heard Ettie's warm laugh. 'Oh love, there'll be a reason behind all this. With Kate, there's always a reason. And once she's figured out how to handle whatever has driven her to this point, she'll come good. She always does. There's gold in the girl, you saw it long ago and so did I. Give her time.'

'How much time, Ettie? And how much more time before we send out a search party? Leaving a defenceless baby . . .'

'That baby will never be defenceless and Kate is fully aware of that. You, me, the reprobates we call a community—we'll take care of her. You know that better than anyone.' He heard her swap the phone to her other ear. 'Let's talk when the sun is up, love. Answers, even to some of the worst problems, can appear like magic in the clear light of day.'

After the call ended, Sam pulled on some warm clothes and returned to the veranda to catch sunrise and that brief, saturated moment of light when the landscape gleamed with a bright metallic aura and promise. In minutes, it flooded in like a tsunami. A shoal of bait fish set the water boiling noisily. A moment later, cormorants appeared like missiles from out of nowhere. The sunlight struck their white throats, turning them gold, like ingots. Two galahs winged past, their bellies throbbing deep pink, wings gilt-edged. A pair of magpies tuned up for their early morning serenade, the most beautiful of songs. He listened as they drifted from a tentative minor key, as if to confirm they'd survived the menaces of the night, into full-blown and triumphant major. *I am here, I am strong.*

Sam dropped his head into his hands. The wonder of it, he thought. It flew above, lingered below, struck at daybreak and slid in serenely at nightfall. Ever shifting, endlessly inspiring: the transformations were a sharp reminder that any tenure on life was fragile and could be revoked at any moment. Kept a man honest, that sort of knowledge.

Again, he asked himself if Kate's sort of formal education led to ambivalence or, more worryingly, dissatisfaction. He gave himself a shake like a wet dog. 'Using some fancy words here,' he said. Light corkscrewed on the rippling water and yachts on their moorings conjoined with their wobbly reflections. It hit him then, that Kate's commuter boat rocked mutely on the pontoon, along with the fancy new tinnie he'd bought after his ancient runabout had carked it in a storm that almost wiped out Cook's Basin at the beginning of summer last year. He raced inside and opened her closet. Her jeans, shirts and T-shirts remained hanging with military precision. He opened a drawer. Her underwear was neatly folded and tucked into bamboo containers of perfectly matching dimensions. He reached to open the bottom drawer, where he knew she kept her most precious possessions: a photo of her father, a necklace given to her on her sixteenth birthday, and other bits and pieces of history she'd never shared. It was all undisturbed. He felt nausea rise and twist his gut. He stepped outside the front door with his phone, ready to dial triple 0. That's when he saw that her backpack was missing, along with her wet-weather jacket and heavy walking boots. At his feet, he saw an envelope half-tucked under the coir floormat. He snatched it up and ripped it open.

Sorry. Sorry. Sorry. I'll be back. I don't know when. K

Sam dropped down on the top step and held the note to his chest. She's alive, he thought. She's breathing. Nothing else mattered.

～

Careful not to alert Sam to her plans, Kate organised her departure from Oyster Bay with clinical precision. She booked Fast Freddy to pick her up in his water taxi at two a.m.: a time she knew Sam would be deeply asleep between the midnight and four a.m. feeds. She also knew that Freddy, if she swore him to secrecy, would prefer to burn at the stake rather than break his word. She considered him her most loyal and least judgemental friend. Aside from Claire, she would miss him the most. It was a connection she couldn't explain. Ettie was supportive, endlessly forgiving and she couldn't wish for a kinder or more talented partner in business. Marcus was a man full of love and joy—which he'd found with Ettie. And Sam? She turned her thoughts away from him before she became consumed by guilt and self-recrimination. Freddy, she thought, radiated a sense of peace and calm acceptance of the frailties that lay hidden in most people. He wasn't a fool. He couldn't be conned. He stood up for his rights when passengers tried to abscond without paying for his services. But he did it in a way that kept emotions under control, even when dealing with the most belligerent partygoers. He was saintly in his Buddhist way and Kate knew that if anything awful ever happened to him, her heart would break.

The other people who lurked on the periphery of her Oyster Bay life were good-hearted enough but there was an edge of self-interested curiosity to them, and her instinct told her to keep her distance or she'd lose her prized privacy. She knew it irked them. So be it.

She packed a minimal amount of clothing in her backpack, grabbed a torch, and crept out of the house to wait for Freddy on the pontoon belonging to Frankie's boatshed, where she'd be out of sight if the boat engine woke Sam. Given the late hour, she knew his seaman's instincts would force him to get up to check all was well . . . or not. As for Frankie, once he laid his head on a pillow, nothing short of a bomb detonating would wake him before the rain, hail or shine framework of his six a.m. start. She wondered if he slept in his Greek fisherman's cap—a thought that almost brought a smile to her lips.

She waited on the pontoon, sitting cross-legged, straining for the sight of an approaching triangle of red, green and white lights. The night dew settled on her shoulders like a damp blanket. She shivered and wished she'd thought to wear a scarf. A sound, like the cry of a baby, brought her to her feet in a flash. Fighting a strong urge to run back, she listened closely and heard the sound again. A bird, she realised, hungry perhaps, or just restless, as Claire was sometimes, if her routine was upset. She wiped a tear angrily with the sleeve of her jacket and stood, chilled to the bone. In the distance, she saw the approach of Fast Freddy and, relieved, threw her backpack over her shoulders and went to stand at the edge of the pontoon where she knew any breath of wind off the water would blow the boat on. She thought of her child, her home, Sam, and how easy it would be to slip back up the steps, return to her warm bed, wake in the morning when Sam brought her a cup of tea, and ask him—as if she'd never even planned to abscond—if Claire had slept soundly. But she'd made her decision.

When Freddy came alongside, his hand holding a cleat to keep the water taxi steady, she stepped on board. 'No questions, Freddy, if you don't mind.' He saw the damp trails of tears on her cheeks, could almost touch the tension that spun off her body like steam, saw a hollowness in her eyes that gave him the willies. But he nodded without a word—what else could he do?—and eased his way into the deeper water of the channel. Together, they rode at a steady pace under a night sky awash with stars. Kate spun her seat to look behind, her white house already small and insignificant, and barely visible in a few more moments.

Freddy was certain he heard a sob so he did his best and reached into his pocket for a handkerchief he hoped was still clean. Without a word, he offered it to Kate, who shook her head and managed a crooked smile. 'I'm good, Freddy. It's all good,' she said, when even a blithering fool could see she was shattering into a million pieces. He stuck to his word and although it broke his heart to help her disembark, he was a man of honour. At the last moment, she bent over the gunnel and whispered in his ear. He nodded sadly and let her shove his boat away from the pontoon with her foot. He set a course for the houseboat he used as an office but decided, instead, to switch off the engine and rock on the water. After a while, he reminded himself that *everything that is born must die* because surely only death would set a young mother off alone in the dead of night without her child? Then he prayed to Buddha to keep Kate safe in her grief—and give her courage for whatever lay ahead.

Kate wandered through a deserted Square, automatically picking up bits of rubbish and tossing them into one of the big bins supplied by the local council, turning her anger towards the people who littered without conscience, as a way of deflecting from her pain. The locked and deserted Briny Café, glowing greenly inside with fridge lights, seemed to accuse her, so she glanced away quickly. She'd had it all, she thought. A good business, the love of a good man, the care and support of Ettie, who'd been more mother and mentor to her over a couple of years than Emily had been in a lifetime. Yet here she was, standing alone with a backpack and nothing but a flimsy forward plan with more holes in it than a sieve. But to stay and live a lie was unthinkable. To leave, even if it cost her sanity, was consolation, an act of decency. She knew she'd be reviled by a community she'd learned to value and even cherish, and despite their universal will to live and let live, she thought they would believe that her behaviour stopped just short of murder.

She remembered the night Sam and Ettie took her dancing by moonlight on the deck of the *Mary Kay*; it seemed like decades ago. She'd never felt happier in her life. She'd found her place to belong. All that joy exploded now by a fuse lit with her own hand.

She told herself Sam deserved a woman who could love him openly and simply, a woman who didn't use mind games as a ruse to hold back affection because to open the door to genuine intimacy—far more powerful than sex—could only end in regret. How often had she cruelly engineered her withdrawal from affectionate conversations as a defence against full commitment? How many times had she scorned the idea of a picnic on a secluded beach when she'd longed to pack a basket and set off; how often had she held back praise for one of Sam's new sausage roll recipes when it tasted good enough to win a prize at the Easter Show? She'd see the hurt look on his face, his confusion, the way he hid disappointment behind a fake smile, but to let him in emotionally ran the risk of exposure. Happiness could make you careless. As her mother, Emily, repeated throughout her childhood, as if it was the only advice worth sharing with her daughter: she'd made her bed, now she must lie in it.

She set off on foot into the night, the sandy track firm with damp, the old black dog of despair trotting at her heels. She found herself wishing for a car to materialise so it would smash her to smithereens, but the feeling would pass. It always did.

As she walked with nothing but the stars to light the way, it occurred to her that death should be embraced, not feared. It was, after all, the only unconditional freedom that existed. Any other autonomy came with a truckload of caveats automatically linked to daily life.

'One step at a time, Kate,' she said out loud, repeating it again under her breath as she looked down at her feet and willed herself to keep going.

One day, the dog would slink back to the kennel and, in time, she would be able to relegate her grief to a remote corner of whatever new life she invented. One day. Right now, thinking beyond the moment was inconceivable.

CHAPTER TWO

BY SEVEN A.M., SAM HAD bathed and dressed Claire and filled a carry-all with enough baby supplies to challenge the might of his sturdy working barge (technically a lighter, but too many lay-abouts made jokes about cigarettes and he'd given up correcting the mistake), the *Mary Kay*. He scratched his head, hoping he'd covered all the bases. There would be a readjustment of his daily schedules, a short settling-in period. As long as Jimmy, his freckle-faced boatswain, a lad with flaming red hair and toe-tapping feet, understood babies weren't as easy or quick to train as puppies, all would fall into place. Sam gave a wry, inwards smile. Longfellow, Jimmy's black and white border collie, might be a bit miffed when Sam rearranged the wheelhouse to accommodate a bassinet, but he was a good dog, and he, too, would settle into a new routine.

He mentally ran through the list of jobs for the day and figured he could delay one or two. Then he slung the carry-all over a shoulder, picked up the bassinet where Claire looked up at him with clear eyes a shade darker than her mother's, which had more green in them, and, whistling to entertain the baby, he made his way down the sandstone steps from Kate's little bayside cottage to the pontoon. Easy as . . .

'Bit early to train the kid for barge work, isn't it?' Frankie asked. The shipwright materialised from the boatshed next door, his Greek fisherman's cap in place, a steaming cuppa in one hand, an egg and bacon roll in the other. Sam's nose twitched and his stomach rumbled.

'Pretty little ketch in the slip.' Sam glanced at the elegant little boat, which was in desperate need of an anti-foul and a new mast, hoping to cut off Frankie's curiosity. 'Haven't seen her under sail around here.'

Frankie gulped his tea and tipped the dregs onto the ground. 'This little lady had a padded pen in one of those fancy onshore yacht clubs. Got thrown up in someone's backyard during that killer storm last year. Owner's had enough of boats. A mug's game, he said. Dollar bills ripped up faster than tops off a stubby on a hot summer day. Bought her for a song.'

Sam, intrigued, put the bassinet out of harm's way, stepped in for a closer look. 'Timber, eh? Beautiful lines.' He ran his hand over the hull. 'You going to keep her or sell her?'

Frankie nodded towards the baby. 'Early morning sun's still got a bite. Tender skin and all.'

'Jeez!' Sam spun around and flipped down the bassinet's fabric sunhood.

'Can't take your eyes off them,' Frankie added. 'Not for a minute.'

'How many kids have you raised, if you don't mind me asking?' Sam said, tetchy with guilt.

'None.' Frankie threw the last of his breakfast into the bay. Disappeared inside the boatshed. The noise of a sander cut through the quiet stillness. Claire began to bawl.

Sam lifted her from the bassinet and held her against his broad chest. Her wailing escalated. He patted her back, paced up and down the crumbling shoreline. One two. One two. 'Cormorants!' he told her, pointing. 'Fish jumping!' Another attempt to distract. A pair of king parrots, red and green explosions, swooped close and got her attention. She calmed to a gentle hiccup or two then invoked their reappearance in vain and the wailing began again.

Sam paced in a small circle. 'Frankie! Get out here!'

Frankie appeared holding the sander. 'No good asking me for help. Never been sure which end goes on top.'

'Ah jeez,' Sam muttered. He dug around in the kit bag for a front pack baby carrier and held it by the straps, flummoxed. Kate put it on so effortlessly. He turned it around a few times, slipped his arms into the shoulder straps. Took it off to increase the length of the waist belt. The kid stopped crying and watched the floorshow. After a while, he stood bow-headed with frustration, a single strap hanging uselessly. Frankie emerged holding the sander and shook his head. He set down the tool, walked up to Sam, nipped, tucked, lifted Claire, and strapped her so she faced forward, fat little legs dangling like loose sausages. 'Need a bit more practice, my friend,' he said, walking off.

'You sure you never had a kid?' Sam bellowed after his crooked back.

Frankie gave a two-fingered response, swung up his power tool, and climbed a ladder to the deck of the yacht. The sound of the sander cut through the peace once more.

Sam boarded the tinnie, wishing he had a built-in pouch like the pesky wallabies that had just about eaten Kate's struggling pot plants down to the roots. He stowed the baby gear out of danger from the rough and tumble generated by a passing boat, and chugged through the moorings in Oyster Bay, his speed so gradual the boat almost stalled. With Claire's chubby little body warm against his chest, he shielded her head with one hand, steered with the other. Babies, he thought, smelled sweeter than puppies. Mostly. He swung the boat south-west into open water at the mouth of the bay and set course for the Briny Café. He needed a coffee. He needed breakfast. Already an hour behind schedule, he needed to delay his first job for the day. He also needed another pair of hands to hold the kid while he wolfed down enough fuel to get him through to dinner. Solo parenting, he thought, might not turn out to be the cruisy experience of his initial expectations. His phone rang. 'Jimmy!'

'Where ya goin', Sam? Ya'r headin' in the wrong direction.' His young offsider's voice pitched a tad higher than usual with surprise.

'Some urgent business to attend to . . .'

'What Sam? How urgent?'

'You have an extra hour to spend on your worm farm, and then I'll fill you in.'

'You promise, Sam? You and me, we're partners, aren't we?'

'To the end, mate.' He killed the call before the kid had a chance to break into another ream of questions. One step at a time. His phone rang again. Ettie. 'On my way, a few delays, nothing serious. Oh, and about Kate? I found a note. She's taken off alright, but sounds okay, all things considered. Be there in five. Triple shot, if you don't mind, and a big breakfast. Feel like I've done a full day already.'

❧

Legs apart for balance as the wash from Sam's boat hit the café pontoon, Ettie felt an almost forgotten hunger stir in her as she held out her arms. Sam released Claire from the sling and passed the baby to her.

'Guess I'm going to have to make a few lifestyle changes pretty quick smart, eh?' he said.

Ettie noted the lightness in his voice. Sam would cope, she thought. He always did.

'Mind her head, eh? Still fragile as a baby chick. But she'll be a strong one, Ettie, I can feel it in my bones.'

'Come upstairs, love, we need to sort out a schedule to keep you and this baby on track.'

'Nah, it's all good. Always told you she'd be a barge baby. She'll have a spot right next to the mutt in the wheelhouse and never be more than an arm's length from her dad.' He straightened from tying the bowline, a grin as wide as his face would allow.

'It won't work, Sam. Not for you. Not for your business. More importantly, it's not in Claire's best interests.'

'You better tell me why not, Ettie, so long as you're quite clear this baby's not going anywhere without me,' he said.

She suddenly felt inadequate, unsure if she had the strength to insist that Sam, whom she loved as much as the chef, but in a completely different way, could not handle his own child and run a cargo business at the same time.

'You and me, Sam, we're grown. Our characters, personalities . . .' she smiled, 'are set in stone. But this baby, she's . . . she's still so new.'

'Not sure where you're going with this, Ettie. Are you saying I'm not fit to look after her?'

'Oh Sam, no. Nothing like that. You're a fine father. But right now, this baby needs stability, someone standing by day and night, ready to drop everything to see to her in an instant.'

'Me, Ettie. That's me. I'd cut off an arm for her. You know that.'

'I do know that, Sam. Of course. But we need to figure out the practicalities. We've got to be realistic.' Ettie looked at the bundle gathered in a perfect fit in the shelter of her capable arms, aware that if she didn't remain firm and inflexible, the consequences could be unthinkable.

They were silent as an incoming tide lapped at the foreshore. Seagulls circled, greedy for easy handouts, cool and elegant but less interesting to the baby after the gaudy drama of the king parrots. No manners, though: the noise from their throats more harangue than song.

'Come inside and I'll cook your breakfast. Make a coffee strong enough to launch you into space. We both need time to think this through.'

Sam felt he was losing control of a situation he believed he was competent to handle alone. Ettie stalled any argument by speaking again.

'Baby steps, Sam, until we come up with a solution that is best for Claire. And you. And the *Mary Kay*, Jimmy and the mutt.'

Sam looked sceptical but gave Ettie the benefit of the doubt.

'You can leave Claire with me today. I'll arrange a temporary crèche upstairs.' Ettie frowned. 'No. Don't look at me as though I've used a four-letter word. There'll be someone close by all day.' And placing her hands behind her back, she crossed her fingers to negate the gigantic fib she was about to fabricate, to convince Sam that she'd given in to his wishes. 'The barge isn't ready for a baby yet. It'll take you a day or two to get organised. I'll watch her like a hawk. Promise.' With Claire getting sleepy in her arms, Ettie handed her back to Sam and he laid her in the bassinet, tucking the blanket tightly. 'Now do you want spinach with your bacon and eggs?'

'Healthy stuff, spinach. Load it up. And a couple of sausos, if you're up to it. A few mushies, too. I'll grab Claire and all her stuff and see you inside.' He ran a hand through his hair. 'Jeez, babies need personal porters, Ettie. The amount of . . .'

'Enough to choke a wheelhouse?' she asked. She slipped inside the café and disappeared from view before Sam cottoned on to the point she'd just made.

As the grill warmed, Ettie dialled her partner, Marcus, retired *chef extraordinaire* and the love of her life. 'How about smoko on the deck this morning?'

Marcus took a moment. 'Is it urgent? Should I fly to your side this instant?'

Ettie laughed. 'Have I told you how much I love you?'

'Well, of course you have, but a man can never hear it often enough from the lips of a beautiful woman, for whom he would . . .'

'Ten thirty. After the brekkie rush. Gotta go. Jenny's just walked in.'

The Briny Café's full-time sous-chef and general dogsbody, Jenny, neat in her uniform of blue trousers, white polo shirt and smart sneakers, gave a salute and fell straight into her morning routine, tying her apron, lining up the tools of trade, firing up the coffee machine.

Sam banged through the flywire door, using his backside to push his way inside: the bassinet in one hand, the bag of baby paraphernalia in the other. Ettie pointed her wooden spoon in the direction of the upstairs penthouse, a fully functional apartment where she'd lived before Marcus—referred to almost universally by the locals as Chef—whisked her away to carry her over the threshold of his home in Kingfish Bay. He'd made her feel like a new bride at a time of her life when she thought the romantic fervour of youth was lost to her forever. 'I'll bring up your breakfast when it's ready,' she said. Sam nodded.

Jenny leaned against the counter, frowning. 'Kate crook?' she asked.

Ettie hummed under her breath. 'A big breakfast, loads of spinach. Coffee with a triple shot.'

'Done another runner, has she?' Jenny asked, eyes cast downwards, getting to work. 'Girl's made a career out of them, Ettie . . .'

Ettie patted Jenny on the back. 'Eggs done?'

'Cleaning up Kate's messes is getting to be a habit,' Jenny said.

'There's going to be a few changes around here, but we'll manage.'

'Yeah. But that woman . . .'

'Kate.'

'Yeah. Kate. Time she faced up to real life.'

'We'll manage.'

'We always do. But Ettie?'

'Yes, love?'

'Sometimes—I'm not saying always—sometimes, too much kindness can be as damaging as not enough. Just saying . . .'

Ettie sighed and shrugged. 'Don't forget to load on the spinach. That man upstairs is going to need all his strength.'

'If I had to make a guess, Ettie, you're the one who's going to need strength,' Jenny muttered.

'Any tips for the winning Lotto numbers, since you're on a roll?'

'Just saying. That's all. Far as I know, it's not a crime to have an opinion.'

Carrying Sam's mega breakfast on a tray, Ettie climbed the stairs carefully, mulling over Kate's history of disappearing. She would always publicly support Kate's behaviour, but would a young woman truly leave her baby to be cared for by others if she wasn't suffering from some kind of stress or exhaustion? Both, she thought, could make a person act weirdly; might even make a young mum think she'd put her baby at risk by staying home. But, she reminded herself, Kate was smart and capable. She'd know if she wasn't coping and she was fully aware there was an army of willing people who could step in to help at a moment's notice. What had driven her to take such a drastic step? She mentally scrolled backwards in time, trying to pinpoint moments that had jarred. There were a few, she admitted, but easily dismissed as new mother nerves. Not one single incident that might have triggered something as serious as this disappearance sprang to mind. Hadn't she seen for herself, over and over, the love in Kate's eyes when she gazed at her child? Hadn't she witnessed her reluctance to hand

Claire into Sam's arms for longer than a bottle feed? Even she, Ettie, strongly maternal and besotted by babies in general, had been given limited time alone with Claire, and her regular offers to babysit were denied kindly but firmly.

Breathless at the top of the stairs (she must talk to Marcus about reducing the number of evening treats), she decided to put all fears and worry out of her mind and focus on the present.

Spying Ettie, Sam tiptoed across the floor to take the tray. He smiled his thanks, sat down, and tucked in with the appetite of a man who hadn't been fed for a week. Ettie sat across from him at an angle where she could see the baby clearly. Such a perfectly beautiful child, she thought, a gift. First and foremost, she'd ensure the baby's welfare. After that, there'd be time to think about the next step.

When Sam finished the last drop of coffee, he stacked the dirty dishes on the tray and planted a kiss of thanks and gratitude on Ettie's cheek as he passed her. She felt a little twinge of guilt at her duplicity but quickly set it aside. Everything would fall neatly into place. Well, perhaps not neatly, but it wouldn't serve any purpose to get picky about the finer details.

∽

Two hours after Sam's exit, Marcus Allenby, the tall, snowy-haired former top chef who'd stepped into Ettie's warm embrace, swept into the café. He carried the scents of earth and sea and an atmosphere of robust good humour about his person. He eagerly scanned the kitchen area where Ettie would ordinarily park her colourful self and found only Jenny. The expression on her face gave the first warning. And then he heard it. The piercing wail of a baby filled the café with the kind of hullabaloo that could break a business in a single day.

'Ah,' he said.

'Couldn't have put it better myself, Chef,' Jenny replied. She pointed upstairs with a kitchen knife. 'The happy duo awaits above. Ettie suggested chocolate cake with your usual tea.'

The chef pressed several fingers to his lips, pondering. 'Yes, yes, I see. This is a serious business. Chocolate will be soothing. Permit me to guess—and a nod in response is all that is required, Jenny.' He tapped his lips again, once or twice. 'Kate. She is not here, is this correct?'

'Bullseye, Chef.'

Marcus patted his girth, rubbed his stomach. 'Please, just the lightest indulgence of a ginger biscuit. At my age, I must consider my weight.'

Jenny felt a lump of laughter rise in her throat. The chef's penchant for exotic little titbits—which could ensure a generous livelihood for heart surgeons—was legendary. 'Ginger biscuit, coming up.'

'Perhaps two, and a double espresso, instead of herbal tea. I will need the extra energy in these circumstances, the details of which I am not yet fully aware, yes?'

He raised his head to look up the stairs. Immediately, silence reigned. He turned to Jenny with a smile wide enough to reach his ears. 'A good omen, surely, that with my arrival, the child senses settled times?'

'Whatever you say, Chef, and hold that thought. Here's your coffee and bikkies. Let me know if you think there's too much ginger in the biscuit. Bit of a fan of ginger, I am, but not everyone is.'

CHAPTER THREE

INSIDE THE PENTHOUSE, ETTIE PACED the lush, blood-red Turkish rug Kate had given her when they first became co-proprietors of the Briny Café. The penthouse itself was in a sense a legacy from Kate: she had created it for Ettie out of a large storage area. Her influence was everywhere, and yet nowhere, as Ettie held the baby draped over one shoulder, and patted and rubbed the tiny back, cooing softly. Swaying now, in one spot, she mimed a gentle 'shushing' to Marcus when his head appeared above the banister.

Content with Ettie's company, Marcus crossed the room and seated himself in a large cane armchair he'd become fond of in the days when he courted her. He pulled a small side table closer and set down his coffee before extracting a ginger biscuit from the paper bag.

Ettie raised her eyebrows. 'Cake?' she mouthed. He shook his head and pressed a palm to his chest. She nodded. Over her shoulder, Claire's curled fist relaxed and Ettie felt the baby's outrage at her missing mother and broken routine flow from her tiny form. She tiptoed to the bassinet and, holding her breath, lowered the baby. After a few moments, she covered the child with a blanket and pointed Marcus towards the balcony. Marcus went outside to wait. Around him, the life of Cook's Basin continued uninterrupted. Glenn went past at a snail's pace, pushing the punt bought by the community after his faithful old vessel was laid to rest in the big storm. Glenn spotted Marcus and tipped the peak of his cap. The chef waved and seated himself at a round outdoor table with a mosaic pattern: one crafted by Ettie before she traded coloured tiles and paint pots for the more lucrative career of cook in a bayside café. A few late commuters chugged past, identifiable from their greetings or dogs: mad waving from Brian; a dignified nod from the German shepherd seated next to Jamie; a one-fingered salute from Col, and so on. He took his customary delight in his surroundings and the people he now knew as friends in the wacky (a description he considered accurate after giving it much consideration) community he'd joined when he bought a rundown house in Kingfish Bay—and innocently agreed to cook dinner for a fire shed fundraiser. It was the unforgettable night he met Ettie as she stood in the fire shed with a cocktail in one hand and a tea towel in the other, her golden hair cascading like Botticelli's painting of Venus. Equally unforgettable was the horrifying sight of a beer-stuffed fridge with no space available for his fragile berry jellies. Ettie had sorted out the issue immediately. He'd later learned that helping with gentleness and generosity was an intrinsic part of her character, although more and more, he wondered if both traits—albeit admirable—might eventually lead to her undoing. He turned as Ettie stepped outside, closing the French doors quietly behind her.

'Phew!' she said, sinking onto the only other chair. 'She wouldn't settle. Finding herself plonked in a new environment without her mother has to be disrupting. It will take a little time for her to adjust.' She turned slightly towards the view that she had found so comforting in some of her darkest moments. Then, taking a deep breath for courage, she gave Marcus a brief rundown of Sam's current difficulties, pausing to read the reaction on his face, before she asked, 'Marcus, my darling, how would you feel if there was a new member of our household for a while?'

Taking his time to form a reply, Marcus ran his fingers over a patch of blue and white tiles representing the ocean on the mosaic tabletop. Then he brushed away a few crumbs, before looking out over the water again. 'Well, first, I must shop for essentials. This is practical, is it not? A baby has needs, yes?'

Ettie let out a breath she hadn't realised she'd been holding. Aware Marcus had very little idea of what was involved in looking after a baby, she knew that to allow him to sign on for an unspecified duration in complete innocence would be deceitful, if not downright criminal; perhaps threaten the foundation of the relationship she valued above all others. The idea sparked a surge of anger. Bloody Kate, she thought, before quickly blocking the direction her mind was taking. 'Babies put pressure on relationships, Marcus. Not enough sleep. Dirty nappies. Tantrums that can drain the joy from a beautifully prepared dinner. They are exhausting, physically and emotionally, and we are not young. The first few days, perhaps weeks, will be extremely difficult and require endless patience. Claire will miss her mother, which means she will cry loudly and at any time of the day or night. Sometimes, no matter what you do, it will seem like she will never stop howling. The sound can send you to the edge of despair and you will want to run from the house before you go mad. Trust me, Marcus, I do not exaggerate. Truthfully, I have no right to ask this of you. If you say no, I will understand.'

Marcus frowned. For a few moments, he looked like a *Diplôme de Cuisine* chef who'd remembered the eggs ten minutes after sliding the cake into the oven. Then his face cleared and he gave the mosaic-topped table two raps with a fist. 'This child needs us. We must plan how to achieve a satisfactory outcome for one and all because you are right, Ettie. This is a task that should not be lightly undertaken. Yes. Hmmm. Planning is the answer.' He stared across the bay as if the majestic gum trees on the far shore might reveal the key to success.

While he watched, a flock of seagulls swarmed over a school of bait fish, and he felt a twinge of regret that his fishing days were probably over for the foreseeable future. A small sacrifice, he told himself, for the sake of a baby in need. He came to a quick decision. 'First and foremost, there is the question of the child's bed. Because, already, yes, the most obvious solution is that Sam will be a weekend parent, and you, Ettie, will care for the baby during the week. While, I, the chef, Marcus Allenby, will once again step behind the counter of the Briny Café . . .'

'You will never know how much I love you,' Ettie whispered, tears in her eyes.

He leaned over and cupped her face in his hands. 'And you, my love, are my whole world. Of course, by this I mean everything . . .' And Ettie was able to cut him short with a laugh, because nothing more needed to be said. Marcus drained his coffee and stood.

'Kate . . .' Ettie began.

'This story of Kate, it will wait.' He checked his watch, clapped his hands. 'The baby emporium must be visited *tout de suite*. If I may suggest, my love, a list please, so *ich kann nichts einsam vergessen.*'

The chef's lapse into his native tongue triggered a shiver of unease. Ettie hadn't a clue what he had said but knew from experience that it might be a ruse to cover uncertainty. She studied his face, searching for signs of reluctance or fear for what lay ahead, but found nothing alarming.

'I was thinking—a lovely oyster pink for the nursery . . .' she said, dreaming of a beautiful environment for a baby she already loved like her own. Together she and Marcus bent their heads over his phone to make a list (so he wouldn't forget anything, he translated for her), and took their first steps towards fostering their new charge.

As, with one hand, he typed in the items required for a new baby in the household, he laid the other lightly over Ettie's and said, 'We are naturally to consider ourselves as grandparents, for however long we are given to guide her.' Knowing how she'd once yearned for a child of her own, he wanted her to understand that Claire could be reclaimed by her mother at any moment. Then he clapped his hands and announced with cheer and genuine enthusiasm, 'I must, of course, learn new recipes. It is good to continue to acquire new skills as one ages, yes? I am thinking, a range of baby food to be provided in the café, Ettie? *Was denkst du?*'

Ettie felt another frisson of unease as Marcus fell back on his first language.

'What do you think?' he asked, this time in plain English. She put aside her doubts. Marcus had made a commitment. He was a man of his word.

'Babies like simple food, Marcus. Mashed pumpkin. Carrots . . .' she replied.

'But I will do it with a flourish. This goes without saying.'

'Wonderful,' Ettie said, rising to a glass-shattering scream from Claire, who had awoken in fright in a strange environment. 'Perhaps,' she said, 'all Kate needs is a rest, and she will walk through the café door in no time.'

The chef kissed Ettie and set off across the Square with a spring in his step, his snow-white hair blown about by a stiff southerly that had sneaked its way into the bays. He shivered and reached for his phone. 'Ettie, I think you will need to find another blanket for the baby. Claire must be kept warm. There is fierceness brewing in this wind. We must be vigilant.'

He ended the call and for the first time felt the iron grip of responsibility for another life. His steps faltered, his earlier boisterous certainty waned. He wondered if he was up to the task, if he really would find the skills he imagined were instinctive in biological parents. 'Because *mein Gott*, babies are mysterious and *mein Gott*, tender like little spatchcocks.'

'You okay, Chef?' asked Seaweed, a Cutter Island tearaway with a hoarder's instinct that frequently tested the patience of his good-hearted neighbours. He was returning with the week's groceries and was concerned the chef might be in a bit of strife, given the panicked look on his face and the fact that he was talking to himself in public.

'Babies,' Marcus boomed. 'So helpless. How is it they survive to become teenagers and even adults?' He raised his arms like a man engaged in serious debate with an enemy force.

'Mate, they're made of iron. It's the parents who are at most risk.'

The chef looked horror-struck and hurried on towards the car park, his emotions in even more turmoil. '*Mein Gott*,' he repeated. He withdrew his phone from his trouser pocket and added 'baby instruction book' to the list. He would become a world expert on raising babies or die in the attempt. Well, perhaps not die.

And spatchcocks, he thought, might be a welcome addition to the menu of the café. Without Kate doing a cost analysis of each dish, he might get it past Ettie and bypass having to consider the condition of the world economy and predictions for global fiscal security for the next decade. Kate, she was a whizz with money, he thought, but Ettie would agree to oysters and lobsters if she thought it would make him happy. Sighing loudly but now mentally tilted more towards calmness than anxiety, he put aside the idea of spatchcocks with less regret than he'd anticipated and focused on mushed carrots and apples with more joy than perhaps they warranted.

Common sense must prevail, he told himself. If it did, then all would be *tickettybootsky*, as his beloved would say.

❧

Late in the afternoon, the door to the café banged open. The chef entered with his arms full of parcels and a triumphant grin on his handsome face. 'Ettie, I must tell you this. And you, Jenny.' He sniffed the air like a terrier on the hunt. 'Is this a new recipe I can smell? Fennel? So distinctive.' The chef set down his packages in an untidy heap. 'But let me describe all that has happened since I departed. First, the car park was full. I waited with great patience in my car until I saw a man walking casually. Too casually. Aha,

I thought. He is being stealthy, so I drove after him. When he reached his car, I made a signal that I would take the space immediately. He indicated a woman in a Fiat, coming from the other direction. I stuck my head out the window and yelled: "I have just had a baby and that car park must be mine!"'

Ettie's eyes sparkled with mirth, which Marcus took as encouragement.

'Ettie, my darling, he dared to say no, so I climbed out and stood in front of his vehicle. I told him, "I will not move until you send your friend away." I was so patient. Patience, it is good, yes? After a while, the woman, she went away. Of course, she was not thrilled. The man, he was quite rude when I stood aside to allow him to leave. But the space, Ettie, it was mine. Mine!' He beat his chest like a gorilla and then—as if he couldn't sustain the silverback swagger—made a little Continental bow. Ettie squeezed his arm and Jenny cuffed his shoulder in congratulations, both laughing at the courteous chef flinging his idea of civility into a strong sea breeze for the sake of a baby as yet unable to utter a word of thanks.

In the wake of their laughter, Sam came in from the deck where he'd tied the *Mary Kay* after hauling supplies and dodging Jimmy's increasingly anxious interrogation about how they would manage a barge baby and deliveries at the same time.

'Sam, I must tell you this right now also,' Marcus said and launched into an account of the increasingly gladiatorial-sounding battle over the quest for a car space. 'It is clear, is it not, that in the case of a baby emergency, I will be reliable, and little Claire will be safe with us?'

'Eh?' Sam stared at them both in confusion.

The chef glanced at Ettie, mortified. 'This plan of ours, it is not yet discussed?' he asked.

'What's not discussed?' Sam asked tersely, aiming his question directly at Ettie.

'Marcus, darling, would you make us a strong brew and a sandwich? I haven't eaten today, and I'm quite sure Sam hasn't had a meal since breakfast.' Before they could move, Jimmy flew inside to join them, chewing his bottom lip. 'I've been measurin' the wheelhouse, Sam, but I reckon Longfella's gunna have to find a new possie.'

He looked at the group clustered on both sides of the counter, his eyebrows raised, his feet tapping like a tom-tom. 'I'm tellin' ya once and for all, Sam, it'll be a stretch with the bub and you can't set the bassinet on the banquette. One monster rock and she'll be spilled out and overboard before you can shout Jack Robinson. Whoever that bloke is . . .'

'Good on you, mate. You're doing your homework, but how about Jenny cuts you a slice of cake and makes a milkshake? You've had a big day,' Sam said. 'Ettie and I need to have a chat in private on board the *Mary Kay*, where I'll . . . er, check the measurements.'

'You're gunna need to extend the wheelhouse, Sam. Sayin' it once and repeatin' myself. Any muffins left, Jenny?'

She nodded and reached for a brown paper bag.

'Put it straight in me mitt and it'll be down me gullet in a second.'

Sam opened the door to the rear deck and stood aside to let Ettie go through.

'Chocolate, strawberry, banana or vanilla milkshake?' Jenny asked.

'Choco . . .'

'Banana!' shouted Ettie and Sam in unison, fully aware that the kid might be eighteen years old, but a hit of chocolate would send him off-grid in a way that would have his mother, Amelia, chasing Sam for revenge.

Jimmy gave a sly grin. 'Ah bugger. Almost got away with it,' he said.

'My boy, let us together tiptoe upstairs to see how baby Claire is adjusting. But watch your language in front of the child,' Marcus said smoothly. 'Bring your milkshake. Be careful not to spill it on the stairs.'

Jimmy eyed the last muffin on the counter. Jenny smiled and handed it to him at the end of a pair of tongs. 'I swear you've got hollow legs, Jimmy.'

The kid frowned and looked down. 'You reckon?'

'This an old saying. I will explain when we are upstairs,' Marcus said, leading the way.

In the penthouse, his bony body bent over the carrier while he searched the baby's face intently, Jimmy asked, 'She gunna look like a girl soon?'

Marcus stood alongside and gazed at the child. 'In my experi-ence, which I must tell you truthfully is limited, despite my considerable age, if two babies dressed alike were placed together side by side, I am sadly aware that I would find it quite difficult to tell one from the other. I am speaking generally, of course, and if one had blonde hair and the other dark, well, that would be an easy point of difference but naturally, many babies are bald, which creates a problem, and I am thinking that I have heard they are born with blue eyes that later change colour, which is another situation that can create confusion . . .'

Jimmy broke in: 'I get it, Chef. But I'm lookin' for signs of Sam and all I'm seein' is a pink blob.'

Marcus straightened and took a deep breath. 'Let me ask you this, Jimmy. Would you want this baby to have Sam's wiry hair? His square chin? His large . . . er, masculine, nose? No, I think not. We must hope this child takes after her mother, who is a beautiful young woman with a sharp brain and, yes, a good heart, though a troubled one.'

'I hear you, Chef, but it's a shame, eh?'

'Give it time, my friend, and you'll see she has Sam's . . .' Marcus hesitated. 'Personality. Yes. This will be the truth, I am sure. Sam's personality.'

Jenny appeared at the top of the stairs in time to hear the chef's words. 'Personality! Oh lord, Chef, that's the best I've ever heard. Now hand me that milkshake container and mind you boys don't leave a mess.' She wrinkled her nose. 'And one of you better change that baby's nappy the moment she wakes up. I can smell it from here.'

Jimmy looked like he'd been struck with an electric prod. The chef took a step back from the carrier, his face pale.

'Muscle up, boys. You're about to set off along the deeply pot-holed track of babyhood,' Jenny said, laughing. 'What a sight you both look. A couple of ninnies terrified of a bit of baby poo.'

She went off, still laughing. Jimmy looked at the chef: 'You reckon it's the same as worm poo, Chef? Worm poo is nothin'.'

The chef, seeing an escape hatch magically open up to him, nodded enthusiastically. 'Yes, yes. Worm poo. We must think of this as merely . . . compost. You are captain of this issue right now, as I descend to the café. My skills are urgently required to make my world-class sandwiches for Sam and Ettie. Good man.' He thumped Jimmy hard on the back.

CHAPTER FOUR

AT THE END OF THE same day, in his soundless, unobtrusive way, Fast Freddy left his water taxi tied at the end of the ferry wharf and slid into the café to softly quiz Jenny. 'Kate's baby? Nothing to worry about then?' he asked.

'Oh no, nothing to worry about.'

'And Kate? Nothing to worry about?'

'No more than usual. That's a joke, Freddy. Settle.'

He nodded, absorbing the information.

'I am making sandwiches for Sam and Ettie who are conferring on the barge,' the chef said, tying an apron around his waist. 'One for you, too, with my best wishes, Freddy. But you must tell me, chicken or beef?'

'Nothing with eyes, Chef, but thank you for the offer,' Freddy said.

'Forgive me, Freddy, my mind is like a scrambled egg. I forgot this point. Perhaps sweet potato . . .'

'Never eat between meals, Chef. A personal rule.'

'Of course. This rule I respect.'

Freddy stood awkwardly, staring at his shoes. 'Takes a lot out of you, I expect, having a new baby,' he said, not wanting to probe but deeply worried that the woman who'd called him to give her a ride to the Square in the early morning hours bore no resemblance to the one he'd grown so fond of since she arrived in Cook's Basin. She'd been as broken as a china doll, with the same vacant smile and glazed empty look in her eyes: he'd thought her baby must be dead and his heart had nearly split in two. He felt like an accomplice in a criminal act when he helped her onto his water taxi as she abandoned that shadowy house where on late-night runs he swore he'd seen ghosts floating above its towering gums, heard their wailing. It wasn't his place to ask questions, but it nearly killed him to leave her alone onshore in the dead of a moonless night.

In a voice dropped to barely a whisper, he leaned closer and said, 'Picked up Kate last night. Dropped her off about two a.m. at the Square. She wanted Ettie to know.' He brushed the sleeves of his jacket, careful not to catch anyone's eye, in case it invited questions he would have to refuse to answer for fear of violating Kate's privacy. He shuffled his feet, studying the laces on his boat shoes intently, while he considered the fine line between care and breaking a trust.

Seeing his uncertainty, Marcus said, 'She needs rest. That is all and, of course, we must support her in this hour of her need.' Behind his back, Jenny gave a disapproving sound, but bit her lip too late.

Freddy nodded, unconvinced. But with his message delivered and nothing more to achieve by standing there, he ducked into the Square once more and made his way to where he'd tied his apple-green water taxi, its vibrant colour failing miserably to lift his spirits. He silently invoked the help of his spiritual guide, Buddha, and told himself to be satisfied he'd done his best. But the words sounded empty and inadequate.

❦

Upstairs, Claire began to cry. Jimmy's panic-stricken face appeared over the banister, seeking Marcus. 'You better call, Ettie, Chef. I'm tryin' to untangle the nappy but it's harder than a crossword. And the bub's gettin' fair dinkum cranky.'

'Ettie!' bellowed the chef through the rear door. 'The baby . . .'

Sam shot off the barge and through the door like he'd been fired from a cannon, rudely pushed past Marcus and bounded up the stairs.

'A dirty nappy. Nothing more and nothing less,' Marcus quickly explained to Ettie. He began to laugh. 'That man. It was like he had flames attached to his backside. *Mein Gott*, babies. They have us completely under *der Daumen*.'

Sam brought a clean and newly comforted baby downstairs, followed by Jimmy lugging all the cumbersome accoutrements that quickly attached to babies. The trio boarded the barge where Ettie waited, the future of a six-month-old baby hanging in the balance. Jimmy, a kid whose life choices revolved around working with Sam, looking after his mum, Amelia, and staying out of the household boarder Artie's way, chattered, innocent of the swirling undercurrents: 'Me mum picked girlie colours for the blankie. Musta known, mustn't she? I wanted her to go for red or orange but me mum said babies don't like shocks. You know, like clappin' your hands loudly or something.'

Ettie nodded. 'Your mum created a work of art, Jimmy.' She reached inside the bassinet and removed the blanket Amelia had knitted in the softest yarns that picked up the colour of Oyster Bay at twilight. She briefly held it against her face then handed it to Sam to wrap around the child. Jimmy saw Sam's face suffuse with tenderness, his eyes fill with a hunger so raw it was painful to watch.

'You gunna blub, are ya?' Jimmy asked, blushing. 'You're an old softie, Sam. Always said so.'

'She's beautiful, isn't she?' Sam said, without looking away. 'Put the bassinet in the cabin, mate.' Seeing Jimmy look from Longfellow's shaggy mug to the bassinette, and fidget around as if something was biting him, Sam added, 'We'll work out logistics later. Okay?'

'Orright. Give us another squiz at the bub, Sam. Me mum'll want a full report when I get home, seein' as how Kate keeps her under wraps most of the time.'

Sam smiled at the boy. 'Here. Have a hold. But be gentle.' Jimmy bent his two skinny arms in a cradle and Sam nestled the child safely. 'Remember, always keep her neck supported. Just to be on the safe side.'

The mutt came forwards and Jimmy dipped to give the dog a sniff. Instinctively, Sam and Ettie swooped. 'Might be best to wait a bit before making a formal introduction,' Sam quickly explained, hoping his heartbeat would return to normal before too long. He disengaged the child from Jimmy's hold. Jimmy did a full spin, his anxiety ramped. Ettie placed both hands on the boy's shoulders to hold him still. 'You were absolutely right. It's a good idea to introduce the baby to Longfellow, Jimmy. But can you imagine how Claire must feel? Seeing a furry face for the first time?'

'Can I have another hold?' he asked. And Sam, realising a second go counted as forgiveness, nodded. Ettie guided Jimmy into the cabin and placed the squirming baby in his arms once more. 'Let's keep her out of the breeze and you can sit while you hold her. Sam and I have a few things to discuss.'

'You gunna give him a few dad tips, Ettie?' Jimmy said, bouncing back to normal.

'He's a natural, love, like you. We've just got to work out a few logistics.' Sensing a packet of questions heading her way, she held up her hands. 'Shh,' she said. 'Babies need peace and quiet.'

'Quiet?' Jimmy murmured to the baby. 'You're gunna have to get used to a diesel engine pretty soon young lady. And that bl . . . bloomin' great crane can make a racket . . .'

Ettie stepped out of the wheelhouse and closed the door behind her.

At that moment, the chef materialised out of the café with a tray and approached the barge, holding it carefully. 'I have taken the liberty of ordering a hamburger for the father, with a large bowl of chips in the event Jimmy wishes also to partake. A simple sandwich for you, my love, of tender ham, melted Gruyère cheese and a ripe tomato. Some salami and olives, plus fresh bread, for something lighter if it better suits your mood. Of course, there is coffee, each made to your personal specifications.' He thrust the tray towards them but felt subdued by the grim expression on Ettie's face, the jut of Sam's jaw. The disappointment in his own expression made Sam and Ettie struggle to their feet. 'You're a star, Chef,' Sam said, taking the tray and placing it on the deck to offer the chef a hand to board.

'No, no, my place is in the kitchen right now,' he said. 'My assistance is required.' He scurried away with his head bent to avoid catching Ettie's eye.

Sam passed Ettie her food and tried to ignore the feeling of a large lump that had lodged in his throat, making food hard to accommodate right now.

Ettie took a sip of her coffee and closed her eyes in content-ment. 'I'll feel human soon.'

'Ettie, the bub . . .'

'I have a plan. Hear me out. Okay?'

Sam automatically picked up a chip. 'Go ahead.'

'Marcus and I will care for the baby together . . . No. Wait.' She held up her hands to silence the protest forming on his lips.

'You know I will love that child like my own. So will Marcus. He is already dreaming up a line of baby food for the café . . .'

'Ah jeez, Ettie . . .'

'It's the only way. You must see that. A new baby on a barge all day? Rain or shine? Wind or rolling seas? With that almighty crane lifting loads that could kill, if one came crashing down? Then there's feeding, nappy changing, establishing a routine . . .'

Sam took another chip, looked surprised to see it between his fingers, and threw it towards a seagull perched on a pylon. The seagull caught it mid-air. 'It'll take a few days, but I'll work it out, Ettie. She's just a little baby. Babies aren't much trouble. Looking after her isn't rocket science.'

Ettie looked at him in disbelief. 'Have you thought about what it will be like when she's teething, sick, crawling, climbing or sticking anything she finds in her mouth? You can't take your eyes off them, Sam. Soon as you do, they've swallowed a bit of plastic they've found on the floor—or the deck in your case—and you're off to the emergency ward while their faces turn blue.'

Sam went white. 'I guess I had no idea how much Kate had to handle,' he said.

'It's a labour of love,' Ettie responded, 'or otherwise no one would take on the job. We wouldn't be stealing her, Sam. On Friday nights, after work, we will hand her into your care for the weekend. If I'm not overstepping the mark here . . .'

'The mark was rubbed out decades ago . . .'

'Spend a couple of weekends in our spare room until you get the hang of looking after her full-time, then she's yours, on your own, for a full two days a week. It goes without saying that we want our home to be home to you both, so if you want to move in, well that's fine, too.'

Sam dropped his face into his hands, swallowing a groan. 'It's too much to ask of you and the chef, Ettie . . .'

Ettie shook her skirt for no reason. 'I can't make you agree, and kidnapping is an offence. But we're a community and communities look after each other. This will work. I know it will. You've got to believe me. More importantly, the baby will thrive.'

Marcus emerged to collect the tray. 'Barely touched? It is enough to break a chef's heart.'

'Thanks, mate, but I can't seem to eat a thing,' Sam said apologetically.

'You have a duty to your child to stay strong, my friend.' He winked at Ettie. 'Of course, if you don't touch this beautiful food, I will have to stand in front of the barge and forbid you to leave. I have learned this strategy today in the car park. It is quite a useful method, is it not?' He laughed, pleased with himself, and Ettie joined him. Sam reached for a piece of bread.

'But I'm not touching the olives, mate, just so you know.'

After the chef returned to the café, Ettie and Sam sat together without saying much. In the cabin, Jimmy swayed from side to side, the baby in his arms, softly humming a tune no one recognised, while at his feet, Longfellow twitched and snuffled in his sleep. On the water and in the Square, the steady pulse of Cook's Basin continued with the quiet sleepiness of early afternoon before the schoolkids arrived to shatter the peace.

'I need to know, Ettie, about Kate . . . She going to come back?'

'Wish I could say yes. Truth is, I have no idea. I don't think Kate would even know at this stage.'

'Yeah. Early days.' Sam placed his great big hands on his knees and pushed to his feet. Helped Ettie upright. 'Might as well get this show on the road, eh?'

CHAPTER FIVE

OVER THE NEXT FEW DAYS, the chef's immaculate, almost surgical kitchen of gleaming stainless-steel benchtops and glossy white cabinetry became a mess of dishes, bottles, an array of measuring instruments and gadgets the man had never even dreamed of. The new order broke all his rules for uncluttered benchtops and a concealed spot for every piece of his treasured equipment. His highly organised pantry, where precious tins of French goose liver pâté were neatly stacked alongside exotic products such as creamed chestnuts, truffles, artisan vinegars, olive oils and spices, was rapidly transformed into a store of baby necessities and as fully stocked as the shelves of the infant section in a supermarket. When Ettie tried to apologise for up-ending his lifestyle, he waltzed her around the kitchen. 'I am at an age when most men reach for their slippers each night. Instead, this home, which was just a house before you entered it, is full to the brim with life.'

'You would tell me if it's too much . . . life, wouldn't you?'

'Ah, Ettie, the child thrives. And when you hold her in your arms, your face . . . it glows with contentment. What man could find it in his heart to deny his beloved such joy?' And he drew Ettie closer into his embrace to make his point. 'Perhaps, though, we might find a more appropriate resting place for the *foie gras*.'

'Where would you like it?' Ettie immediately asked, wanting to make up for the disruption of his kitchen.

'Right now, we must remove many tins of baby formula to lay our hands on one small can. I was thinking . . . somewhere within easy reach. If we are hungry and wakeful in the night after you have fed the child, a few spoonfuls on a warm piece of toast to lure us back to peaceful rest? Is this a good idea?'

Ettie laughed. 'You always make me feel like a prize no matter what I ask of you.' It wasn't until much later that she realised Marcus had avoided the question of whether he was delighted by the arrival of Claire or simply accepting the inevitable under the circumstances.

∽

A week later, Sam delivered the *Mary Kay* to her mooring, jumped in his tinnie, dropped off Jimmy and his dog on Cutter Island and made a beeline for the white timber house in Kingfish Bay, where his child was beginning her life in a room that had been quickly repainted and swathed in softly coloured fabrics chosen and arranged by Ettie.

If the child slept, he sat by her crib, content to watch the rise and fall of her chest. When she woke, he scooped her into his arms and gazed into her eyes, willing her to understand how loved and cherished she was by him and the people around her.

In between, Ettie wrote a schedule for his weekend watch, told him routine made for happy babies and if Sam broke it for any reason, she would know by a sudden restlessness and she would come after him on her broomstick.

'Thank you, Ettie. For too much to mention,' he said, late one evening when their dinner table was strewn with empty plates and he felt too fat and full to move. 'You, too, Chef. You're a hero.'

The chef tilted his head in acknowledgement and raised a glass of his post-dinner digestif of honey mead, which he'd recently adopted as his habitual late-night tipple: he'd found a decent slug of cognac interfered with his new early morning routine.

Sam's mobile buzzed. He apologised for the interruption, checked the screen for an emergency call, then sighed and picked up, walking away from the table.

'Can't you sleep, Artie, or is it book-club night for Amelia?'

'As you know,' Artie said, 'I am not a man who interferes in the lives of others.'

Sam almost choked. After a stroke made his legs useless, the old bloke invested in a pair of binoculars and knew more about the infidelities, small criminal acts and petty pilfering (also known as *borrowing*) in Cook's Basin than the local coppers.

'However, suffering as I was last week from insomnia, I happened to see Fast Freddy ferrying a passenger who was a ringer for Kate, whom I'd recognise on a moonless night, which was fortuitous as it happened to be one, not too long after midnight. In the sole interest of untwisting the knot of worry in me gut, so I can catch up on me beauty sleep, you wouldn't like to give a bloke a subtle hint about what the bejesus is going on, would you?'

'Mate . . .'

'Me lips would be sealed if that's what you want. But the rumours are flyin' thick and fast. Add in the fact that Ettie is missing in action and the chef is bellowing orders behind the counter like he's back in that swanky two-hatted restaurant he hailed from: it has people worried. Most worryin' of all, young Jimmy refuses to discuss the matter and we all know he's a kid who runs off at the mouth without the least encouragement. Say the word and helpin' hands will be there forthwith. Say the word, mate. That's all you have to do.' Artie gave a little puff as though the speech had knocked the air out of him.

'Life a little dull on the Island, mate?'

'Bad as that, is it? You can't even give a man a straight answer when you know I care about that girl with all that's left of me worn out heart?'

Sam was beaten and he knew it. 'She needed a break, mate. That's all she said.'

'Postnatal depression, that's what they call it, isn't it? Hits mums out of the blue and knocks them for a six. Read all about it on me new phone after Kate went on me personal missing list for more than a couple of days.'

Sam floundered. 'Er, no diagnosis at this stage. Keep it under your hat, though, if you wouldn't mind. The bub's thriving and there's nothing to worry about.'

'Wouldn't know about that from the criminally limited information you've sent my way, but I'll take your word for the time being. And mate, me lips are sealed, but if I were you, I'd spread the word 'cause it won't take long before the louts and layabouts that make up the crowd that passes for a tight-knit community decide nothing short of murder and mayhem has taken place. I'll tell you that in the interest of saving you a lot of trouble down the pike.'

Sam ended the call and returned to the house where the table had been cleared, the kitchen swizzled, and the chef and Ettie were close on the couch.

'What was all that about?' Ettie asked.

'Artie's worried about Kate. Says he hasn't seen her since he clocked Freddy taking her ashore a week ago. Says I should inform the locals before the rumours start.' He looked around for his windcheater. 'One last check on the bub and I'll leave you two in peace.' In the nursery, he kissed the tips of his fingers and laid them lightly on the sleeping child's cheek. Raised the same hand and laid it over his own jam-packed heart, hoping it didn't burst.

⌇

Ettie walked Sam to the end of the jetty and stood on tiptoes to kiss his cheek. 'Artie's right,' she said. 'We should get Jenny to spread a suitable story, okay? Kate's having a break. She's been called away on family business. Whatever. She's forfeited all rights to any say in what happens, and we'll have to come up with a cover story sooner or later. Now's as good a time as any. Now, off you go, and we'll talk tomorrow night. Marcus is planning veal cutlets for dinner, unless the weather ramps up to a real taste of winter: then it's cassoulet or Irish stew.'

'Where does that man find his energy?'

'He tells me love powers his every move.' She smiled, crouched to hold the gunnel.

Sam jumped aboard and turned the key with only a faint tinge of nostalgia for his old pull-start.

At the lounge lizard purr of his spiffy new four-stroke engine, Ettie gave the boat a little push with her foot, and Sam cruised slowly home under a sky blitzed with stars.

By nature, he was a fixer. Saw a problem and wore it away with bull-headed determination. But he had no idea where to start with Kate. Every possible strategy led to a seabed strewn with mines. He shook his head and tried to clear his brain. Bottom line, he thought, Claire's best interests would drive every decision. There was no other option. He rolled the words around in his head, searching for a similarly solid point of reference in his relationship with Kate. He was jolted by the knowledge that he no longer felt full responsibility for Kate's welfare and that his concern for her, once the prime driver of each new day, lagged well behind what he felt now for the small group of people he'd always called family in Cook's Basin. He waited for the shock of loss to hit him, but felt only relief. Postnatal depression, he thought, and in an inner segue beyond his control, he returned to dread for the mother of his child. 'Concern, not dread, you mug,' he insisted loudly to the dark open waters, 'nothing more.' He knew he was lying to himself. He wasn't over Kate. Not yet. Maybe not ever.

Behind him, the foaming wake glittered green with sparkling phosphorescence and he found some solace, as he always did, when his spirit was soothed by the living sea.

CHAPTER SIX

TWO WEEKS AFTER CLAIRE'S ARRIVAL in the household, and as the year slid towards April, Ettie began a morning routine of walking the back tracks with the baby. Unused to the domestic entrapment demanded by infants, she'd begun to feel odd bouts of cabin fever. With Claire strapped into a papoose against her chest, it was as good a way as any, she explained to the chef— who feared for her wellbeing on isolated trails—to shift the extra padding that her hips had gained from his tender ministrations during a bout of flu some months earlier.

'But even a small rock, Ettie, could trip you up. What if the child lay under you, suffocating, and with no hope unless a passing bushwalker might stray by . . .' Marcus said, worried in the way of any first-time parent.

'And what, after all,' Ettie insisted, 'is the point of a mobile phone, if not to use it for emergencies?'

'And this phone? It works when you are alone on the escarpment?' Marcus asked, deeply suspicious.

Ettie quickly changed the subject but knew she hadn't fooled him for a second.

As Ettie walked out one fine morning, when the black cockatoos were feasting on casuarina nuts and the white cockatoos were strafing a small goanna as it endeavoured to raid a nest, Lizzie, who lived in the renovated house at the end of Stringy Bark Bay with seven other like-minded retirees, rounded the corner, staff in hand, immaculately dressed in chinos and a white cotton shirt, a red and blue scarf tied at her neck. She almost ploughed directly into Ettie. The two women, taken by surprise, let out little yelps. After a moment or two to steady their pulse rate, they walked to where a table-sized flat rock provided a good seat with a spectacular view to Cat Island and way beyond to the ocean. Ettie extricated the baby from the papoose and Lizzie took the child onto her lap to give Ettie a break. 'I'm not very good with babies,' Lizzie said, 'but I feel like I have a vested interest in this one.'

'Part ownership. No doubt about it.'

Lizzie had been right there at Claire's birth; had even played temporary, involuntary midwife.

'And part blame. I told Kate first babies are never early, and let her join me up on the escarpment, never dreaming it could end in catastrophe. Madness.'

Ettie, keeping her own counsel, reached out to stroke Claire's little fist with her finger, quietly reassuring her that she wasn't going anywhere.

Lizzie gave Claire a few gentle jiggles on her knee. 'Without Cliffy to manage the delivery like the good dairy farmer he is, I hate to think what could have happened.'

'But here she is, our little storm baby.'

Both women looked at the child, their faces softening. Claire gummed her fist, kicked her legs, happy to be free from the carrier. Way below and in the distance, two yachts elegantly under sail made their way to open waters. Once, Ettie would have yearned to be aboard as a passenger, a deckhand, a navvy, a cook: anything to escape the shrinking potential of her island life. Until a sick old man decided to sell her the café for a knockdown price. And Kate appeared like a good omen, to run the business side. And Marcus cooked a feast for the fire shed fundraiser dinner, then had a fit when he saw the fridge jammed with beer, dooming his berry jellies to melt in the summer heat. Ettie had taken him for a stroll along the seafront until he regained his equilibrium, and the whole community watched as they fell in love right before their eyes. Now, there was Claire. A blessing for a woman who'd been unable to conceive after a pregnancy went horribly wrong.

'How is Cliffy?' Ettie asked, bringing her mind back to the present.

'Still recounting to anyone who'll listen how he safely delivered a baby during a maelstrom, while a woman with a broken ankle boiled water and the shack rattled in the wind, until it was almost reduced to toothpicks. Greatest night of his life, he says. Barring his marriage to Agnes.'

Ettie was curious. 'Did you ever meet Agnes?'

'Lovely woman. Died too young.'

They were silent for a while, the ghosts of those who'd died *too young* floating through memory. Ettie said, 'How's it going with the other residents in your new home? Still glad you made the move from your old shack?'

'That shack was almost unlivable after the big storm. Moving into GeriEcstasy—which, it must be said, is gold-plated communal living with like-minded people—was like being handed a gift. A miracle, really.'

Ettie rolled her eyes. 'A few glitches, though.'

Lizzie sidestepped the allusion to a strange, chaotic episode in her new home: when one of the other residents threatened her life. 'We're planning a bushwalk. I'm on a mission today to rediscover the landmarks of my youth so I don't get them hopelessly lost. The bush changes so subtly over time that it's best to note a split rock, a copse of casuarinas, a clump of xanthorrhoea as sign posts.' She shifted the baby a little and stretched out her legs to avoid a cramp.

'Looking back, would you change anything?' Ettie asked, less out of curiosity than a desire to know whether regrets, like those still haunting her in her fifties, followed you like a dark shadow into old age.

Lizzie passed Claire back to Ettie, untied a shoelace to free her left foot. 'A blister. Old skin, it lets you know when it's had enough.' She fished around in her backpack and found a bandaid. 'Discovered the old reservoirs today. Bit leaky but still holding water after more than one hundred and fifty years. Not bad, eh?'

Ettie took the hint and swallowed her questions about why Lizzie had chosen to live like a hermit in the shack on the escarpment. 'What was it like when you first came here?' she asked instead.

Lizzie pulled on her sock, eased on her shoe with a grimace. 'Fewer people, fewer houses. Mostly folks doing it hard and trying to live cheaply.' She frowned, thinking. 'There were two fancy houses, though. One owned by the daughter of a politician and the other by the daughter of a retail king.'

'Two women living here alone?'

'Well, not quite. It was way before my time but I understand they had caretakers and housekeepers. Legend has it that neither of the women wanted to marry. In those days, a woman's property automatically became her husband's when they tied the knot.'

'Smart girls,' Ettie murmured. Claire became restless and Ettie hoisted her over her shoulder, lightly patting her back.

'You and the chef, taking on a baby. Oh, don't look at me like that. It's common knowledge Kate is on leave of absence. Either way, you deserve sainthoods.'

'Kate will return when she's ready.'

Lizzie raised her face to the sun and closed her eyes. 'If there's one thing I've learned in nearly eighty years of living, it's that there are no certainties.'

The child squirmed and wriggled, then twisted towards Lizzie with a beatific smile, followed by an explosion that instantly wiped out the clean, fresh scent of eucalyptus. 'Oh, lord,' Lizzie said, turning her face away, holding a hand over her nose. 'Oh, dear God,' she added.

Ettie stood and laid the child on the bare earth to change her nappy. 'The chef's baby food. He's still on a learning curve.'

Lizzie caught Ettie's eye. The two women laughed uproariously. Lizzie spluttered, 'He hasn't been feeding her *foie gras*, has he?'

Ettie, negotiating her way around a clean nappy, shook her head. 'Not as far as I know.'

'I'd check, if I were you,' Lizzie said, pink-faced, standing and waving the air around her before moving away a little. 'Oh God, that is rank. Might head off and leave you to it, if you don't mind.'

'Before you go,' Ettie said, folding the dirty nappy with close attention and placing it in a bag, 'moving in with the GeriEcstasies, all good?'

Lizzie sighed, succumbed to the pressure of Ettie's curiosity. 'No complaints, Ettie. None at all.'

'The Days of Donna gone forever.'

'Seems like a hundred years ago,' Lizzie said, stepping forwards into clean air once again, to run her index finger along the smooth ridge of the baby's nose.

'Does anyone ever talk about her, about what happened? You know, around the dinner table, after a couple of glasses of wine?'

'What takes place or is said under our roof stays under our roof. House rules. Now, I better get going or I'll be late for cocktail hour.' Lizzie set off with a wave, a walking stick in one hand, her silver head bent to watch the ground for hazards.

Ettie sat there a while longer, her thoughts snagged on Donna, a sad, mad old actress who, after Lizzie joined the household, nearly killed her. The household, essentially, was a group of loyal friends trying to protect Donna and keep her out of circulation and out of institutions, after she had already committed at least one violent crime. After Donna's own death, no one expected the residents of the optimistically named GeriEcstasy to stay on in the big house near the mangroves in Stringy Bark Bay.

Yet the land and sea, the turquoise lagoon, the forest of mangroves, the magnificence of the escarpment, the wonder of the physical world, had worked their magic, and now Lizzie was part of a household of seven similarly aged people intent on living independently, until the end. Lizzie had a sound roof over her head, solid walls, reliable hot water and a family without strings attached. GeriEcstasy resurrected, Ettie thought, hoping it was true.

She nestled Claire back in the sling against her chest and, on the way home, murmured stories about the bush into the child's ear, pointed out special trees, giving them names: blueberry ash, cheese tree, grass trees, scribbly gum, apple gum—so many, she thought, marvelling at the way relaying information lifted the blinkers of familiarity.

At the fork, where the track split to follow the coast or the ridge, a baby echidna nuzzled the dirt with its long snout. Claire was fast asleep, a warm weight against her chest, and Ettie felt the extra poundage dripping off from her efforts. I'm blessed, Ettie thought, holding Claire's head steady when it was time to descend the steps to the house she shared with the chef. Quickly, she laid her hand flat on the wood of a nearby tree. Just to be on the safe side.

ᢙ

At home, Ettie put Claire to bed, then tiptoed around the house, doing light housekeeping. She prepared the baby's food, tasting the chef's sweet potato concoction to check if it was to blame for a smell that would have felled lesser women. Not the culprit, as far as she could tell. Puzzled but unworried, she looked in on the child. She was still deeply lost in her dreams. Fresh air is more effective than a sleeping draught, Ettie thought.

She made a cup of Earl Grey tea, which she drank at the kitchen bench. And in that rare moment of solitude, she had time to reflect on the strange conjunction of events that had up-ended her ordered existence and now threatened the ongoing viability of the Briny Café. A sharp edge of anxiety about Kate's future role in the café wiped the gloss from a lovely day. It's the not knowing, she thought and felt a rare surge of anger against the young woman for whom she'd made excuses since they'd become partners in the Briny Café. Ettie had always defended her against any critics who felt a responsibility to point out Kate's failings in a bid to protect Ettie from disappointment. But Ettie had a history of plucking aimless or destitute strays from the crowd and finding their strengths. Of course, there were failures. Kate wasn't one of them, though. No way. Even so, a postcard, a short note—anything—just to let the people who cared about her know she was safe . . . surely that wasn't too much to ask?

Claire stirred. There was the muffled sound of a kick against the crib wall; a suspended toy rattled by a balled fist; silence—and two minutes later, a wail that could wake a sleeping city. Ettie sighed loudly and slipped into the nursery to greet her charge, wearing a happy face in the hope Claire would pick up the feeling. Marcus would be home soon with his great smile, to touch her lightly and lovingly, as if to prove she hadn't evaporated in his absence.

She turned on soft music, lit a candle to fill the house with the calming scent of lavender. Then put it out. It clashed violently with the briny scent of seaweed at low tide. Anyway, lavender made her soporific. She gathered the child in her arms and marvelled again at the sweet heaviness of Claire's warm, pliant body. What she'd give to be as supple.

'Here we go,' she said, nuzzling Claire's chest and making loud blurting noises to the baby's delight. 'Bath time. Best time of the day. Well, it will be soon. I guarantee it.' She slipped Claire into warm water, holding her safely. 'Your mother is missing out, baby girl. But her loss is my gain.' She pulled up short, shocked by the selfishness of the thought, and focused on soaping the baby, washing her fine hair. When she'd finished, she wrapped her in a huge white towel and returned to the nursery to wrangle her into her pyjamas. A nightly tussle. Part fun, part resistance. She was a strong baby, though, and the battle gladdened Ettie's heart. She heard the unmistakeable purr of the chef's boat engine and scooped up the child. Meeting him at the end of the jetty with Claire in her arms had become a ritual.

'My two beautiful girls,' he said, stepping out of the boat and reaching for Claire with one arm, slipping the other around Ettie's waist and leaning to kiss her cheek.

'How did things go at the café today?' Ettie asked.

'So many stories to tell it is difficult for even me, a brilliant raconteur, to know where to begin.'

'Then I will pour you a glass of wine and we will sit for a while before dinner, while you tell me everything in your shy and modest style,' Ettie said, smiling. The irony swept past Marcus's head without disturbing a single strand of his hair.

'But first, I must confess, I have café leftovers for our meal tonight. The veal for the chops: it was more likely from a beast that was a student of university instead of kindergarten. I could not, in all conscience, sell it over the counter to your treasured customers. Tomorrow, I must talk to the butcher.'

'But they are *your* leftovers, Marcus, and therefore they will be wonderful.' Ettie, about to say more, paused; she worried she might be falling into the habit of praise without judging whether it was truly deserved. It was a trait she'd noticed in long-term couples, as though they'd decided peace was preferable to war, even if it meant seriously testing the boundaries of truth. But then . . . false modesty was just as bad, wasn't it? She refocused her attention on Marcus. 'They will be deliciously wonderful,' she added firmly.

'Yes, of course, this goes without saying. Now I will pass to you this precious package and take a shower.' He turned towards the empty boat. Slapped his forehead. '*Ach, ich bin ein Dummkopf.* I have left the victuals on the deck of the Briny. I must go back this instant. Forgive me, my love.' His face was a picture of frustration. Halfway into the boat, his phone rang. Ettie watched as Marcus waved his arms, threw back his head, and heard him bellow his thanks. He returned to Ettie at a slow trot. 'Sam has saved the day. To be accurate, Jimmy is the saviour. He glimpsed on the deck an icebox that had been apparently abandoned and fearing a bomb left by a terrorist—these are Sam's words, you must understand—he demanded Sam investigate before there were injuries. I ask you, how this has come to pass that a young boy in this paradise of Cook's Basin should have in his mind the worry about a bomb . . .'

'All is well. The evening meal has been saved,' Ettie said, attempting to get the chef back on track. 'And look, there's Sam.' She nodded towards the mouth of the bay, held up Claire's chubby arm in a wave. 'Here comes Dad,' she told the child, pointing out Sam's boat as it peeled a path through water turned coppery in the final gush of evening light. Sam cruised into port, tied up and leaped sure-footed onto the jetty. He held out his arms, clapped his hands, and his daughter squirmed in his direction, her own arms outstretched. Ettie untangled the baby blanket from her arms, handed Claire over, and then helped the chef with the heavy icebox.

'Are we expecting an army tonight?' she joked.

'We must be prepared always for this,' responded the chef seriously. Ettie pondered whether instinctive generosity or a child-hood of scarcity triggered his tendency to over-cater before deciding it was generosity coupled with kindness and a healthy dose of ego.

In the kitchen, after a moment of Claire's stubborn resist-ance—kicking legs, writhing body—Sam settled the baby in her highchair. Ettie handed him a bowl of warmed sweet potato, tasting it first to test the heat. Remembering Claire's earlier response, she turned to the chef and innocently asked, 'This sweet potato, Marcus, it has a flavour I can't identify. Enlighten me?'

The chef, who'd abandoned the idea of a shower, was busy transforming the leftovers into the ingredients for a spectacular potluck dinner. He shrugged. 'But it is only the potato, Ettie. Your tastebuds are in error.'

Reassured, Ettie handed Sam the spoon. 'More down the hatch than down on the floor, if you can manage it,' she said.

'My mum used to pretend the spoon was an aeroplane,' Sam said. 'Worked a treat.'

'Give it a go,' Ettie encouraged. She went to the fridge and withdrew a beer, holding it up for Sam to see. He shook his head. 'Later. After Claire is in bed.'

Ettie nodded and reached for a bottle of white wine.

'You are a genius,' Marcus said warmly. 'Tonight, only a white wine can do justice to this miracle of flavour and textures I will concoct. Cooking the veal a second time should bring it to adequate tenderness, although, I fear, never to a point of velvet.'

Ettie caught Sam's eye and they both held back laughter. 'Your modesty is overwhelming, Chef, as usual,' Sam said, failing to keep a straight face. 'Bullseye!' he shouted as an entire spoonful of sweet potato swung through the air and landed intact in Claire's mouth. 'Clever girl,' he told her, trying not to use the baby voice that Kate found so offensive.

Suddenly, the chef slapped his forehead. 'I am becoming old and forgetful. The sweet potato. I added a small, tiny, *infinitesimal* pinch of cumin and coriander to begin early the process of educating Claire's palate. You were completely correct, Ettie, and I am an old duffer, yes. This is the right word, I believe. Duffer.'

'Ah,' Ettie said, nodding and casually removing the bowl of food from Sam's hand. 'Perhaps it's time for Claire to try the pumpkin and potato combination. Have you tweaked that recipe in any way? A subtle spice, or perhaps . . . ?'

Marcus looked at her, frowning. 'Of course not, my love. These vegetables are a match made in heaven and a pinch of salt suffices to bring out their flavours.'

Ettie discreetly swapped the bowls. Sam raised his eyebrows in a question. Ettie shushed him with a finger to her lips. Sam shrugged his shoulders and resumed his food game.

Later, when Claire was in tucked in bed, her eyelids drawn like a magnet towards her cheeks, Ettie whispered in Sam's ear. 'The spices were a little too . . . rich for Claire's tummy. Might be wise to keep the food very simple for another month.'

Sam grinned. 'Bet it was an eye waterer, eh?'

Ettie smiled. 'We were outdoors, thank goodness, but I reeled.'

CHAPTER SEVEN

MEANWHILE, IN THE TUCKED-AWAY NOOK at the end of Stringy Bark Bay, Lizzie helped clear the dinner table at the GeriEcstasies' communal residence. She rinsed the plates and passed them to Daisy without her usual care. Daisy, moving her wheelchair a little closer, said, 'You seem distracted.' She took an extra moment to jiggle around the crockery in the dishwasher to make more room before she caught Lizzie's eye.

'Sorry. I'm off with the pixies tonight,' Lizzie said.

Daisy, a retired cattle farmer who'd lost the use of her legs when she'd inadvertently stepped between a cow and her new calf, gave Lizzie a look that would cut through hard cheese. 'If there's something on your mind, I'm a good listener and not a gossip.' She paused. 'Not regretting joining us, are you?'

Lizzie placed a soapy hand on Daisy's shoulder. 'Not for a minute.'

'It must be difficult, though. The rest of us . . .' Daisy gestured towards the table where the other residents were lingering over their glasses of wine, 'we've been friends for decades. It would be easy to feel like an outsider, occasionally.'

Lizzie handed Daisy the last plate, pulled the plug and wiped her hands on a tea towel. Daisy finished stacking and closed the dishwasher but didn't move. 'You didn't exactly receive a blue-ribbon introduction to the household, either.'

'All in the past,' Lizzie said reassuringly.

'Forgiven, though?'

Lizzie hung the damp tea towel on the handle of the oven and spun Daisy's wheelchair towards the others. 'Of course. Otherwise, I wouldn't be here.'

Daisy put her hands on the wheels, braking. 'What is it then? You don't have to tell me. That goes without saying. But sometimes it helps to talk about . . .'

'In this case, it would mean breaking a trust. I can't do that.'

Daisy nodded slowly. 'Ah, so it's Kate, isn't it?'

Lizzie's eyes widened in surprise. Daisy caught her expression. 'I thought so. You and Kate, there was a bond. Anyone could see it.' Daisy glanced over her shoulder. 'Let's head over to the window. Leave this lot to their chitchat. I'll tell you what I think is going on. If I'm right, nod. If I'm wrong, call me a silly old fool who should know better than to make up scenarios without any facts to work from.'

As the women prepared to move, Mike Melrose, who handled the body corporate finances for the GeriEcstasy property (originally designed for five retired couples), called out, 'We need your votes to make a decision. Should the fire be lit on any cold evening, or should we hold off until winter officially begins?'

'I'm the wrong person to ask,' Lizzie said. 'I kept the fire going in my old shack right through summer.'

Mike pushed back from the table and stood. He walked over to the two women and took control of Daisy's chair. 'Which way to do you want to face? Outside or inside?'

'Outside, please,' Daisy said.

Once Daisy was in position, Mike turned to Lizzie. 'Through summer? Didn't you roast?' he asked, pulling over a light cane chair for her.

'It . . . simmered, kept the place dry during humid spells, which made it impossible for mould to grow, and I liked the sight of flames in a stove after the sun dropped.'

'Daisy? What do you think?'

'I'll go with the majority vote. However, I do enjoy an evening in front of the fire on a cold night, any time of year.'

Mike nodded and walked back to the table. 'Looks like we need to increase the supply of firewood in the household budget.'

'Sam delivers,' Lizzie called across the room. 'Best to put in an order before the real cold hits and the queue gets rock-concert long.'

Mike resumed his seat at the table. Daisy leaned towards Lizzie, keeping her voice low, not noticing that Sheila, who once wore five-inch heels that could double as deadly daggers, shuffled towards them in sheepskin slippers. 'She's living in your old shack, isn't she?' asked Daisy.

'Who?' Sheila, not known for her tact, immediately tried to muscle in.

Lizzie sighed. Daisy smiled. 'If I hadn't dropped my voice, no one would have tried to listen. Tactical error. Sorry.'

Across the room, chairs scraped on the timber floor as they were pushed back from the table. 'Who?' Sheila repeated, firmly. She turned to look over her shoulder. 'Gavin, I need a chair.'

'Yes, my love,' her husband replied. 'I am, as always, your slave.'

'A lifetime in crippling stilettos for the sake of your business. You're getting off lightly.'

'*Our* business, if memory serves.'

Lizzie looked on helplessly as Mike helped Gavin set up a semi-circle of chairs that faced a large window filled with the black of night. 'An outside spotlight . . .' he murmured, a finger thoughtfully on his lip. 'No!' Lizzie almost shouted. He turned towards her, surprised by her vehemence.

'Darkness is a luxury,' Lizzie added, her tone more subdued.

'I get it, Lizzie dear,' Sheila said sotto voce, as though they were members of an undervalued sisterhood. 'The lighting bills for the shops were crippling.'

Daisy caught Lizzie's eye and smiled. 'Not quite the point, Sheila, but no matter,' Daisy said.

One by one, the household took their places: the cheesemakers; the shoe-shop owners; the cattle farmers; Mike Melrose (widow of the troubled, violent Donna), and Lizzie herself: a retired playwright, who'd once lived high on the escarpment, writing in a tiny, timber house she'd inherited from a beloved friend and mentor.

'Wait!' Sheila held up her hand for attention. 'Are we about to embark on some new adventure? Is there a lot to discuss, or are we celebrating? Do we need to uncork another bottle of wine?'

Corralled by people she'd grown to love and respect, Lizzie tried to tone down the moment with a careless shrug; but, aware she'd been trapped into revealing more than she felt was wise, she warned, 'Whatever is said here tonight remains in the cone of silence. Not a word of this conversation leaves the house. Clear enough?'

Sally Kinnane, a sensible, organised woman, whose love of colourful clothes and clunky jewellery sometimes led to her intelligence and dependability being overlooked, glanced at her husband. 'We're on board,' she said, after David indicated with a barely perceptible tilt of his head that he'd follow her lead.

Lizzie made a steeple with her hands, pivoted, locking eyes, one by one, with the rest of the group. 'Do we have consensus? No matter how much pressure is applied by other interested parties? Okay. As Daisy has already guessed, this is about Kate. I'm sure everyone is aware she's disappeared and that Ettie, Marcus and Sam are sharing baby duties.'

Heads nodded. Mike, sensing a long discussion, rose and went to the fridge for the bottle of wine. He passed around clean glasses and carefully filled them one by one, until he reached Daisy's husband, Rob, who placed a hand over the top of his glass. 'Red, if you wouldn't mind?'

'And for me,' Gavin added, relieved. 'White at this time of the night gives me heartburn.'

Sheila rolled her eyes. 'Nothing to do with the little nip of whisky you have as a nightcap, is it?'

Before Gavin had time to reply, Mike was back with a bottle of shiraz. 'Full of antioxidants and healthier than . . .' he floundered.

'A tonic, I'd call it,' Gavin said, rescuing him.

'About Kate?' Daisy said, steering the conversation back on track.

Lizzie accepted her glass from Mike, lowering it carefully. 'She's living in the shack. Oh, it's a wreck since the storm. Not fit for human habitation, really. But Cliffy—remember him? My dear old neighbour with the dairy herd . . .'

'Of course, we remember. He delivered Kate's baby. Lovely man,' Sally said. 'Typical dairy farmer. Works his guts out and takes better care of his cows than he does of himself. Knew dozens just like him when we made cheeses for a living.'

Her husband, David, nodded. 'Working with dairy cattle. There's no room for airs and graces. Never met one who didn't have his feet solidly anchored to the ground,' he said.

Lizzie continued. 'He called a week ago. Said he went over to the shack when he saw smoke coming from the chimney, lights on after dark. Thought he'd find squatters or—as he put it—farmers of illicit herbs. Instead, he found Kate, who made him swear to secrecy. It took him a week to decide that someone else needed to know where she was. In case he dropped dead, he told me.' Lizzie rubbed at the knuckles on one hand, ill at ease at breaking a confidence.

Mike took a large gulp of wine and investigated the bottom of his glass as though it might hold the collected wisdom of the world. 'Kate is a tough, independent woman who can look after herself. She'd call someone if she got into trouble.'

'That's the thing,' Lizzie said, turning towards him, her face wreathed with concern. 'Cliffy said she's broken. That's the word he used. Broken. Like her spirit has gone to join others in the ancient past and only her shell remains on earth. His words, not mine.'

Sheila harrumphed, dismissive about what she considered esoteric rubbish, though Sally's eyes filled with tears. Daisy gave her useless legs a light whack as if force and sheer will could bring them to life. Mike, Rob, Gavin and David were quiet at first, then dived into their wine, none of them comfortable with emotion. 'Bit extreme,' Mike ventured, when the silence in the room stretched out like a long road on a moonlit night.

Rob, a slight, immaculately dressed man with thinning grey hair who usually relied on his wife, Daisy, to speak for him, as if he trusted her to read his mind accurately, said, 'Interfering in a young woman's life . . . I don't know. . . '

'At this stage, none of us knows what should or could be done to help her, dear. Let's keep our minds open to suggestions. You'll see things differently after a good night's sleep, I'm sure of it.'

'I don't know about that, Daisy,' he said, his eyes dark with doubt.

'We have to get her out of there,' Mike said. 'If the house is a wreck and she's unwell, it's the only solution. Perhaps Sam, Ettie and the chef . . .'

'Cliffy has broken her trust by telling me,' Lizzie said. 'And I've broken his by telling you. She needs help. But whatever I do has to look coincidental, accidental.'

'We, dear. Whatever WE do,' Sheila said. 'You have joined a commune. One for all and all for one.'

Hear, hear.

Lizzie smiled yet felt the drag of worry in all the small muscles of her face. 'Thank you, but Kate is not your problem . . .'

'Don't be silly,' Daisy said impatiently. 'Do you really think we could just sit around playing at being busy in our retirement when there's a . . . *broken* . . . young woman who needs our help? Criminal to turn our backs on her. Frankly, I already have a bucket full of regrets and I don't want any more.'

'Daisy!' Rob said, wringing his hands anxiously. 'What regrets? You've never said anything.' He struggled to his feet, looked around for somewhere to place his glass.

'Not you, Rob, never you,' she said, reaching out to him. 'You are the light of my life—and that's as sentimental as I'm going to get. Now sit down. We need to figure out what to do.'

Hear, hear.

'This calls for a refill,' Gavin said heartily.

'You've had enough.' Sheila stood to remove the glass from his hand.

Lizzie, sensing a shift in the general mood, said, 'It's late. Let's all sleep on it. Come at the problem fresh in the morning.'

Daisy nodded approval. 'It might be wise for us to consider that this young woman needs help beyond our skills.'

Lizzie's eyes filled with tears. 'It's tempting to blame postnatal depression. But in my opinion, the problem was brewing even before the baby was born. Maybe it's beyond us to make a difference, but just like Daisy said, it would haunt me if, one day, I stood by a grave with the words "if only" ricocheting around my skull.'

Hear, hear.

One by one, and with varying degrees of grunts and groans, the residents struggled to their feet. With murmured goodnights, and a light touch on an arm here and there, they made their way to their suites, each wondering at the erratic and unreliable good fortune that had carried them to this point of comfort and contentment in their own lives.

Melrose and Lizzie were the last to go through the door. 'I know all the best mind doctors in the country,' he said. 'If it comes to that . . .'

Lizzie paused and leaned against the wall in the hallway. 'Donna,' she said. 'Do you miss her?'

'I don't miss the constant feeling of anxiety, or the fear of what she might do next, how she might hurt someone else in one of her rages. But all of us here, we did our best. As it turned out, it wasn't enough. It cost a dear friend his life. Meddling, if that's what we end up doing, even with expert advice, well, there are no guarantees it will solve Kate's problem.'

'Ettie says she saw gold in her the first day they met. I saw that same quality when she looked after me so beautifully after I broke my ankle. I cannot give up on her. But the responsibility is mine. As we all know—and you more than anyone—even the noblest of intentions can end in tragedy.'

Beside her, Mike stiffened. 'For what it's worth, everyone knew Donna's state of mind and could choose whether to help or not. No one hesitated. I'll leave you with that thought. Good night.'

Lizzie watched him turn from the hallway into the corridor that led to the suite he'd once shared with Donna, an incandescently beautiful woman: a household name for her role as a star on a long-running soapie. She was violently unhinged, yet he'd protected her from life in an institution. Lizzie felt she could see the cost of caring for Donna in his slow progress along the corridor, and she sighed. Dorothy, who'd left her the shack, had a saying: 'Bad stuff happens fast.' She knew a thing or two, that magnificent woman.

In that moment, Lizzie decided she would hike to her former home the following morning. An innocent visit: to check how it was faring in the aftermath of the storm that had rearranged the coastline and left a corridor of destruction high on the escarpment. To wallow briefly in nostalgia, she would explain, if Kate was suspicious about her arrival; to visit Cliffy, her dearest friend; to pay silent homage to Dorothy, to whom she owed a debt beyond calculation. From there, she'd didn't have a clue what to do. She would play it by ear. But she was damned if that young woman was going to deteriorate any further on her watch.

In the luxurious quarters she now called home, she sat for a while in the old leather armchair that she'd shipped from the shack. Nestled into its wide arms and creaky cushion, she breathed in the smells of her past life—wood smoke, her father's vanilla-scented tobacco—trapped in the upholstery and recalled how Dorothy had shown her the magic of the bush, the life in the earth, the hilarity of the wildlife. 'You be right, daughter,' she told Lizzie. 'You be right. You come with me.' Lizzie looked out the window to where the mangroves shone silver in the night. Now it was her turn, she thought. Her turn to save a life.

CHAPTER EIGHT

THE NEXT MORNING, HIGH ON the escarpment, Kate shuffled around Lizzie's garden, picking up broken branches for kindling to relight the kitchen fire that had gone out overnight. Letting it die was a betrayal of the old woman's rule that the fire should smoulder even on the hottest summer day: it made her feel as though she'd broken a sacred trust. It didn't matter that Lizzie had virtually abandoned the shack, that there was no one to point a finger at her shortcomings and pick away at her self-esteem, as her mother had from the moment she was old enough to speak and understand her first words. Lizzie's shack, Lizzie's rules. She had a duty to fulfil them, even if she couldn't quite understand why they were so critical, when Lizzie no longer lived there.

When her arms were full, she made her way back along the pathway where the large waxy leaves of the dendrobiums spilled over the edges, and the ti trees bent towards the sunlight, which had moved further north and left them partially in shade. She kept her eyes on the ground, alert for the stony-eyed brown snakes that Lizzie said had filthy tempers when riled; and the red-bellied blacks, shy and timid, that slithered out of sight if you gave them space to retreat. She'd met a tiger snake basking in the sun a day after her unsanctioned arrival and stood still with shock until it gave chase and, jolted out of her apathy, she'd sprinted off. But summer was over and even though it was only early autumn, she told herself, soon the reptile world would hunker down for the winter. She turned to take the pathway that led to Lizzie's vegetable garden, which was snugly encased in a wire house called the Birdcage to protect it from wildlife. She'd scavenged the remaining scrappy produce, finding barely enough to sustain her.

On the whole, though, her familiarity with the idiosyncratic quirks of the tank-water system and solar-power supply from her time caring for Lizzie had eased the transition from Oyster Bay to shack living. Each day passed in a blur of basic household chores and finding enough sustenance to keep from starving. But Lizzie's old tea caddy was almost empty and, while she wasn't too fussed about food, brewing tea gave her a sense of control: warm the pot, boil the kettle, measure the tea exactly, pour on hot water while it still bubbled, spin the teapot three times and wait three to five minutes—no longer or the taste would turn bitter. Tea-making at specific times of the day kept her mentally anchored. At night, though, her ears were still attuned to a child's cry, and she woke instantly when a bird whimpered, or a bandicoot squealed. That's when it hit her like a punch in the stomach: her baby was no longer in her care, her Oyster Bay life was in ruins. All that was left was a catastrophic mess of her own making. With no one to hear, sobs turn into howls until, exhausted, she fell asleep as the first feathered revellers announced the break of day.

About to return to the shack with her load of kindling, Kate heard noise erupt from the henhouse. She stood still and listened, puzzled. The chooks had gone to new homes when Lizzie vacated. It was unmistakeable, though. Wing beating, clucking hysteria. She saw Cliffy then, with a brown hen in his arms, stroking her feathers while three more scrabbled, scratched and pecked, vying for supremacy.

'G'day,' Cliffy said. 'Meet your new girls.'

'Cliffy . . .'

'No thanks needed. Nothin' beats a fresh egg first thing in the morning. Sit it on a slice of bread toasted in the smoky heat from the kitchen fire and I reckon it's a meal fit for gods.'

'Cliffy . . .'

'Now, now lass. You can't deny an old man his indulgences. A sin to see the henhouse that Lizzie built like the Taj Mahal empty. She took better care of it than the roof over her own head. Look after the girls, lass, and they'll look after you.' He placed the fourth hen inside the coop with a gentle clucking sound. The argy-bargy among the other three ceased as they rushed up to him and squatted, looking for attention. He gave them all a single stroke along their feathered backs then stepped outside, pulling the wire door closed behind him. 'Let 'em settle in for a week before you turn 'em loose to forage. There's grain in the tub over there. A couple of handfuls twice a day until they can free range.'

'Cliffy . . .' Kate tried again.

'A cuppa wouldn't go astray, lass. Took the liberty of droppin' off a bottle of Clarabelle's milk. Fresh this mornin'. Know how to milk a cow? 'Cause she's comin' back here, soon as I can manage it. The Jerseys are sick to death of her. Only took her on to ease Lizzie's mind.'

Kate made a gesture of surrender.

'If you don't mind me sayin', you're lookin' skinnier than a blade of grass,' Cliffy said. 'As I recall, your scone-makin' skills were right up there after a couple of days under Lizzie's instruction. No. Don't say a word. Not expectin' a scone when I've called in out of the blue like this. But I'm goin' to town this arvo and if you give me a list I'd be happy to drop off supplies on me way back. Take it you'll be needin' flour for the scones?'

Carrying the chook basket, Cliffy babbled all the way to the shack. Inside, he took the kindling from her and dropped to his bony knees in front of the old stove, blowing on the ashes to see if there was a spark. 'Cold as,' he remarked, shaking his head. 'Gunna take a bit to get goin', but you'll be warm through till next summer once you get the hang of keepin' it simmerin' through the day and buildin' it up at night to last through to mornin'.' He looked up at Kate. 'I take it you're not goin' anywhere for a while, eh?'

Kate turned away and filled the kettle, grateful as always, that Lizzie had kept the shack equipped in case she felt like a break from the GeriEcstasies—or they needed a break from her.

Cliffy rummaged in the wood box and found matches and firelighters, then he made a hole in the ashes the size of a soup bowl and set the kindling over the natural firelighter cubes. He went outside to Lizzie's wood heap and returned with a few smaller pieces that he balanced in the shape of a teepee over the kindling. 'Reckon that'll go,' he said, striking a match and leaning in to set fire to the fuel. 'Leave the door ajar for a minute or two, to get the oxygen in. Not too long, mind, or you'll smoke out the house. That cuppa ready yet lass? I've got the thirst of a horse in the desert.'

Kate set a tray with mugs, milk and sugar, which she remembered Cliffy enjoyed in a brew *strong enough to stand up a spoon*. She put the kettle on to boil. When it was ready, she filled the teapot and led the way down the hallway, where the pale outlines of what was once Lizzie's art collection made a pattern on the walls.

Cliffy, following on her heels, popped his head into the parlour and checked the ceiling. 'Tarp's holdin' out the rain but it won't last forever. That roof needs a proper fix if you're plannin' on movin' in for the foreseeable.'

They settled into the old cane chairs on the veranda in a routine honed when Kate cared for Lizzie with her broken ankle: a time that resulted in Kate giving birth during one of the worst storms in living memory, the baby delivered by Cliffy with the confidence of an obstetrician and in the dead of night. A baby, as he'd learned from Lizzie, that Kate had abandoned for reasons known only to herself.

'Thanks for not asking any questions,' Kate said, as if she'd read the turn his mind had taken.

'None of my business, but I've a good pair of ears for a fella of my slowly advancin' years, if the mood takes you.'

Kate laughed, a small and metallic sound, but it seemed to strike Cliffy like music. 'Lizzie says you're a spring chicken, compared to her,' she said.

'Fifteen years between us, not that we ever counted. All in the mind, anyway, if you ask me.'

'What is?'

'Age. A good day in the paddock or the garden and it's like havin' the years stripped off you.'

'Refill?' Kate held up the teapot in a query.

'Nah. Better get home to finish vacuumin' before I head off to the shops.'

Kate looked at him, astonished. 'Vacuum? Pictured you as more of a straw-broom bloke myself.'

'Heh, heh. Not much of either, if you want the honest truth.'

'Cliffy? Thank you.'

'It's nothin', lass. Glad of the company. Put the spring back in me step, you have.'

Without another word, Cliffy hitched his overalls, adjusted the braces and pulled on the boots he'd removed before entering the house. With a wave over his shoulder, he set off down a sandy track that wound through dense bush. Less than a kilometre further along, the scrub suddenly opened to wide green pasture with the signature aroma of well-fed cattle hanging in the air like heavy pollen. 'Think of the hilltops in *The Sound of Music*,' he'd once proudly explained to Kate. 'That's where I grow the best milk this side of the Divide, although there's always some ignorant blighter ready to argue the point.'

After he'd gone, Kate remained seated in the morning sun for a long time, unable to find the energy to tackle any chores, to create order out of chaos. She felt the subtle shift in a south-easterly and caught the whiff of smoke. She jumped with a start, thinking, the fire. She rushed inside and threw on the last of the kindling to bring back enough heat to keep the logs burning. Then she turned down the airflow knob and checked her watch. Two hours and another log would have to go on. The wood pile would need restocking for cold weather. Recalling seeing an axe in the ruins of what had been Lizzie's shed, and without making a conscious decision, she headed there to begin sifting through the rubbish: tidying up; searching for tools she'd need to get through the winter and make small repairs to the shack. The hours slid by, until she realised it was too dark to continue.

After a dinner of fried tomatoes and two fried eggs courtesy of Cliffy's industrious ISA Browns, she sat in front of the fire, tamping down self-recrimination, guilt, self-loathing, the awful knowledge that, all along, her relationship with Sam had been a betrayal, the baby a constant reminder of her duplicity.

She woke in her chair in the middle of the night. Outside, the masked lapwings were arguing like rabble-rousers at a protest meeting. She stoked the fire, which had reduced to a bed of glowing coals, and went to bed, her cheeks scaly with dried tears, a tight band around her chest that she felt might cut off the oxygen to her lungs at any moment.

⌒

In Stringy Bark Bay the following morning, the GeriEcstasies gathered at the kitchen table in colourful pyjamas, several of them feeling a high dose of enthusiasm they'd believed lost to them forever. 'We've got lots of ideas to throw in front of you,' Sheila said, eyes bright with purpose, when Lizzie entered the room.

'Coffee anyone?' Daisy asked, giving Lizzie, already dressed in her daily outfit of khaki trousers, a white shirt and baby blue cashmere sweater, time to settle.

'I'll make a big pot,' Mike said, pulling out a chair for Lizzie. He rose, dignified in a navy-coloured silk dressing gown with red paisley lapels. His slippers, tan calfskin, made a slight flapping noise as he crossed the floor to the kitchen area.

'Not for me, thanks Mike, I made one earlier, and that's my quota for the day,' Lizzie said. 'Makes my heart race if I overdo it.'

'Now Lizzie,' Sheila said firmly, 'we've all agreed this is an opportunity. Let's face it: we're bored. We live in paradise, a privilege, yes, but we're used to being busy, ticking over the little grey cells. We've become fluffy-headed with contentment, which as anyone over the age of seventy knows is an open invitation to entering the possibly joyful—but more likely terrifying—world of doolally. When I say joyful, every moment is a new moment, I've been told—although the person in question *was* talking about one of her cats.'

'Just call it dementia, Sheila,' Daisy said.

'We need a project to stop the atrophy, and this is it,' Sheila continued without acknowledging Daisy's input. 'We're all in. Whatever you need, we'll make it happen. Oh, this is already fun and we haven't even started! A happy snap to mark the beginning of the adventure.' She raised her phone; Gavin snatched it away.

'For God's sake, Sheila, it's not even eight o'clock.'

Lizzie spread her hands on the table, unable to meet anyone's eye. 'So kind. All of you. I don't know what to say. It's just . . . we need to go slowly. There's no rush . . .'

'Oh but . . .' Sheila began.

'Cliffy is keeping a close eye on her. Too much interference at once will scare Kate. She'll bolt—who knows where.'

Daisy joined in. 'We might do more harm than good, Sheila. None of us wants that.'

Lizzie watched the excitement drain out of Sheila.

'Nothing wrong with making plans, though,' Lizzie said, hoping to placate.

Sheila brightened instantly. 'Yes, yes. Can I tell you what we've been thinking?'

'What *you've* been thinking,' Rob muttered.

Lizzie smiled her encouragement and Mike brought over a tray of mugs. Coffee for one and all except Lizzie. He'd prepared a herbal tea for her. David withdrew a notebook from a pocket. Sally passed him a pencil and an eraser. 'We thought we'd jot down any ideas that come up,' she said.

Sheila unfolded an A4 piece of paper covered in scribbled notes. 'I'm ahead of you,' she said, waving it in front of everyone like a flag.

Rob, morose, sat with his eyes downcast. 'I'm not sure about this. Yes, we all want to help. But look at us, a bunch of people with a poor track record, and on the brink of our ninth decade. We're dangerous even to ourselves!'

Daisy reached out to take her husband's hand. 'That's why you couldn't sleep. You've been worrying all night?'

He nodded and scrabbled for a handkerchief within the voluminous folds of his red and green tartan dressing gown, which Daisy suddenly noticed was inside out. He blew his nose loudly. 'We did our best for Donna but the consequences were dreadful. Cameron would still be sitting here with us if we'd had the guts to do what needed to be done. I'm sorry Mike, but that's the truth.'

On the other side of the table, Mike went pale under his tan. Daisy lifted Rob's hand to her cheek and held it there in a gesture of such tenderness and support that Lizzie's eyes filled. 'I'm sorry,' Rob continued, almost stuttering with the strain of what he had to say. 'I will not be part of any plan to interfere in this young woman's life, no matter how noble the motives.'

Sheila was the first to respond. 'But there's a big difference between Donna and Kate,' she insisted. 'Kate has a future. Donna . . .'

'No need to go into details,' Mike said unhappily. 'As for guilt about what happened, I carry enough for all of us.'

Everyone spoke at once, voices rising as each one struggled to reassure Mike that the blame should be shared: they'd known the risks. And while it was clear Donna could be violent, they insisted, no one ever suspected she was capable of murder.

Lizzie remained silent, witnessing emotions that had rarely been articulated after Donna's death: shame, horror, helplessness, the fear they'd been too old to be trusted with the task. 'The worst thing about age,' Sally said, picking at a thread on her sleeve, 'is the humility and indecisiveness it brings.'

'That's why we need a project,' Sheila said, thumping the table.

'Your enthusiasm is wonderful,' Daisy said, 'but let's not forget this is about Kate, not us. Our lives are . . .'

'Regrets are futile,' Sheila said, her voiced raised slightly, 'and death is irreversible. We can't let the past hold us back.'

Lizzie stood and retied her sweater around her shoulders. 'How about we all be guided by what Cliffy has to say? I'm going to hike to the shack today on the pretext of checking how it's holding up. I'll make a full report at dinner. It's my turn to cook but . . .'

'Leave it to me,' Sally, a passionate cook, said. 'There's a new recipe I want to try.'

Rob cleared his throat. 'As long as everyone is quite clear that I will have nothing to do with this. Naturally, Daisy is free to make up her own mind.'

Any last traces of the early euphoria in the room were now well and truly dispelled.

'What's the recipe?' Sheila asked Sally, to distract from rising gloom.

'Chicken and rice, heaps of ginger and garlic. A purple vegetable to nourish our slowly atrophying brains. That's a joke, Sheila. Found it in a magazine at the dentist and photographed the page with my phone. Healthy as.'

Daisy looked around the gathering and declared that it was time to get dressed for the day. 'There is nothing helpful nor cheerful,' she said, 'about seeing elderly folks wandering around in their pyjamas after ten in the morning.'

CHAPTER NINE

LIZZIE ASKED MIKE TO FERRY her to Kate's abandoned Oyster Bay house by boat. It would cut the walking distance to her old shack by more than half, and it was the most direct route when there was daylight to show the track. 'I am not as youthful as I like to think,' she said.

Mike nodded. 'None of us are. Although in my mind's eye, I see myself as an eternal forty-year-old.'

'Me, too,' Lizzie replied. 'It's one of the few kindnesses old age bestows.'

They set off with the wind at their backs. The new commuter boat—bought in unanimous agreement after Lizzie said she would happily captain, instruct and navigate until other would-be sailors felt confident—bounced forwards on a choppy sea.

'No whitecaps yet,' Lizzie shouted over the engine noise, twisting to look behind where the wake from the boat frothed. 'But they'll appear by afternoon unless the wind drops.'

Mike shifted the throttle down a couple of notches. 'How long to do you think you'll be?' The boat quieted and slowed, but the wind and a following sea kept it on course to Oyster Bay.

'You handle a boat so well,' Lizzie said. 'Not the novice I was led to believe you were.'

Mike slipped into neutral. 'Think about it, Lizzie. Not many landlubbers would stumble into Cook's Basin on foot. Even fewer would find the gem where the estuary meets Stringy Bark Bay and see the potential in an old ruin of a building.'

Lizzie gave Mike a long, serious look. 'Do you want to talk about it?'

'Here?'

'Well, private conversations are tricky at the house. As much as I love the place, I always feel as though there are ears flapping in shadowy corners.'

Mike laughed. 'Sheila has an insatiable thirst for information, but she's well-meaning.'

'Up to a point,' Lizzie said. 'I detect small hints of narcissism occasionally.'

'She craves attention, that's all. Gavin was . . . not always fully attentive during their marriage.'

'I've never heard infidelity described so delicately,' Lizzie said.

'Are you shocked?'

'Of course not. I'm curious, though. You and Donna . . .'

'I never went off-piste, if that's what you're asking.'

Lizzie rummaged in her backpack and pulled out a bottle of water. 'Forgive me, it's none of my business. You were about to reveal how you found Stringy Bark Bay.' She offered Mike a swig, but he shook his head. She took a deep drink and wiped her lips with the back of her hand. 'Not very elegant but . . .'

'I was a young newspaper reporter. I was asked to write a story about a headless body that washed ashore . . .'

'I remember!'

'I never forgot the beauty of the bays. Came back every time Donna spent time in . . . care. Took sailing lessons, learned to thread bait on a hook and gut a fish without losing a finger.'

'I've forgotten, did they identify the body—a woman, I think? Did they find out who killed her?'

Mike pushed forwards the throttle and they picked up speed. 'Yeah. She was a sex worker, trafficked from Thailand. One of her clients . . .'

Lizzie held up her hands. 'That's right. Awful. Do the others know about your long-term links with Cook's Basin?'

'Stopped coming here about thirty years ago. And when Donna and I returned together, I saw no reason to dig up the past. Anyway, she needed to be kept ignorant of any earlier connections for our plan to work.'

'Kate noticed your ability with knot-tying when you first arrived. Made her curious and suspicious. People who try to hide things make her hair stand on end, she told me.'

Mike asked, 'Any idea what's going on with Kate?'

'I'm not a fan of guessing. I'll know more when I return.'

'Call when you're close to Frankie's boatshed on the way back. I'll pick you up.'

When they reached the mouth of Oyster Bay, Mike slowed, hugging the open navigation channel between yachts hanging off their moorings. Sheltered from the wind, the bay, deep green under an overcast sky, rippled. A parade of xanthorrhoeas stood at attention, spears rising straight and strong from wide grassy skirts.

'You'll be careful, won't you?' he said, sliding alongside Kate's pontoon and reaching out to grab a cleat.

'The cold weather will slow down the snakes. And I could walk that track in my sleep.'

'Still . . .'

'It's kind of you to worry. Here we go: the infamous Lizzie disembarkation roll.'

At the boatshed next door, the shipwright Frankie put down a can of paint and dashed along the foreshore, calling, 'Kate's not home, before you kill yourself! Oh, it's you, Lizzie. Didn't recognise you on all fours. Kate's gone, though. A while now.'

'Haul up an old woman, would you?'

He offered two strong hands and Lizzie shot to her feet. 'Thanks,' she said, brushing her knees. Mike inclined his head, acknowledging Frankie, then passed over a backpack and walking stick. He gave a little salute before pushing away from the pontoon, reserving a stellar smile for Lizzie. 'Call me when you're ready,' he repeated. Lizzie waved and turned to Frankie. 'Taking the short cut to check on my old shack,' she explained.

Frankie lifted his Greek fisherman's cap and scratched his scalp, the skin white as bleached bone. 'Nothin' to see, is what I heard on the grapevine.'

'The shack is okay. Sort of. The shed was demolished.'

'Ah. Bloody grapevine. Less reliable than ever. Fancy a cuppa before you head off? Kettle's not long boiled.'

'Best get going.'

Frankie nodded. Halfway back to the boatshed, he turned and stared to where Lizzie had paused for a breather before tackling the cabbage palm tunnel. 'Watch yourself!' he shouted. 'Pains me to mention it, but you're no spring chicken.'

Lizzie made a rude sign, noticed an ever-increasing constellation of brown marks on her hands. Age spots: although since *age* had become a dirty word, they were probably called something much more exotic these days.

∽

Lizzie scanned the landscape, quickly separating wallaby tracks, which led to dead ends, from the walking track: which was, however, in such poor condition it could easily be mistaken for an animal trail. Satisfied she'd read the signs correctly, she strode forwards at a steady pace, pausing every so often to catch her breath and to look back the way she'd come, to make sure her bearings were still on target. Soft living, she thought, did no one any favours.

With every careful step, she struggled to devise a strategy to handle Kate, imagining one script after another. Talking out loud occasionally, as she once did when she wrote plays, to test the sound of words, the truth in them. By the time she reached the scrubby outer perimeter of the land she'd once called home, she'd given up trying to predict what might happen and how to respond to any situation. Anyway, Kate homed in on lies like a long thin needle jiggled in a borer hole until the grub had been fatally pierced. Lizzie didn't relish being skewered and exposed as a fraud.

She emerged from the last of the scratchy bush, caught sight of her shack and almost wept with nostalgia for a youth that could never be recaptured, not even in her dreams. The awful irony, she thought, was that the times she feared would break her were now tinted to softness, the pain dulled to nothing, leaving her bewildered and mystified by what had once seemed so critically important it might suck the marrow from her backbone.

She would try to convey that perspective to Kate, if the right moment presented itself. Or perhaps numbness to the past was one of the few blessings bestowed by ageing? She sighed inwardly, threw back her shoulders and walked towards the veranda where the

French doors were wide open. She swallowed the impulse to call out and announce herself and clattered down the hallway to alert Kate to a visitor. As it turned out, the house was empty, although the fire flickered lazily in the kitchen and a kettle murmured on the hob.

'Did Cliffy tell you I was here?' Lizzie spun around. Kate stood in the doorway, her face twisted with fear, her hands clenched around the handle of a shovel.

'Good God, Kate. You almost gave me a heart attack.' Lizzie sank into a chair at the kitchen table.

'I thought you were a murderer. Or something,' Kate said, dropping the shovel and going to the sink to wash her hands.

'So this is where you've ended up. You know the whole of Cook's Basin has a theory about whether you've . . .' Lizzie held up the fingers of her left hand and ticked them off. 'A: Done a runner. B: Jumped off a cliff. C: Gone off to live like a hermit in the red centre of this parched and godforsaken land. D: Sorry, I'm getting carried away.' She smiled, trying to lighten the moment, desperate to deflect from implicating Cliffy. 'If you must know, I came to check on the shack. It calls me back, always has. And while I still have two good legs . . . I see the kettle has boiled. I could murder a cup of tea.'

Kate hesitated, then the fear and fury seemed to drain out of her. 'Do you mind me being here?' she asked. She reached for the teapot, measured three teaspoons into it. 'Bugger. Forgot to warm the pot.'

Lizzie searched for signs of the broken young woman Cliffy had described but beyond her thinness and a sort of febrile intensity at odds with the person she remembered as clinically calm, there was nothing to suggest Kate had lost her will. Lizzie also figured that if she truly meant to cut off all future contact with Sam and her child, choosing to flee to the shack was an odd way of doing it. Respite, she wondered? A cry for help?

'You won't get any complaints from me,' Lizzie said, letting her shoulders relax.

'I didn't think you'd ever come back,' Kate said. 'Milk, no sugar, as I recall.'

'Perfect.'

'I can leave, if that's what you want.'

Lizzie accepted a mug and blew on the top to cool the brew. 'I've given up any rights to the shack so make the most of it. As long as you're aware that, eventually, someone will come along to claim it.'

Kate nodded. 'Cliffy called you, didn't he?'

Lizzie sighed, resigned. 'Yes.'

'Does Sam know? Ettie?'

'I haven't told either of them. That's your call.'

'Cliffy . . .'

'Told me because he wanted someone to know in case anything happened to him and he couldn't keep an eye on you. He knew I wouldn't betray you.'

'I should be grateful . . .'

'Yes. You should.'

Silence fell like a heavy blanket as each woman held back from saying things she might later regret. After a while, Lizzie stood, rinsed her mug and went to the back door. 'The dendrobiums. Are they . . . ?'

'Slowly recovering. I've given them some orchid food. Well, Cliffy came by with a bag. Said you'd haunt him for eternity if he let them die on his watch.'

'Would you mind if I took a walk around the garden?'

Kate opened the door and stood aside to let Lizzie go first. 'You were here first. Clarabelle is back with her calf.'

'That awful name,' Lizzie said, rolling her eyes. 'Cliffy has a knack for terrible names. He has a Pansy, Tansy, Flossie and I've forgotten what else. Rabbit names, I think, like Flopsy and Mopsy.'

'Serious?' Kate asked, scrunching her face in a comic gesture of distaste.

'And they're the least ridiculous of them!'

Lizzie could think of a thousand questions but held back, not sure how to handle this hesitant version of a woman she'd always considered to be tough-minded and independent. She worried Kate could easily close down emotionally and she'd be left without a way to ferret out the reason behind her fleeing to a shack that was barely habitable in summer. Let alone winter. So she held her tongue and, in silence, the two women toured the garden, still showing signs of storm damage but bouncing back in places with green-tipped vigour. Every so often, Lizzie plucked a dead bloom, pulled strappy yellowed leaves from the spider lilies, picked up dead branches on the pathway and threw them into the bush. She wished she'd brought along secateurs. It was the perfect time to prune.

When the silence became uncomfortable, Lizzie halted and turned to face the young woman.

'What exactly are your plans, Kate? Any idea? I'm not prying. It's just . . .' And Lizzie suddenly had what she later told the GeriEcstasies was a brainwave. 'I've started a fitness regime with my fellow housemates. Long bushwalks, a little bush regeneration where it's needed. I'd hoped to bring them here one day.'

'If you want me to go, say so,' Kate said tersely. 'Right now, Lizzie, the world is my oyster . . .'

'Cliché, Kate. Sam once told me you were appalled when he fell back on them to make a point.'

'And yet here I am, already falling into bad habits. Is that what you mean?'

Lizzie found a place to sit on a rock wall, crossed her ankles, folded her hands. 'You're a young woman with more talent than anyone has a right to. What are you going to do? Live like a hermit until you wake up one day and realise how many precious years have slipped by unnoticed? I don't want to preach . . .'

'Then please don't.'

'But I'm going to anyway. There's a whole lot of people who love and care about you and who have given up their freedom and careers to pick up after you. Ettie . . . no, don't interrupt. Ettie has taken on a baby when she should be running a business. Marcus, who'd retired to go fishing and live out his golden years in peaceful contentment, is on his feet twelve hours a day cooking to keep the café viable—a café in which you have a financial interest. As for Sam . . .'

'Leave it, Lizzie,' Kate snapped. 'You've made your point.'

'The thing is, Kate, all the people around you are in damage control. At some point, though, even the best intentions collapse under pressure.'

'I don't have to listen to this.'

Lizzie, torn between compassion and a desire to force Kate to be practical, grabbed Kate's arm when she tried to walk away. 'Yes. You do. The others, they're afraid to speak their minds because they love you and would never hurt you. I care about you, too. But truly? I have no idea what's going on here. I don't know much about postnatal depression, but surely if that's at the root of blowing up your life you'd have enough sense to get help. You're one of the smartest women I know, Kate, so this . . . this . . .' She struggled to find the right word. '*Situation* is beyond my comprehension. If you're ill, I beg of you, get help. We will all support you for however long it takes to get you back on track. Please, you must understand that running away isn't the solution and . . .'

'It's not Sam's baby.' The words spat out, like poison, Kate's face red with anger and remorse. 'Okay? Get it? It's all a lie, Lizzie. A great, big, fat, ugly lie.'

Lizzie felt the blood drain from her face. She stared at Kate, the ground, Kate, then rested her head in her hands. 'You're sure?'

'So you see, I am no different from the mother whom I despised and judged, jeered and condemned. In a way, I am much worse. She was a child when her father began abusing her. She didn't know right from wrong. But I knew exactly what I was doing the night Claire was conceived—oh, I don't mean it happened deliberately. When I realised I was pregnant, I was appalled. So yes, I took the cowardly and selfish way out. I couldn't bear the thought of hurting Sam, disappointing Ettie, seeing locals look away every time I walked past. I am not fit to be among good people. You see that, don't you? You must see that.'

Lizzie remained seated. In the trees, birds twittered. Above, the sky, vast and empty, clean and uncomplicated, throbbed blue. This is nothing in terms of the universe, and yet it is everything, she thought. 'Give me a hand up, would you?' she asked, stretching out an arm. Kate, remembering the days when she cared for Lizzie, placed her hand under a shoulder and gently hoisted instead of yanking. Lizzie looked at the young woman before her, the deep shadows under her eyes, the painful thinness of her body, the sea-green eyes dark with despair. In the end, feeling inadequate but unable to think of a way to proceed, she said, 'It's a bit of a mess. Why don't you tell me about it over another cup of tea.'

'That's a hell of an understatement for a woman who once made a living as a writer, if you don't mind me saying so.' Lizzie recognised a clumsy attempt at humour to disguise guilt, shame and what she guessed was more deep-seated self-loathing than postnatal depression. But she was unequipped to diagnose the underlying issues leading to Kate leaving her child. As always, when stumped for an answer, she took refuge in practicalities. 'No one died, Kate. That's irretrievable. This situation is not. Now, run ahead and put on the kettle. I am parched. And if you don't mind, I might spend the night. These old bones are creaking in ways I've never heard before. I imagine you have a spare set of sheets somewhere. I do like a crisp bed. You see, Kate, how the biggest problems are inevitably reduced to human needs and comforts?' She patted the young woman on the shoulder and sent her off with a light push in the small of her back, then waited a while, struggling to absorb the information.

Eventually, when she figured the tea would have brewed, she texted Mike.

Have decided to stay the night. Nothing to worry about.

And that, she thought, accompanied by a loud sigh, was the greatest understatement of all.

CHAPTER TEN

LIZZIE DAWDLED OVER GETTING HER room ready for the night, as the full impact of Kate's revelation began to weigh on her.

Kate, who'd bought two of everything for her own bed when she first became a squatter in Lizzie's old territory, tried to insist on getting the room ready. 'Find a perch in front of the fire,' she'd said. But Lizzie couldn't let it happen. It felt too much like the first shuffling steps towards dependence. Her few months of absence from the shack had opened her eyes to the shabby, barely stitched together framework of her former existence. She was torn between feeling proud she'd hung on for so long, and ashamed that she'd let things deteriorate to such an extent, hiding the worst of it with wicker chairs, soft floral cushions and pretty 'bugger-it' baskets in which to fling untidy odds and ends. She felt every day of her current age as she tucked in the sheets and flailed around, trying unsuccessfully to stuff a doona into a cotton cover, eventually opting to fling a blanket over it instead. When it was done, she sat on the edge of the mattress and considered the evening ahead.

Poor Sam, she thought. Poor, idealistic, good-hearted, kind and self-sacrificing Sam, who'd never done anyone a bad turn in his life and who seemed to trigger catastrophe with every good deed. Knowledge of Kate's duplicity could kill every generous instinct in his body. As for Kate, she wondered if revealing the background to abandoning Sam and her child might have helped her towards . . . what? Healing? Acceptance? Or even more deeply entrenched guilt and despair? If she had to guess, Kate's mental health might flip either way and Rob had made a valid point that interfering could do more harm than good. But Kate's spirit was not truly broken, she was sure of it. Lizzie tried to imagine how she might feel in the same situation. Recalled the sadness and regret that she'd lacked the courage to raise a child as a single mother and, instead, had chosen to terminate a pregnancy in the days when it was illegal and dangerous. She recalled the grief that followed that decision and, more than sixty years after the event, had to fight back tears. She lay on the pillows, intending to rest her back for a moment or two and woke with a start half an hour later when Kate tapped on the door. 'Are you okay, Lizzie? Dinner is ready.'

'Coming,' Lizzie called, struggling to gather her woolly thoughts. Where to begin, she wondered. Where the bloody hell to start unravelling a story that could shatter so many lives. And what— if anything—could she do about it?

Kate was standing at the bedroom door when she opened it, holding a tartan wrap in her hands. 'It's a chilly evening, even in front of the fire. You'll need this.'

Lizzie, surprised by Kate's thoughtfulness under the circumstances, examined the garment and smiled. 'Where on earth did you find it? I haven't seen it for years.'

'There was a box under the bed in the spare room. I didn't think you'd mind if I opened it.'

Lizzie frowned, trying to remember the origins of the shawl. 'I bought it on a trip to Scotland, I think, in a summer more than thirty years ago, on an afternoon that felt like our coldest winter day. It looked ridiculous when I wore it here.'

'It's very beautiful,' Kate said.

'I must have loved it once. Only my favourite things went into that camphor laurel box.'

'There's a matching hat, sort of a beret thing.'

'Oh God. Leave that where it is, please.'

Kate led the way to the kitchen, which was dimly lit by a single lamp on the dresser. The fire blazed and the smell of pork, mushrooms and spices simmering in a cast-iron pot on the stove made Lizzie's mouth water. 'You're turning into a real cook.'

Kate made a deprecating movement with her head. 'Cliffy keeps dropping in with food parcels.'

'I can honestly report that in all the decades he and I have shared this tableland, he never once appeared holding a pot of stew. I wasn't even sure he knew how to cook!' She lifted the lid and stuck her nose in the pot. 'I can smell cinnamon, star anise. Who knew the old boy had it in him.'

'What's his background?' Kate asked. 'I tiptoe around him, afraid to bring back memories of Agnes, so I know almost nothing.'

'Been on the farm since he was a boy. Taken in by Agnes's parents to help with the dairy. He was an orphan, I think. Or a foster child. I remember Agnes telling me the clothes on his back were all he owned, not even a pair of shoes, when he arrived.'

'So that's where it comes from,' Kate murmured.

'What comes from?'

'That rare combination of toughness and forgiveness found in people who know what it's like to do it hard.'

'Sam did it hard after his parents were killed in a car accident,' Lizzie said. 'The story of how he went out to sea in a leaky dinghy followed by the Misses Skettle, who had no intention of letting him die on their watch, is now legendary in Cook's Basin.'

Kate ignored or failed to recognise the implication in Lizzie's words and reached for a white bowl Lizzie didn't recognise. She looked around with fresh eyes. New things leaped out from ancient, bendy shelving. Bowls. Crockery. Even a vase, old-fashioned wavy glass, but not from the stash she had left behind. The mantelpiece, stripped bare of the mementoes she'd carried to her new home, had a different personality. Pictures in silver frames of a baby. Ettie and Marcus. Sam. Jimmy. A man Lizzie didn't recognise. She almost reeled when she suddenly understood Kate's departure from her child and Oyster Bay hadn't been the irrational act of an emotionally unbalanced and stressed young mother but planned with precision and care.

Taking her life in her hands, Lizzie picked up the photograph of the unknown man and held it towards Kate so there could be no mistake. 'Who's this?' she asked.

Kate gave a faint smile, immediately understanding the subtext of the question. 'My half-brother,' she said. 'He lives in England.'

'I didn't know . . .'

'My mother had a child as a result of being abused by her father. The baby ended up with adoptive parents on the other side of the world. She told me about him just before she died. No details, just that he existed. Finding him became a sort of holy-grail quest. Turns out, he's a lovely man, and has all his fingers and toes, in case you're wondering.'

Before Lizzie could react, Kate added, 'It's a long story, Lizzie, not particularly pleasant.' She ladled a generous serve of stew. Passed it to Lizzie. Did the same for herself, although the amount barely covered the base of the plate. Despite the circumstances, they sat at the kitchen table set with silverware, bread and butter plates, even paper napkins.

Lizzie wondered how long it had taken Kate to smuggle in all the accessories she clearly believed necessary for a civilised existence. If she'd used her car, she thought, Cliffy would have been alerted. Then it hit her: Kate knew Cliffy's routines, the day he went shopping every week, the timing of his early morning milk deliveries.

Where to find the key to the entrance gate to the National Park. She could have done it all in one trip.

Night closed in, a dark curtain. The hoot of an owl echoed mournfully. The clink of forks on porcelain. Lizzie scraped the last of the sauce with her finger, smiling in apology. 'Too good to leave a drop,' she said.

Fire shadows danced on walls. Every so often a gust of cold air slunk under the door, wrapping around their ankles. Lizzie fetched a towel and pushed it hard against the gap. 'Never be too proud to stuff the cracks in the floorboards with newspaper, too,' she said. She looked towards the fire, missing the presence of her father's leather armchairs. Big and solid and Art Deco in style, with arms so wide they could seat two extra adults, they had resided by the hearth until she removed them to her new home. 'I wonder if Cliffy's hoarded something more comfortable than these kitchen chairs in his shed? A fire always needs an armchair or two. I'll ask him in the morning.'

Kate cleared their empty plates and quickly washed them in the sink, leaving them to drain. Lizzie stoked the fire and pulled a chair nearer, stretching her legs so her feet were close enough to soak in the warmth. Kate filled the kettle and placed it on the hob. 'Tea?' she asked.

Kate also offered store-bought ginger shortbread, then paced around the room, fiddling with inconsequential details: readjusting a mug handle on the sideboard so it faced outwards, riddling cinders with the poker, adding a fresh log.

Lizzie waited, feeling Kate's earlier revelation still cannon-shot-loud in the silence. She bit into the biscuit with a loud crunch and, as the wind picked up outside, she looked at the ceiling.

'The leaks in the roof . . .'

'I've been getting quotes from builders,' Kate interrupted, defensive now.

'I could never find a contactor brave enough to tackle the sand tracks while carrying a load of building materials.'

'I have two blokes coming next week. Yes, I've cleared it with the rangers. I hope you don't mind, Lizzie. I know I'm taking liberties.'

'I'm happy to see the old shack being brought back to life. But Kate . . .'

'Yes?'

'You do know this can't go on forever.' Lizzie brushed crumbs from her lap.

'Yes, of course. But I wondered . . .'

'Yes?'

'If you continued to list this place as your primary address I could be your tenant . . .'

'But it's not true, is it?'

Kate visibly slumped as she made the tea. Tears filled her eyes. 'No. I'm sorry, I should never have suggested it.'

Lizzie scrambled to find a solution. 'On the other hand, you're investing in the preservation of the property. That must give you certain rights.'

Kate looked directly at Lizzie for the first time. 'Do you think so?'

'Well, yes. Perhaps.'

'Thank you, Lizzie.'

'Kate . . .'

The young woman bent her head, her dark hair fell forwards, hiding her face.

'All this tiptoeing . . . what you said. I understand now. The anguish, I mean. Uncertainty. Even . . . the running away.' Lizzie accepted a mug of tea from Kate. Steam spiralling upwards, the earthy scent almost masked by a heavy citrus addition to the brew that she was unable to identify. 'Is there any of that cognac lying around?'

Kate shook her head.

'Ah, well, if you want to talk, we'll do it stone cold sober. *Do you want to talk?* It's nobody's business but yours. But we are all here to help, if that's what you need. I'm sure you know that.'

Kate's fists clenched. Released. Expressions whipped across her face. Despair. Regret. Shame. Somewhere deep, the pressing need to unburden, the weight of secrecy unbearable. 'I don't know what to do, Lizzie. Sam is such a good man . . . but if I say there were days when I wanted to shake loose his moral certainty and hit him over the head with it, would that make any sense to you?'

'I once had a friend who could never admit defeat. During a power outage caused by torrential rain and flooding, he managed to hook up his house power to the battery of his car. I remember his words: *a crisis is always an opportunity if you look at it the right way.* I recall at the time, I wanted to punch him.'

Kate gave a small laugh. 'Yes. That's it exactly.'

Lizzie looked at her watch. 'It's still early. Neither of us has anywhere to go . . . nothing you say, of course, will ever be repeated.' She indicated Kate should pull up another chair and join her in front of the fire.

Kate sat primly, hands folded in her lap. After a minute or two, she tweaked the fabric at the knee of her jeans and, with a shudder, looked directly at Lizzie. 'The lies, the duplicity and, underlying that, the shame, it eats away at you.'

Lizzie nodded but remained silent.

'Have you ever been in love? Madly, irrationally, insanely in love?'

Lizzie smiled sadly. 'Once. It nearly killed me.'

Kate exhaled. 'You'll understand, then.'

'Why don't you start at the beginning. And Kate? I'm not here to judge. Only to help.'

Lizzie gave the young woman time to organise her thoughts. She considered Sam, the betrayal of a good man, his adoration for a child that held none of his DNA, whether there could be any acceptable resolution to an age-old impasse that was so often based on ego and ownership, blood bonds, inheritance, instead of love and care. Humans, she thought, with their never-ending capacity to summon emotional havoc, were blind when passion overrode common sense, and they became convinced the only person who could ensure happiness was also the individual who had done them the most harm.

Kate began in a small voice. 'I was eighteen years old. A first-year cadet on a financial newspaper. Eager to make a mark. I rubbed shoulders with workmates who had university degrees, experience, track records that included Walkley Awards for investigative journalism, and colleagues who had access to the private phone numbers of powerful politicians and business leaders of hallowed financial institutions.'

Lizzie tried to cut short a snort. Kate smiled. 'I know. Hallowed? But that's how they were seen until the world economies started to crash. I was in awe of those seasoned journalists. Left breathless by their inside knowledge of scandals and rorts, corruption and fraud. They talked about back-room deals that never made it into the news. Inside knowledge, they called it, that could bring a paper to its knees if it was published because—as I was reminded, over and over—in Australia, truth is rarely a defence in a libel suit. The gossip seemed so glamorous, and I inhaled it, that rich perfume that colludes with power. I was dizzy with it.'

Lizzie understood instantly. Hadn't she fallen for the lure of fame as a young playwright only to wake up one day to realise fame was nothing but ephemeral nonsense?

'One day, I interviewed a fitness junkie who'd called the newspaper with claims that a gym—one of a chain of gyms—was defrauding clients. The chief of staff handed over the details and told me to investigate it. I failed to check with the CEO of the company and wrote a story reporting the allegations. A chance chat with a senior reporter who'd chased the same story a few years earlier revealed the fitness junkie had a longstanding grudge against the CEO who'd had an affair with his wife. I nearly vomited. I'd failed to follow the most basic rules of investigative reporting, a fireable offence. I told the senior reporter what I'd done, and he took care of the whole debacle in a way that saved me from a humiliating fiasco. The story was pulled before it went to press. That night, I met the senior reporter at a bar to buy him a drink, as a way of saying thank you. He wouldn't let me pay. Instead, he pulled out a notebook and wrote down a ten-point list of rules. Then he patted my shoulder, kissed the top of my head, and asked if I needed a taxi to get home. He made me feel safe, protected. A rare feeling. I watched him leave, and it seemed to me that the sea of yabbering wannabes with flushed faces and shiny eyes parted before him. I wanted to chase him, call him back to my side, never lose sight of him again.'

'*Coup de foudre*,' Lizzie said softly. 'The bloody French always find the perfect words to explain irrational romantic responses. He was married, of course?'

'How did you know?'

'Oh, Kate, in these situations, he so often is.'

As Kate described what came next in a dead tone, Lizzie's mind drifted. She knew the backstory without having to hear it. Remembered when she'd been found in the bush by Dorothy as she'd sat sobbing high on a rocky ledge overlooking bays stroked gold by the late afternoon sun. Her words: 'You be right daughter, you be right, you come with me.'

Dorothy, who'd turned away when Lizzie spoke falsehoods, but who smiled widely with love and understanding when, stripped of pride and ego, she spoke the simple, devastating truth. Accepted Lizzie's own love affair for what it was: sordid, destructive, soul destroying. Understood she'd squandered, beyond retrieval, everything precious. That's when the healing began, Lizzie remembered: after she'd rid herself of the gnawing secrecy. The warmth, Lizzie recalled, of Dorothy's large rough hand when she held it out to help her rise. It felt like she'd been offered a lifeline. It had been enough to call her back from a brink she couldn't bear to think about at this end of her life.

'Why do some of us believe there can only ever be one true love?' she asked, interrupting Kate's narrative. 'And why is it almost always in an impossible situation? The contrariness of most people never ceases to astound me.'

'He was beautiful,' Kate whispered, 'in mind, body and spirit.'

'He sounds like a user, Kate. He took the best of you and left you stranded.'

'It wasn't like that! *I* left! *I* quit my job. Quit my city life. Quit everything I knew. I found a dark little corner in Oyster Bay with a rundown house where I could guarantee I'd never get a knock on the door from an uninvited guest whom I'd find impossible to turn away.'

Lizzie, puzzled, mentally scrolled through the timeframe. 'But you've lived here for more than two years now, with Sam for most of the time. Claire is six—nearly seven—months old.'

Kate stood and paced the small kitchen, her face suffused with redness from both the heat of the fire and the shame she felt. 'There was a single night. After my mother died. I called him. Mistake. Big mistake. He wrapped his arms around me and there it was again: safety, as though nothing terrible could touch me.'

'Ah,' Lizzie said, nodding, understanding the power of belonging, even for a moment, in safe arms.

'We were together in a hotel room for less than two hours. He had to go to his daughter's confirmation ceremony. A big event in the Catholic faith. I understood, of course. I always understood. That's what the third person in a relationship does, right? She understands or she risks losing the little she has. Am I right?' she asked for the second time.

'Last in the queue,' Lizzie agreed. 'Until the bitterness outweighs the sweetness and all that's left is bile.'

'He paid the hotel bill and, for the first time, I felt cheap. I never contacted him again, and other than a couple of phone calls, he never made any effort to see me, either. When I realised I was pregnant, I panicked. Sam always used contraception. One night, I told him birth control was my responsibility. A throwaway line that altered everything.

'I knew Sam would make a good father, I knew he longed for his own family. I told myself I could live with the lie for the sake of the child.' Lizzie saw the struggle on Kate's face: her earnest desire to be understood. 'As it turned out, my duplicity became part of a much bigger issue. I became terrified for Claire's safety. The first time I found her lying on her stomach, I almost threw up.'

Lizzie raised an eyebrow.

Kate explained. 'It increases the risk of sudden infant death syndrome. God, Lizzie, after that, I felt I couldn't take my eyes off her for a second. I barely slept for an hour straight for weeks. Soon she'd crawl, then toddle. The bay is at the foot of the garden. What if I turned my back for a moment too long and she drowned? Suddenly, everywhere I looked, I saw hazards. When Sam offered to help, it seemed like a godsend. Instead, seeing him with Claire on a daily basis made me sick with guilt.

'I felt like I was slowly dying . . . drowning in lies, questioning my ability as a mother, increasingly convinced Claire would be better off without me. Coward that I turned out to be, I ran away. I know she will be safe with Sam. He was born to be a dad. Look at the way he took on Jimmy when the kid was lost and vulnerable. How he looked after Artie when he lived aboard a boat with more leaks than a sieve. Show him a stray dog, and the next thing, it's living with him.'

'What about you, Kate? What about your hopes and dreams?' Lizzie asked.

'I ran away, Lizzie, and gave away all my rights.'

Lizzie tried to find words of comfort but knew instinctively it would be pointless.

'If you don't mind me asking . . .'

Kate leaped in before Lizzie could finish the question. 'I told you, I never contacted . . . that man . . . again. Never. He has no idea.'

'Are you still in love with him?' Lizzie asked, laying her hand on Kate's arm.

'I'm not sure what the word means anymore. But I am sure—without a shadow of doubt—that if I passed him in the street today, I would struggle to recognise him. He belongs to a world I've left far behind.'

'But, if he spoke to you, would the electricity, that addictive rush of adrenalin that hooks us more powerfully than a drug, would that still be there?'

Kate took a long time to respond. She fiddled again with a fire that was dying: riddling, stoking, filling the room with another puff of achy smoke, so much of it already embedded in the wobbly DNA of the shack.

'I must have been mad,' she said, taking a seat once again. 'Or else my mother's history is so deeply ingrained in me . . . '

'That's ridiculous, and you know it.' Lizzie watched Kate's eyes fill with tears and knew she'd been too harsh. But for Kate to grab hold of an idea like that would justify her current position and potentially rule out any solution. 'How about we concentrate on one day at a time?'

'We? This is my problem and I can handle it.'

Not alone, Lizzie thought, seeing a valid reason to involve the GeriEcstasies in Kate's welfare that went way beyond patching a few gaps in the floorboards and fixing the leaky roof. 'Let's sleep on it,' Lizzie said placatingly.

'I did this to myself, and I will sort it out myself. End of story.'

'As you wish,' she said, to keep the peace. Six months would be long enough to judge whether rest and a good diet, the potentially irksome company of a bunch of oldies and Cliffy's benign influence were having a beneficial effect on Kate's mental and physical health. If these efforts failed, she would personally engage the services of a specialist and drag Kate along for therapy—by the scruff of her neck if she had to.

The fire kicked into new life. Shadows danced on the walls. Outside, night sounds ramped up a notch. Thump of a wallaby. Hoot of an owl. Two bandicoots argued over who knew what. Muted, like a distant horn, Clarabelle called her calf.

'The calf's wandered,' Lizzie said. She stood and went to the back door to listen. 'Something's not right.'

Clarabelle's piercing wail sounded again, high-pitched. Then came the hair-raising sound of howling.

Lizzie spun on the spot. 'Wild dogs,' she said. 'Let's go or the calf will be nothing but bones stripped clean by daybreak. Grab a waddy from the back door. They're still there, aren't they?'

'What's a waddy?'

Lizzie was gone. Kate saw her waving a length of poly pipe, grabbed one for herself from the collection she'd only half-registered at the shack's rear exit. She followed at a sprint, holding a torch. They ran towards the noise. Clarabelle hurtled towards them, bellowing. Kate almost stopped, frightened of being trampled, but Lizzie kept going so she continued, too, slipping and falling once.

'Shine the torch around,' Lizzie shouted. 'Try to pick out the calf. There! Over there! On the wrong side of the fence. Stupid animal.' The torch picked up the sandy coat of a large animal slinking into the night. 'Bastard,' Lizzie shouted, but she dropped her voice, as she slowed to approach the terrified calf, her words calm and soothing.

'C'mon little miss, c'mon. You're okay, it's all okay.' She climbed through the fence carefully, murmuring quietly the whole time. Then she slid an arm around the calf's neck, felt the quivering fear rippling through the warm soft body, and gently propelled it along the fence towards Clarabelle. The calf saw Clarabelle and charged through a gap in the fence wire, galloping up to her mother with such force that Clarabelle was almost knocked flying.

Kate held the wire further apart for Lizzie to climb through, watched as the old woman ran her hand along flanks of the calf, under the stomach, whispering as though to a small child. 'Your mamma's here, little one. She'll look after you now. You're safe with her.' Without looking at Kate, she ordered, 'Shine the torch on her body. Any wounds and she'll need a dose of antibiotics.'

A few minutes later, Lizzie declared the calf unhurt. She straightened up, her fist clenched in the small of her back, groaning. 'She'll live, but I hope she's learned a lesson. Are you sure there's no cognac lurking in the house somewhere? I think I've pulled a muscle.'

The two women followed the yellow beam of light back to the house. Inside the warmth of the kitchen, they washed their hands, drank some water, stoked the fire for the night. Then by silent consensus, they headed to bed. At the door to her room, Kate asked, 'Wild dogs. See many of them around here?'

Lizzie, exhausted, replied, 'They come and go. A radius of about two hundred and fifty square kilometres. You never know when they'll turn up. Is that cow shit all over your backside? Slippery stuff, isn't it? Good night, Kate. Thanks for your help.'

'Lizzie . . .'

But the door was already closed. Kate heard one shoe, then another, hit the floor, and a groan as Lizzie fell on the bed, making the springs squeak. Kate grabbed her pyjamas and tiptoed to the bathroom where she threw her filthy jeans into a bucket to soak. She scrubbed hard under the shower but the stewy stink of cow poo lingered in her nostrils. In bed, she vowed to cut out her tongue if she ever again felt the urge to lay bare her soul.

⌒

Unable to sleep and aware that her revelations had given Lizzie an opportunity to interfere, Kate rose long before the first light crept above the horizon. Her breath steamed in the frigid room and the floorboards felt as cold as ice. Lizzie had warned her that winter came early to the shack, but she hadn't really understood the wide temperature gap between the coast and the escarpment. She listened to the low murmur of a lazy wind rustling leaves before creeping through the floorboards and curling around her ankles. She hurriedly slipped into warm clothes and sheepskin slippers, hoping that Lizzie had been snug through the night.

As she made her way down the hallway to the kitchen, she heard the wind pick up. In the kitchen, she followed her house-keeping rules: stoke the fire, sweep the hearth, dust tiny grey smoke particles from all surfaces. Fill the kettle. While the water heated, make the bed, sweep the hallway and kitchen floors, run a cloth around the bathroom sink, tub, refresh the loo. By the time she'd completed the chores that formed the framework of her existence, Lizzie was stirring. In the kitchen, Kate warmed the teapot and set out breakfast, fighting the urge to bolt. The memory of her confession the day before sparked a new wave of embarrassment and fury at her lack of restraint. Hearing footsteps in the hallway, she made a racket of tending the fire.

'Morning,' Lizzie announced, her voice slow and drowsy, shuffling past the kitchen door to the bathroom. Kate made the tea, giving it time to brew, and then cracked eggs into a bowl, whisking them with a spoonful of sour cream. She figured Lizzie would need a solid meal to sustain her during the homeward trek. There was an awkward silence in the kitchen when Lizzie reappeared and the two women took their places at the table.

'I'm sorry, Lizzie.' Kate offered Lizzie a plate of scrambled eggs, made toast for both of them. Poured two mugs of tea.

'Great eggs. Not overcooked, which is an art,' Lizzie said.

'Ettie taught me to remove them from the heat when the eggs were just coming together. Cliffy's girls are enthusiastic little layers. Lizzie . . .' The old woman held up her hand for silence. Finished her food. Dragged her chair from the table and returned to her possie close to the warmth of the fire.

She rubbed her hands together, leaning closer to the heat. 'Signs are pointing to a long, cold winter,' she said.

Kate began. 'I should never have burdened you . . .'

'No burden.'

'Lizzie . . .'

'The thing is, Kate,' Lizzie interrupted, 'you, Sam, the issue with Claire's paternity? Only you can sort that out.'

Kate cast her eyes to the floor, feeling a faint flush rise from her neck.

'If you decide to stay here, though, the shack will need some pretty extensive rehabilitation and some serious cash to make it livable. Are you sure you want to take it on?' Lizzie asked, without taking her eyes off the fire. Kate exhaled.

'I would like to, if it doesn't cause you any trouble.'

'Why, Kate? Explain why.'

Kate got up, her chair scraping the floorboards. She walked around the small space of the kitchen. Fists clenched at her sides. Face muscles pulled tight. 'I don't know how to explain it,' she said, after a while. 'Something here calls me. Has done since the first day.' She met Lizzie's gaze, shrugged. 'Probably sounds mad.'

Lizzie gave a resigned sigh. 'The shack always needs maintenance and repairs. Bad weather can cut you off for days. You need to be able to read the bush when it suddenly goes silent, judge the danger of a hot westerly wind. A whiff of smoke, how long to prepare—or get to safety. A distant grumble—do you bring in the washing—or batten down the hatches and take shelter under the kitchen table? And always, like a monkey tapping your shoulder, the certainty a brown snake might get you and you'll probably die.'

'You managed alone,' Kate said, determined.

'I had a teacher. Dorothy.'

'And I have you and Cliffy,' Kate said. 'Don't I?'

CHAPTER ELEVEN

TWO SIPS OF TEA AFTER Kate's plea, Lizzie knew she had the power to make a deal Kate couldn't refuse. It came to her in full-colour images, each one rounded and fully formed, like cartoons in a comic book: a deal that would engage the GeriEcstasies; call on their experience, skills and knowledge; and ensure the young woman was surrounded by amiable guardians until she regained her equilibrium.

Driven by a desire to see Kate return to caring for Claire (any other outcome was too sad to contemplate), Lizzie set down her cup with such force she had to watch it didn't spill—but then she leaned forwards, resting her elbows on her knees, clasping her hands in a way that resembled fervent prayer. 'Everyone needs a teacher, Kate. Here's the deal and be under no illusions. It's non-negotiable.'

She led into her plan with a description of how ageing corroded wellbeing unless you were distracted from the stark reality of time reducing in small bites, then gulps, by being useful. She said there was a shitload—yes, shitload, she wanted to shock Kate into listening intently—of talent contained in a perfectly beautiful house, in a perfectly idyllic location, but that meant diddlysquat, unless the residents had goals and meaningful jobs. Of course, there were daily essentials to be addressed. But old people rose early and covered the bases by smoko. After that, well, the whole day stretched emptily before them. Scrabble (and really, the words allowed these days made a mockery of the game). Walking in the bush. Conferring on the dinner menu or shopping list. Long chats about events from the distant past: even the worst recounted with gentle hilarity now that time had erased heightened emotion, even distress. There was more to retirement, of course, but it boiled down to filling in time until death tapped you on the shoulder and told you your time was up: a thought that could take a vice-like grip if you spent more time dwelling on it than was healthy.

During what Lizzie later considered a worthy monologue, Kate remained as still as a statue, seated in her straight-backed kitchen chair, arms folded across her chest as if to keep any words from accessing her heart.

'I can't see how all this is relevant to me,' Kate said, when Lizzie, ragged from her own fierce point-making, paused for breath. 'And what's non-negotiable?'

'The shack is in a very poor state. It needs fixing, and for a long while now I've known the GeriEcstasies have needed a project.' She paused to remove a tiny dark speck of tea leaf from her mouth; wryly remembered the old saying, *you'll get spots on your tongue for lying.* 'The non-negotiable part is that if you stay on here, you will take on a pack of oldies with much to give. And, if I'm being strictly accurate, much to forgive. Old people are not easy to be around. Especially old people who have made a success of their businesses. We are used to giving orders, not following them. We have firm ideas about the way things should be done. Some people call it inflexibility. I prefer to think of it as the wisdom of experience. We take things slowly. Do them right. It's a way of conserving energy. Won't be exactly what you want, sometimes, but you'll need to hold your tongue. Old people act tough, but they can be easily wounded. Lose confidence. Creep back into the safety of their shells.'

Kate's eyes widened incredulously. Lizzie cracked a grin. 'Of course, our group may be the exception to that rule.'

'But what's the plan, Lizzie?'

'We GeriEcstasies will get this old girl of a shack upright on her bunioned feet, reframe her sagging body and restore her faded beauty. It will take time. You will need to learn multiple cake recipes. There will be clashes of opinion. Bottom line? It is still my shack and . . .' Lizzie paused, chewed her bottom lip, thoughtful. Came to a decision. 'It will be mine until the day I die.'

'I thought . . .'

'A little white lie to keep away property developers. I own the freehold. Cliffy owns his land. The title is mine until the day I die. No caveats. So I will have the final say on every decision that needs to be made.'

'If I may be allowed . . .'

'Yes!' Lizzie was curt.

'I would like to oversee the budget.'

Lizzie's face lit up, the ferocity gone in an instant, her quiet good humour restored. 'I hear you're very clever with money,' she agreed. The two women rose from their chairs and shook hands. 'This calls for a fresh cuppa. I've talked the other one cold. And if I'm not mistaken, that distant whistle signals the imminent arrival of Cliffy. I swear that man can smell a fresh brew before the kettle is on the hob.'

As Kate filled the kettle, Lizzie frowned at her hands, picking at a chipped nail for a moment. Then she said, 'Mike Melrose is our collective money man and to turf him off this job might be a tactical error. Do you think you can work with him?'

Kate hesitated, aware they'd reached a critical point in the negotiations. It was not and never would be in her nature to let go of the purse strings. Her track record of restoring her Oyster Bay home under budget and turning the once barely profitable Briny Café into a thriving business was now woven into local lore. Let go? Hand the responsibility to a man she barely knew and for whom she had scant respect? She wasn't sure she could do it.

Lizzie's hubris evaporated on the back of a long-drawn breath. 'This is make or break time, Kate,' she said, taking the kettle from Kate's grip and plonking it roughly on the hob.

'I'm not a team player by nature . . .'

'That's that, then,' Lizzie said, ready to annul the offer.

'But I am a quick learner. What worries me, Lizzie, is how I'll be seen by your crew. I am a woman who has dumped all her responsibilities. Claire, Sam, Ettie: they're all carrying a load that should be mine. The GeriEcstasies will probably despise me.'

Before Lizzie could answer, Cliffy thumped down the hallway and entered the kitchen, his nose red, cheeks like varnished apples. 'See you're expectin' me,' he said, nodding towards three mugs lined up on the table. He took in the sight of Kate's white face, Lizzie's seriousness. 'Good time? Or should I come back later?'

Lizzie went over and pulled him into a hug. Kate stoked the fire, noticing Cliffy's hands were blue with cold. She pulled a chair closer to the heat and told him to sit down and warm up, wrapping a scarf around his neck. Cliffy blushed, embarrassed. 'You're makin' me feel like an old man, Kate, and as far as I can tell, I'm still a long way off a nursin' home.'

Lizzie made the tea, and the shack filled with the comforting clink of cutlery and crockery. 'Wind's straight off the South Pole,' she said, and in a subtle gesture, she handed Cliffy his tea and removed the scarf, laying it on the back of the chair.

Kate noticed a frail look about the old man that she'd never seen before. She'd make chicken soup, a cure all, according to her father who cared for her each time Emily took off from the family home, sometimes for months, without leaving word of where she'd gone or when she might return. The awful mockery of her life-long habit of condemning her mother's selfishness, while her own behaviour mirrored it, was not lost on her.

Lizzie cooked more toast and slathered on butter and store-bought strawberry jam. The cheesemakers, she thought, might be persuaded to turn their hand to making jam.

'If you don't mind me sayin' so, you two looked like you were off to a funeral when I walked in,' Cliffy said, glancing at each woman in turn.

'Tell me,' Lizzie began, choosing her chair. 'Would you say the elderly are judgemental?'

Cliffy's face wrinkled. He gave the question serious thought. 'You're askin' me as an observer of the aged, seein' as how I'm nowhere near the condition meself, right?'

'Naturally,' Lizzie responded, struggling to keep a straight face.

Through the kitchen window, the trees were now still. Birdsong stretched out from branch to branch. The sub-zero draught that had been nosing under the doorway ceased.

Cliffy shifted uncomfortably, as if aware there was a truckload of undisclosed stuff riding on his answer. 'Worst thing for old folks is too much time on their hands. Gives them an openin' to feel the aches and pains. Worry a cough might turn out to be more than a cough. But judgemental? Nah. Most of us . . . them . . . carry a swag of lapses in judgement so they're in no position to point a finger.' He broke off, beaming, pleased with his considered response. He slapped his knees and got to his feet, pausing to toast his backside in front of the warm glow of the fire. 'Better be off then. Headin' to the shops later, Kate, if you need anythin'.'

'All good, Cliffy, thank you.'

'Could give you a lift to the Square, Lizzie, if you fancy a trip in Bertha.'

'That old Vauxhall still going?'

'Sweet as the day she cruised off the showroom floor.'

'Love is blind,' Lizzie said.

'Just as well,' Cliffy responded.

'No thanks, all the same.'

Cliffy muttered something about a cow that needed tending. He patted the two women on the shoulder and told them to stay put in front of the fire. The weather wasn't fit for humans. He grabbed an extra piece of toast and set off.

Kate, worried the weather might turn nasty, suggested Lizzie stay another night. Lizzie shook her head. 'I'll be sheltered from the wind for most of the way,' she said. Longing to regain her privacy, Kate didn't try to persuade her to change her mind. She handed over the staff, long and biblical with a curved handle at the top, and stood back. 'Do we have a deal?' Lizzie asked.

Kate nodded. 'If I think your money man is wrong, though, I will argue the point.'

'Goes without saying,' Lizzie said.

'Will they accept what I've done?'

'They might not understand your decisions, Kate, but they'll accept they are yours to make.'

Halfway back to Oyster Bay, where a narrow opening between two massive boulders signalled a turn to the left on the track, Lizzie called Mike to organise a pick-up at Kate's pontoon.

'How did it go?' he asked.

'Put a bottle or two of bubbles in the fridge.'

'Consider it done,' Mike said, already on his way to the shelf in the pantry where the booze was kept now that it no longer had to be hidden from Donna.

∽

The word spread through the corridors and rooms of the five suites and a gentle euphoria filled the house. Soon, doors opened and closed, feet pattered towards the kitchen, a low hum of conversation rose and in less than half an hour, the rich scent of a celebration chocolate cake cooking in the oven drifted enticingly in the air. After-dinner Scrabble was cancelled. There were decisions to be discussed. Only Rob remained unconvinced by their interference in Kate's life. 'It will end in disaster,' he told his wife.

She shrugged and rebuttoned his shirt correctly. 'Maybe. But you've got to help if you can, don't you?'

With the fire lit early, the GeriEcstasies gathered half an hour ahead of schedule, a small crowd babbling excitedly, faces alight with expectation. Lizzie was the last to arrive. A dramatist, she was aware of the impact of a late entrance.

Sheila rushed over and threw an arm around her shoulders. 'Mike has been so secretive, we're still half in the dark. But he said this was a celebration dinner and we've all guessed the reason.'

Mike came towards Lizzie with a champagne glass filled to the brim, the fizzy scent of yeast rising with the bubbles. She met his eyes with a wordless thankyou and drifted towards the group scattered around the fire, soaking in the warmth. She couldn't help thinking of a scene out of an English novel where the family gathered on icy nights for a sherry before a dinner of steak and kidney pie, plenty of mashed potatoes and the odd Brussel sprout. The thought made her ask, 'What's for dinner?' Seven pairs of eyebrows were raised in her direction.

'Dinner?' Sheila asked.

'Mmmm. I can smell something delicious. It's distracting,' Lizzie said, drawing out the suspense.

'Oh, right,' Gavin said. 'Ruled by our stomachs, eh?'

'It's a wickedly rich cassoulet made from brisket and pork belly with a hint of chilli and a few cannellini beans,' Sally said with a hint of pride.

'Celebration fare,' her husband, David, explained. 'Not an everyday dish at our age.'

'Smells fabulous,' Lizzie said, taking pity on her assembled housemates and hoping the plan to engage in Kate's welfare ended in success and not disaster. One of Sam's favourite clichés sprang to mind: *no good turn goes unpunished.* She sent a silent prayer for guidance to the spirits in the mangroves, then smiled at each person in turn, lingering just a fraction longer on Mike.

'Cheers,' he toasted. They clinked glasses in a festive room, a pool of bright light in the furthest corner of a cold, dark bay.

'There is a question . . .' Lizzie began.

'Yes, yes, ask away!'

'Everything depends on your answers.'

Heads nodded, faces subdued now, faintly apprehensive.

'How do you feel about Kate?' The tone of her question stole the bubbles from their glasses, the fizz of excitement from the room.

Daisy, attuned to underlying agendas, was the first to speak. 'This plan you've come up with, it's not allowed to be about her, is it?' A few gasps. Rob surprised. Gavin frowning. Unsure where this was leading.

'Yes, yes, it is. Who else?' Sheila insisted.

'She has to believe it's about our needs, doesn't she? As far as Kate is concerned, she just happens to be the catalyst. That's the story, right?' Daisy caught Lizzie's eye and shrugged with a wry grin. 'I've spent a lifetime trying to read animals. People are so much simpler.'

She gets it, Lizzie thought, relieved. Steer away from the personal. No value in it. Stick to the practical.

'But . . .'

'No buts, Sheila,' Daisy said firmly. 'Kate's old enough to look after herself. All of us trying to give her advice at once would lead only to confusion, hurt and perhaps even more damage. Best to get on with the job at hand, don't you think?'

'Hear, hear,' endorsed the room, over Sheila's dismay.

The discussion had to pause for a while, as Sally left to check on dinner and David followed to help, returning a few minutes later with a clean tea towel over his shoulder. He made a mock bow and waved his arm to usher everyone through the door and into the formal dining room. 'Dinner is served,' he announced, in a fair imitation of an English butler.

For the first time, Lizzie wondered how they would cope in a small, draughty old shack with one loo and not a single window that shut out the cold. What would happen if the challenge was beyond them, if they failed to make a difference to Kate's existence? As if reading her thoughts, Mike whispered in her ear, 'If the plan doesn't work, we'll withdraw. No harm done. Think of it as a calculated gamble. No guarantee but plenty of blind faith. But tell me, how's her mental state?'

'Fragile, but keep that to yourself. I reckon we'll know soon enough if she needs more help than we can give her.'

'I'll look into options but hope it doesn't come to that.'

Daisy went into the dining room first, Rob pushing her wheelchair. Lizzie and Mike were next, heads bent, talking softly. Sheila and Gavin, in the rear, squabbled: Gavin, frustrated, turned to his wife and said loudly enough for everyone to hear, 'The protocol is in place. Ignore it and you'll be back here rearranging your clogs until the day you die.'

'What's a protocol, Mr Smart Arse?' Sheila bent to fiddle with a strap on her shoe.

Gavin sighed. Took her arm and led her into the dining room. 'Try listening for a change. You never know, you might even get to like it.'

As everyone sat down to dine, they were happily distracted by the food: meat swam in a shallow bowl of aromatic sauce, underpinned by crusty bread, and served with apple salsa on the side to cut through the richness. The applause was genuine—and the diners grew so absorbed in the flavours of Sally's beautifully considered meal that the conversation about Kate was suspended, until the lull between main course and dessert.

As the men dealt with the clean-up, the kitchen filling with clatter, banging and male laughter, Daisy wheeled her chair next to Sheila and said, 'Kate will run like a rabbit if you say one word about what she's done. No. Listen. Even offering understanding and compassion will launch her off to who knows where. Not a word, Sheila, not one word. We will help to rebuild Lizzie's old shack. For Lizzie. Not Kate. She just happens to be there. Do you think you can manage that?'

'It's for the best, Sheila,' Sally said, an ear tilted towards the sounds from the kitchen. 'I'd better go and check on the next course. Those boys sound too happy for their own good.'

After a dessert of molten chocolate cake and late Queensland strawberries macerated in Tia Maria, the GeriEcstasies regrouped in the sitting room with snifters of cognac for the men and Lizzie, and a sticky dessert wine in delicately etched glasses for the other women. Once again, Lizzie had the feeling she'd stepped back into a more civilised era, an age of gentility and time stretching lazily under bowers of dripping purple wisteria. The patina of nostalgia, she thought, that conceals unpleasant chips and scratches. What would the aged do without it?

Mike picked up a clipboard from a side table, withdrew a pencil from under the clip and placed it on his knee. 'Where should we start?' he asked, directing the question at Lizzie.

Gavin swirled his brandy in its glass. 'At the beginning, mate,' he replied for Lizzie. 'Where else?'

Lizzie exhaled, feeling a mixture of wistfulness and heaviness. 'The real beginning would be with Dorothy,' she said.

And so her new companions gathered around, like Jane Austen characters listening to a poetry reading in an old English drawing room, while she gave an account of finding her mentor, a woman who was all heart and soul, and who taught her the secrets of the landscape and left her the shack for her use until her death. 'She was a mother, sister, aunty, and in her final year, child, to me,' Lizzie said. 'I asked her once, why she'd been so kind to a stranger she'd found crying in the bush. *You needed fixing*, she said, amazed I'd had to ask the question.'

She knew from the ripple that went through her audience that they understood they were the fixers now. Their hearts opened with compassion, and in that beautiful room of soft sofas, cosy armchairs and a gallery of art hung on the walls, any remaining vestige of condemnation flew off to be inhaled by mangroves and exhaled as clean, pure oxygen.

'Fixers,' Mike murmured, draining the last of the honey-coloured spirit in his glass. 'Sounds about right to me.' He considered a second cognac but resisted, only slightly mourning the necessity of moderation as the years piled up.

CHAPTER TWELVE

WHILE THE GERIECSTASIES MADE PLANS to revitalise the shack, Jimmy hopped around the *Mary Kay* like a cat on a hot tin roof. Sam watched him, mildly exasperated, but figured if something was bothering the kid, he'd spill the beans soon enough. He grinned to himself. Two ripper clichés and no one around to criticise him. He checked the weather forecast on his phone and figured if all deliveries and pick-ups were finished by two p.m., they'd avoid the icy southerlies that were due to sweep into Cook's Basin by mid-afternoon. An imminent cold snap, according to the experts, which could rewrite the record books for this time of the year. He checked his work list and moved the two moorings due for a service to the head of the queue. If predictions were accurate, gusts could reach up to eighty kilometres an hour. He didn't want to be responsible for a couple of yachts snapping loose. There'd been enough damage done in the big storm and the resilience of the locals might be extraordinary, but everyone had a breaking point.

'Jimmy!' he shouted, leaning out of the wheelhouse so the kid couldn't fail to hear. 'Alert and focused, mate. We're going to hit top speed. First stop, Blue Swimmer Bay.'

Jimmy gave a ragged salute before joining Sam in the wheel-house, his ever-faithful mutt, Longfellow, following close on his heels. 'You reckon Kate's ever gunna come back?' Jimmy asked.

Taken off-guard, Sam hesitated. Not sure where the kid was headed. 'I dunno, Jimmy.'

'S'pose she broke your heart 'n' all, scarperin' like that in the dead of night.'

Sam, who tried to avoid all conversations about Kate, shrugged. 'She must've had her reasons, mate.' He trained his eyes on the water, willing Jimmy to drop it.

'I've been thinkin' about love, Sam . . .'

'What kind of love, Jimmy? Love for your mum, love for Artie . . .'

'Artie! Not Artie. He's me mate. You couldn't love Artie, the cranky old bugger, although me mum reckons she's brought out his soft side 'n' all.'

'Artie's all mush. Always has been.'

'Spends half his life with those binoculars of his screwed to his eyeballs. Knows more about what's goin' on in Cook's Basin than the rest of us put together, if you ask me.'

'No one's asking you, Jimmy, and Artie can't do much else with his busted legs.'

Jimmy scraped the deck with the toe of his boot. 'Yeah. He's orright. He keeps me mum busy. I'll say that for him.'

Sam spun the wheel and eased back the throttle, turning the nose of the *Mary Kay* into a breeze that had already cooled and stiffened. Jimmy licked a finger and stuck it outside. 'Temperature's dropped heaps,' he said, nodding his young head with the certainty of untested youth.

'Two moorings here, then we're into Oyster Bay . . .'

'Kate's back!'

Sam shook his head, and knew he couldn't ignore the comment. 'Nah. Not yet. Maybe never. We're picking up twelve bulka bags of rubbish from that reno on the sunny side of the bay. The builder says there's heavy stuff and watch out if a bag breaks. You listening to me, Jimmy?'

'Yeah, Sam. Watch out if a bag breaks.' His tone was sad. 'Never, you reckon?'

'No way of knowing.'

'Sad, eh?'

'It's life, Jimmy. Relationships don't always work out. You deal with them the best way you can, even if it breaks your heart.'

'I'm here, Sam, aren't I? We're mates, aren't we?'

'Of course we are. Living in Cook's Basin, where everyone's a helper, makes a real difference.'

'There's only one Ettie, right?'

'You got it. Now hook up the mooring and let's hoist it aboard to see what needs fixing.'

The kid hesitated in the doorway, chewing his bottom lip. The dog, sensitive to every mood, leaped out of his bed and sat at Jimmy's feet, leaning hard against his leg. Jimmy rubbed a furry ear, his face pensive.

'Something else on your mind?' Sam asked gently.

'Nah. It's all good. It's just . . . I was wonderin'. How do you know if you're in love?'

Sam laughed. 'Mate, that's a story that's going to take longer than we've got today, tomorrow and the rest of the year. Hop to it, or we'll be hauling cargo till midnight.'

The kid did as he was told but with a reluctance Sam had never seen. It struck him, like a blow to his solar plexus, that young Jimmy, one of the best and 'goodest' of the innocents, might be growing up. Had he found a girlfriend? A sliver of cynicism and uncertainty slipped into his head. Jimmy had a hefty bank balance: all due to a series of fully paid television appearances he'd made, following his stellar role in the fight to save Garrawi Park, a pocket of dreamy rainforest (where, according to folklore, half the kids on the Island were conceived), from developers. He could be attractive for all the wrong reasons.

Sam craned the mooring on board, set to work stripping cungies from the anchor chain, and made a mental note to have a long conversation with the kid at the end of the day, but first, he'd call Artie. The old man would know the score.

When the moorings were done, and Jimmy had hosed down the deck, Sam found he was unable to hold his curiosity in check. 'You met a girl, Jimmy?'

The kid's face looked like it had suddenly been struck by a shaft of heavenly light. 'Yeah. And she's a beauty.' He did a little jig, his feet tapping to a beat only he could hear. He grinned, spun, high-fived the air, then punched it with barely contained joy.

'She got a name?' Sam asked.

'Aw Sam, if I tell you, will you keep mum?'

Sam made a zipper gesture across his mouth.

'Orright then. But I'm breakin' me word to her, just so you know. She says it's too early to go public 'n' all that.'

'Have I ever let you down, mate?'

'Nah.' His face flushed red, he stared at his feet, then looked up at Sam from under his brows. 'You know her, Sam. It's Cindy.'

Sam's heart sank. The girl was five years older than Jimmy, and a renowned island party animal with expensive tastes.

'Cindy?'

Jimmy nodded.

'With the purple and pink hair, the nose and lip piercings?'

Jimmy nodded, smiling. 'She's got style. You gotta say that about her.'

'Man to man, Jimmy, you want to tell me how far this romance has moved along?'

'Like I said, early days. But Sam, me heart leaps when I see her, me stomach turns over and me words come out more back to front than usual. I've flipped, Sam, and I feel pretty good.'

Sam, fearing Jimmy might launch into a detailed account of his fledgling romance, changed tack. 'Right. Well let's do the pick up from Oyster Bay and call it a day. Whitecaps are coming in and it's colder than . . .'

'A witch's . . .'

'Cold as the South Pole, which is where that wind started. We'll need to rug up tomorrow. Big delivery. Two fireplaces, the internals for a new bathroom and enough bookshelves for a library.'

Jimmy scratched his head. 'It's got me flummoxed. Two fireplaces, Sam. What's a house need two fireplaces for?'

Relieved that he seemed to have headed off a detailed account of his evening with Cindy, Sam replied, 'Not sure, mate. Let's ask when we make the delivery.'

❧

As the man and the boy secured the barge against strong winds, Sam mulled over the dangers of falling in love. Why, he wondered, does one person trigger a reaction that can only be diagnosed as irrational, while another fails to make an impact of any kind? He consoled himself with the fact that throughout history much wiser men than he had been unable to provide an explanation beyond *chemistry*.

He'd felt it for Kate, but when he lay awake at night thinking about how their relationship had gone so wrong, he had to admit that it had felt one-sided from the start. Without their baby, they'd have long gone their separate ways. His lips rose at the corners when he thought of his child. At least, he thought, something fine and good had come out of the wreckage.

With the barge secured, Sam jumped into the tinnie, started the engine, and waited while Jimmy released the buoy and leaped onto the bow. He dropped the kid at Triangle Wharf and, after reminding him they had a dawn start, he motored home slowly.

In the kitchen, he made a hot chocolate and pulled a stool up to the kitchen counter. He dialled Artie.

'I know what you're gunna say,' said the old man, without bothering to say hello. 'And I'm pulling me hair out.'

'Amelia know?'

'Not bloody likely and best we keep it that way to prevent a homicide on Cutter Island. A murder hasn't happened here for nearly two hundred years, after that rum smuggler got caught . . .'

'Save the history lesson. We need a plan.'

'My oath, we do, or his mum will end up back in the clink for all the wrong reasons this time,' Artie said passionately. 'I'm rackin' me brains but short of payin' the girl to stay away—which would be pointless, because she's the sort that'd take your money and hang around anyway—I've come up blank.'

'Er, Jimmy. Amelia's talked to him about birth control . . .'

'Don't be bloody stupid. Amelia still thinks he's ten years old. Best get Ettie onto it, mate, before there's a disaster.'

'You couldn't . . .'

'You're dead right, I couldn't. Outside me frame of reference, not to mention me skill set.'

Sam killed the call and stripped to take a hot shower. The cold weather brought out the aches and pains in a body he'd overused in his youth. He stood sideways and looked in the bathroom mirror, appalled to see the early stirrings of a paunch. Too many dinners with Marcus and Ettie. Marcus, a man who treated every dish like a work of art and whose generosity was overwhelming. Sam struggled to think of a way to repay his kindnesses and realised the debt was insurmountable. He felt a stirring of anger, which he thought he'd managed to put aside, at Kate's disappearance. Squashed it down. Rage was pointless.

Pulling on warm underlayers to cross the water for his evening catch-up with his daughter, Ettie and the chef, he reminded himself he was a lucky man and if he was any judge, Kate had only bleak times ahead. The desertion of their child would tug at her heartstrings forever, if she was halfway decent, and she was. He pulled on a sweater, wrapped a scarf around his neck, tugged a knitted beanie down over his head and closed the door behind him.

On the cruise to Kingfish Bay, he tussled with the idea of breaking the kid's trust and telling Marcus and Ettie about Jimmy's romance. The idea of spelling out the mechanics of birth control to the kid himself made him nervous, considering his own efforts with Kate had failed miserably. Not that he'd wind back the clock, even if it were possible. The thought of little Claire ironed out the creases in his face. He pushed the throttle forwards. A few waves broke over the bow but he remained sheltered and dry in the cabin. He could feel the weather building, though, and the threat of an early winter already sucking the last warmth from the sea. He tried to recall where his winter socks were stored. His house? Or still at Kate's? In a rare philosophical moment, he contemplated the fact that possessions held on long after humans had departed and he wondered if monuments were a stab at immortality. A pointless exercise considering the current trend for toppling statues and the crumbled remains of ancient cities being dug up all over the world. Sensing he was close to his destination, he strained to see through clears thick with salt, to get his bearings, then slid slowly alongside the pontoon and reminded himself to thank Marcus for tying his boat out of the way. He leaped onto the pontoon, 'Like a gazelle,' he said, his mood lifting as it always did, at the prospect of holding Claire in his arms.

'Permission to come aboard,' he called out, sticking his head through the door and feeling the warmth of an open fire, smelling the char of burning wood, letting his eyes take in a room that enfolded all who stepped into it. Overlaying everything was the rich, winy fragrance of a beef stew. Or cassoulet, as the chef would say.

Marcus appeared before him, his arms outstretched in welcome, his face split by a smile that said a million times more than any words. 'My friend,' he said, greeting Sam with a slap on the back, 'you are just in time. The sauce needs an expert opinion and although my Ettie has the palate of a chef, she also has the heart of a lover, so she cannot be trusted to tell the truth.' He laughed, delighted. 'I am grateful, of course, but there are times when judgement must be unbiased . . .'

'The stew, mate, I can smell the magnificence from here,' Sam said, anxious to see his daughter.

'Stew! This word, it lacks . . . elegance,' Marcus said, horrified. 'What I have made is a concoction of gently braised beef and mushrooms, by which I mean fresh, but overladen with the intensity of dried porcini; sweet, sweet onions and a few carrots. I will serve it on a bed of mashed swedes, naturally . . .'

'Only way,' Sam said, resigned to the fact that he would be tightly corralled until Marcus had said his piece.

'Well, of course there are other ways. Many. But tonight . . .' He kissed the air in a sign of ecstasy and finally turned towards the kitchen. Sam followed, his neck craned around the bulk of the chef for the first glimpse of his daughter.

In the kitchen, he grinned like an idiot, held out his arms. 'How's my best girl?'

'Pass the parcel,' Ettie said in a singsong voice. Claire squirmed out of her grasp, leaning towards her father, and Sam's heart almost exploded.

A long time later, as a golden moon rose above the water, fading to silver high in the sky, the three adults stared into the fire. Marcus patted his stomach with a sigh of satisfaction and reached for the little glass of honey mead Ettie had placed on the small stool near the arm of his chair. She slid off the sofa and threw down a cushion on the floor to be nearer to him, resting first an arm and then her cheek on the big man's knee. 'It's late,' Sam said, reluctant to move.

'There's no hurry,' Ettie responded. Sam's shoulders relaxed.

'Winter is when I remember,' Marcus said in a soft voice.

'Remember what, my love?' Ettie asked, twisting so she could see his face.

'It is the fire, you see. The flames awaken a sadness in me that grows with the passing of years.'

'Sadness?' Ettie asked, worried, reaching for his hand, holding it tightly in both of hers.

'My mother. Her cough. Years of frost like snow. Draughts that sneaked like an evil spirit under the door, slithered through gaps in the window frames, turning to ice where moisture gathered. How she would have loved this fire.' Ettie struggled to her feet and nestled into his lap, pulling his head against her chest and stroking his mane of white hair.

Sam saw the exhaustion in the man, felt responsible for it, and had no idea what he could do to make it go away, barring putting on an apron and jumping behind the counter of the Briny Café. Or stowing his baby in the wheelhouse without fearing one lapse of judgement might put her in jeopardy. He rubbed his fists in his eyes and felt the moisture. It was all such a bloody mess and he was as helpless as a baby himself.

Hoping to deflect from the sadness that filled the room like a thick fog, he blurted, 'Jimmy's got a girlfriend!'

Two heads instantly swung towards him. 'What? Jimmy?' Ettie said, shocked.

'It's a secret,' Sam said, feeling a stone sink in his gut.

'Not anymore,' Ettie said, rushing to extricate herself from Marcus's lap and standing in front of the fire, lifting her skirt to warm the backs of her legs. 'Who?' she asked grimly.

Sam instantly wished he could haul back the information. 'You're not going to like it.'

'Who?' Ettie asked even more forcefully.

'Cindy.'

'Out of the question,' Ettie snapped, pacing the floor, almost knocking over the stool holding the chef's honey mead. 'How old is she? Thirty and not a day younger. With the worst reputation on Cutter Island. She'll chew Jimmy up like a prawn and spit him out like the shell.'

Marcus reached for Ettie's arm as she passed. 'The boy is nineteen, my love, and he is feeling things that cannot be held back.'

'She's twenty-three,' Sam said.

'Twenty-three. Thirty. What does it matter? Jimmy might be nineteen, but he has the innocence of a ten-year-old.'

'The thing is, Ettie, we're looking for someone to have a birds and bees kind of discussion, and Artie and I reckon there's no one better fitted for the job than you.'

Ettie's eyes looked as though they might pop out of their sockets. 'The boy has a mother,' she said. 'Amelia . . .'

'Who will try to eviscerate Cindy at the first opportunity if she finds out what's going on,' Sam said.

Marcus stood with a grunt and held his hand over his mouth to hide a yawn. 'If you will excuse me, both of you. Sleep is calling me, and I cannot resist the temptation, even though the question of Jimmy's romance is undeniably a topic that deserves my full attention. Forgive me . . .' And he shuffled from the room.

'I need to go to him,' Ettie said, staring at the empty space where Marcus had sat until a few moments ago. 'Jimmy will have to wait. But frankly? The job of educating Jimmy falls squarely on your shoulders.'

'Jeez, Ettie, that's so far out of my comfort zone it doesn't bear thinking about.'

Ettie paused. 'Tell me, Sam. Who explained the basics to you?'

Sam looked affronted. 'Well, how the hell would I know? It's just something kids pick up along the way.'

'Maybe Jimmy is more aware than you think. Suss it out. And close the door on your way out. Softly. We don't want to wake the baby.'

CHAPTER THIRTEEN

THE FOLLOWING MORNING, UNDER AN iron grey sky and a lazy
wind that cut into flesh with the sting of a sharp knife, with the
sea foaming white but charcoal in its depths, Sam ordered Jimmy
into the wheelhouse. The kid's nose was red and dripping, his
hands blue; so Sam poured the lad a hot chocolate out of a thermos.

'Chocolate! Musta done something right, eh?'

'Cold weather. You deserve a treat.'

'Can't feel me fingers, Sam,' said the kid, trying to hold his
jaw steady but failing.

Sam rummaged around the storage space under the banquette
and came up with a pair of woollen mitts of dubious ancestry.
'Put these on, mate, till the drink thaws you.'

Jimmy opened his mouth to protest but shut it again after a
look from Sam designed to make his gonads shrivel.

'Amelia won't thank me if I send you home with pneumonia. And if you don't mind me saying, the bags under your eyes are packed like you're heading off on a long trip. Or you're just back from one.'

Jimmy shuffled, suddenly shy. 'Cindy and me. We stayed up talking till late then she sent me home. Said Amelia would tan her backside if she didn't.'

'She got that about right.'

Sam dithered over the day's work list while under his feet the impatient thrum of the *Mary Kay*'s diesel engine prodded him to get a move on. He made a quick decision. 'Okay, mate, you warm enough to let loose the mooring? After which, you and me, we're heading to the Briny Café for a sit-down brekky that's as good as you'll find in a five-star Parisian establishment on the Left Bank.'

'Aww, Sam, Kate used to say that.'

'Yeah. Never did quite get it, not having been to Paris or . . .'

'Cindy reckons travel gives you the best education.'

'That so?' Sam replied, his eyes narrowing. 'The mooring, mate. Time is of the essence.'

'Eh?'

'Just get the mooring!' Sam ordered, anxious to get the morning over and done with. He rubbed his forehead, trying to come up with an opening line for a discussion about the joys and dangers of an active sexual life. As they tied up at the end of the Briny's deck, he decided he'd need a double shot in his coffee and a double dose of jalapeño pickle on his scrambled eggs, for inspiration.

Jimmy beat him through the flywire door into the café. Jenny looked up from making lunchtime sandwiches. 'Your mum know where you were last night?' she asked the kid.

Sam did a double take. Jimmy looked like a rabbit caught in a trap. 'Didn't think so,' Jenny added.

'You're not gunna tell on me, are ya?' Jimmy asked, hippity hopping.

'You bet I am,' Jenny said, without a hint of humour.

The kid looked ready to cry. To change the direction of the conversation, Sam ordered his food, asked Jimmy what he wanted. The kid said he'd lost his appetite. Sam asked for a bacon and egg roll, double dose of barbecue sauce, a banana smoothie, then propelled him onto the deck where he pulled out a chair and forced the kid to sit.

'She's gunna kill me,' Jimmy said, almost sobbing.

'Who? Your mum?'

'Cindy. She's gunna kill me.'

'Why'd you reckon she wanted to keep it a secret—you and her, I mean?'

Jimmy, slumped in his chair, kicking a table leg, said, 'I dunno.'

Sam reached across the table and grabbed the kid's forearm. 'Mate, we're talking Cutter Island where a secret lasts a nanosecond. You didn't stand a chance in a million. If she's got a decent bone in her body, she'll understand.'

'Nah. She won't. We're done. Made it plain, she did. One word and we're done.'

A tear trickled down a cheek red raw from the wind. Jenny appeared with their food, warned them to eat fast or it would freeze in front of their eyes. She spun around quickly and disappeared inside the café.

'Tuck in, mate. Nothing gets resolved on an empty stomach.'

Jimmy broke off a small piece of bread, nibbled it, then picked up the roll and demolished it in three bites. Sam let out a hiss of double relief: that his plans for a heart-to-heart were put on hold indefinitely, and that the kid was not so heartbroken he couldn't find the energy to eat. He sent Jimmy back to the *Mary Kay*, then gathered the plates and took them inside to the sink.

'Tipped him out the back door and let Freddy Stillwell in the front,' Jenny said, without being asked. 'Girl has issues. Mostly to do with ensuring a solid supply of weed.'

'Expensive habit.'

'When there's no money coming in from gainful employment.' Jenny raised an eyebrow expressively and Sam gave her the thumbs up. 'I'll sort it,' he said. 'Not a word to Amelia, okay?'

Jenny shrugged. 'She'll know by now. The gossips have been at it since dawn.'

In the wheelhouse, Jimmy turned his back but Sam heard the sniffles and decided it was time for a slow cruise, no destination in mind. He made a couple of quick calls, citing uncooperative tides teamed with uncooperative winds, and ditched the work schedule. Then he pointed the nose of the *Mary Kay* towards a cove where the sun would shine and the sharp jut of the landscape would block the wind. This time, when he tried to mentally rehearse his speech, the words came easily.

Halfway to the cove where the rainforest crept down a gully of rocks and a waterway gushed after rain but went dry soon after, Jimmy got up from his possie beside Longfellow. His hand crept into Sam's and he held on as though to let go might send him spiralling into a vortex with no one on the edge to yank him to safety.

'Your mum call you?' Sam asked. The kid nodded. 'She said a whole lot of stuff you know is true but didn't want to hear?' Jimmy nodded again. The dog crept between the man and the boy, sitting at attention, eyeing first one, then the other, as if following every word.

'Love hurts,' Jimmy said, in a voice so small Sam struggled to hear.

'Oh yeah, mate. It hurts alright.' He steered a steady course. 'See that escarpment over there? It's old. Been around since the beginning of time. You and me? We're just passing through this world pretty damn quick so it's best to let go of stuff that doesn't do you much good and get on with the stuff that makes you feel . . .'

'Mum reckons she was only after me money.'

'You give her any?'

'Nah. She asked for me pin but only me mum knows that. Made her pretty bloody cranky, I can tell you.'

'Did you ask her why she wanted it?'

'Nah.' Jimmy slipped his hand out of Sam's grasp and wiped his nose on his wrist.

'Worked it out for yourself, I'll bet.'

'Told her I was gunna buy a ute one day. Wouldn't be seen dead in one, she said.'

'Woman has no class,' Sam said, grinning. 'Get ready to throw down the anchor. You and me, we're going to spin out the day, while the sea rocks us, light fades and even the birds decide it's time to find a toasty perch for the night. You with me?'

'All the way, Sam.'

⁓

When the boat was settled, Sam spread a blanket on the bow, found a couple of cushions and poured the last of the hot chocolate into two mugs. He and Jimmy sat side by side, facing the land, while steam curled lazily, and their drinks went cold. 'Let's talk about women,' Sam said.

'Ah jeez, Sam, everyone on the Island reckons you've got the sense of a gnat when it comes to the female species.'

'Female species?'

'Yeah. And the sense of a gnat. That's what they say.'

'So, my friend, let me leave aside the gnat issue, which I assume is based on my long-gone youth, and give you the benefit of my experience with the female species. I will try to explain where the delightful insanity of infatuation can land you if you're not careful.'

'Me mum beat you to it.' He slipped a hand into his pocket and pulled out a gaudily wrapped condom. 'I was wonderin', though, how you and Kate slipped up . . .'

Sam swallowed a quick, lighthearted response. 'Accidents happen, mate. So it's wise to choose your partners . . .' He hesitated. 'Ah jeez, drink your hot chocolate before it turns to ice.'

'You reckon Sally Butler is a good sort?'

Sam stared at the kid. 'More your age group, if that's what you're asking, but mate, you might want to steady up for a week or two before . . .'

Jimmy slapped his thigh. 'Just kiddin'. Had you goin' but.'

They weighed anchor. Outside the shelter of the cove the wind peeled the skin off their faces and the roll of the sea tested the serenity of the *Mary Kay*. Despite a satisfactory talk with Jimmy, Sam felt a cramping, roiling anxiety in his gut. In the end, he put it down to rough weather and let his uneasiness fly out the door of the wheelhouse to be dispersed by the elements and rendered harmless. But it was there again when he filled the kettle in his kitchen. It followed him into the shower, and then on to Kingfish Bay for his play hour with Claire, his dinner with Ettie and the chef. Coming up to tax time, he finally decided. It was enough to drive anyone's gut into turbulence.

CHAPTER FOURTEEN

MARCUS STOOD ON THE DECK above the café and stared across the water. His feet hurt. He had a blinding headache, and he was ashamed. A chef never left his post until the last dishcloth had been rinsed and here he was, upstairs in Ettie's old penthouse, feeling every one of his sixty-three years and almost tearful with fatigue before the lunchtime rush had even begun. He felt stripped of his manhood, assailed by intimations of mortality, and fearful that he might grow to resent the custodianship of beautiful baby Claire, because it was robbing him of the retirement he'd dreamed of during his pressured years of intense and stressful restaurant work. He tried to remember the last time he'd set off on an incoming tide with an icebox full of bait, a simple ham and cheese baguette— the best ham, and only Swiss cheese, of course—and a thermos of thick soup (perhaps pea and ham) to keep him warm if the fish were slow to bite. Weeks? Months? A year? Well, certainly not a year, if he intended to stick to the facts like an honourable man.

He would do anything for his darling Ettie and if he were twenty years younger, he would embrace it all, with enough energy at the end of the day to take out the boat by the light of a full moon, rod ready to haul in whatever bounty the sea was willing to offer. Now, he could barely keep his eyes open by dinner time, the highlight of his day, when the child lay sleeping and he reached for Ettie's hand and recounted (with what he hoped was a degree of hilarity for her delighted entertainment) the day's events.

Hearing a rising note of voices from downstairs, he took a great heaving breath of briny sea air, threw back his shoulders and prepared once more to enter the fray. Pulled up short at the bottom of the stairs when he saw Kate's former workstation and the accusing screen of her computer, *Mein Gott*, he thought, giving himself a mental slap on the wrist. Perhaps, when he boiled it down, it was just the increasing calamity of the accounts that was wearing down his customary ebullience. Nothing to do with the café, the child or the workload. Just those dastardly emails covered in numbers that he chose to ignore because he was a man, after all, who had done business in the days of paper invoices, cheques and handshakes.

'Jenny!' he yelled downstairs. 'We must, this instant, find a clear-headed person to do the accounts before the bailiffs arrive to close us down. Do you know someone who can fill the shoes of Kate until her return?' He clomped down the stairs to find a sea of curious eyes staring in his direction. 'This is no concern of yours,' he told the queue at the counter with a sweeping gesture of his arm. He marched behind the counter and raised his wooden spoon. 'Which one is the first in line?'

'Good on ya, Chef. Bacon and egg roll, thanks mate, heavy on the relish.' And so it went on until early afternoon, when Jenny made him a short black and took him aside to tell him Jane, an Island mum, would be a suitable replacement for Kate for the foreseeable future. The creases between the chef's brows smoothed in a moment and he turned his smile towards his stalwart colleague, whom he would have been proud to have alongside—well, perhaps a little behind—in his two-hatted restaurant. 'This Jane, she is good with figures?'

'Genius,' Jenny said.

'She is also capable of sliding a little this way and that way to accommodate a chef's creativity occasionally?'

Jenny screwed her face thoughtfully. 'Can't lie to you, Chef. She'll make Kate look slack. But she'll get the accounts back in order in a flash.'

Marcus sighed heavily. 'We must take this one footstep in front of the other. First the accounts. Then, when the moment comes, I will turn my great charms upon her. She will succumb instantly and we will reach a happy rapport that will bring great flourishment to the café.'

Jenny waggled her head in doubt but remained mute. The accounts were a shambles. She hadn't been paid for a couple of weeks. The chef was pushed to the limit and Ettie's occasional visits to the café only confused everyone. 'If Jane could start with my salary . . .'

Marcus slapped his forehead, a look of horror on his face. 'I have been distracted for too long. I will attend to this right now and ask your forgiveness.'

'Nah. Wait for Jane. She's on her way.'

'You are ahead of me, Miss Jenny. I can see that now. Yes, yes, Miss Jane, she will put all to rights and we can resume . . .'

'Gotta go, Chef. Dentist. You good to handle Jane and lockup?'

Marcus made a fist and stepped forwards like a boxer ready for battle. Then his face crumpled. 'But I must ask Ettie her permission for this new staff member to be on the payroll.'

'All done, Chef. Ettie's cool.'

Marcus opened his arms wide, head tilted to the side. 'You are ahead of me once more. Perhaps, after all, I am beginning to show a little sign here and there of behaviour to match the colour of my hair . . .'

'I'm outta here, Chef. See you in the morning.'

༄

Jane, a small, neat woman who favoured short spiky haircuts, an athlete's shirts and shorts regardless of the weather, settled into Kate's swivel chair as though she'd been waiting all along for Ettie to come to her senses and hire the right person. She'd been the frontrunner in Jack the bookie's list of contenders for the job: Kate not even listed on the board. Ettie's choice of the snooty former journalist had left Jane feeling hurt and undervalued and the inhabitants of Oyster Bay, who'd put their hard-earned cash on her certain victory, reeling in shock and uncomfortably out of pocket. When Jack bought a fancy new TV with his winnings, it took a community invitation to watch the Rabbitohs in the football grand final to accelerate his forgiveness.

Jane worked long after closing time, entering the chef's shambolic paperwork into the system and sussing out the sneaky little orders he'd tried to slip through on his personal credit card without any trouble. She tapped her finger on her bottom lip, wondering whether exposing Marcus's tiny frauds might be politically unwise, coupled, as it was, with Ettie's hazy confusion when it came to adding up. She would mull over the problem overnight. Or perhaps over a glass of wine when she got home. She picked up the empty cake plate next to the keyboard and carried it to the sink. Café work might turn into a dangerous business if she frequently succumbed to the dizzying seduction of sugar combined with eggs and butter. She checked her desk was neat and tidy, ready for her arrival the next morning, turned off all the lights and locked up. In the Square, she gave a little jig of joy. The stars, she thought, were aligned correctly at last, and good fortune had tapped her on the shoulder. She'd have a gentle word with Chef, just firmly enough to let him know she was on to his little tricks. It's what she loved about numbers. They never lied.

⌒

That night, Marcus and Ettie lay side by side in bed, the night sky through the window brilliant with stars. Despite his earlier conviction that the neglected accounts were all that lay at the heart of his growing discontent, Marcus knew there was more to it. He confessed his exhaustion, his growing fear that the years were compressing and time running out.

Ettie raised herself on one elbow. 'Time for what?'

He rolled over and gathered her in his arms. 'For life, Ettie, what else?'

'But . . . but what are we doing together, if not living life?' she asked, her breathing scatty and shallow. 'Marcus. Are you not happy with how we are together?'

'Do I not show you how much you are to me each day?'

'I don't understand . . .'

'I am wearing out, my love. I wish to be all things to you always, but I also wish to go fishing. I wish to lie beside you on a tropical beach while some kind person delivers trays of cocktails. I wish, Ettie, to be free to make choices. This is what I have worked for my whole life.'

Ettie swung her feet out of bed and reached for her dressing gown.

'I have offended you, my love, but mustn't I be truthful in all things? Isn't that the only correct path between a man and a woman?'

'I need some fresh air, Marcus. Time to think.'

'Ah yes. Time. That is the essence of what I am trying to say. We are running, you and I, like spooked deer, when the thoughtful pace of a turtle is better suited to this time of our lives.'

Ettie leaned over the bed and kissed Marcus's cheek. 'Give me a little . . . time . . . my love, to digest what you are telling me.'

'May I accompany you on this midnight walk?'

'Perhaps it's better if I am alone. Within ten minutes, there would be a delicious little nibble on a tray and a glass of some-thing delightful in my hand and we would pass the time—yes, yes, that word—distracted from what is a very serious issue. I love you with all my heart, Marcus, but there is so much more to consider.'

Ettie pulled the bedroom door closed behind her and made her way down the dark hallway, through the shadowy sitting room and onto a deck slippery with moisture from a low sea mist. The damp night air settled on her shoulders, clung to her face and hair. She turned on the dock light, smiled at dew drops hanging like diamonds from the rail, and turned towards the low-slung house where she and Marcus had made a life that she'd thought was more than enough for both of them.

She understood, of course she did, his desire to be free of all commitments and to swan around the world at whim, indulging every wish until the bucket emptied. Hadn't she felt the same way for years, without the funds to turn the dream into a reality? She'd hankered after a garret in Paris where she would paint masterpieces. A *pensione* in Italy where she would study the secrets of Italian cuisine. An island shack where she would dive with whales or dolphins in the deep blue sea. A desert where she would ride a camel along the ancient Silk Route, meet a sheik and have a brief, tempestuous affair. Or perhaps gaze up at the Himalayas from Everest's base camp with a Buddhist monk alongside to divulge the secret of happiness. Happiness? That blinding, ephemeral, short-lived rush of adrenalin—so much more seductive than solid and reliable contentment. Quickly forgotten but eternally yearned for. Was Marcus unhappy?

She wandered to the end of the jetty. A tinnie emerged from the murk of the sea mist, etched by frail starlight.

'Turn on your nav lights,' she called out. A torch came on.

'Shouldn't you be in bed, Ettie?'

'That you, Harry?'

'Yep.'

'Prawns obliging tonight?'

'Two tiddlers. Chucked them back to reach their teens. About to head home.'

'Keep the torch on, love. Not everyone has X-ray vision.'

Harry pushed the tiller away from his body and made a U-turn. In the dark, Ettie missed his farewell salute. She heard footsteps, then arms encircled her.

'What are you asking of me?' she whispered, leaning into Marcus's comforting bulk, hearing the steady beat of his strong heart.

'A holiday, my love. You and me. Alone.'

'But Claire? The café?'

His arms dropped away. The shuffling sound of weary feet made their way back to the house. Cold air rushed to take his place.

A breeze kicked in and shoved the mist along. Winds of change, Ettie thought. A metaphor for life. She shivered and waited until he'd had time to climb back into bed and then followed, careful not to disturb. The lonely sadness that had dogged her until the miraculous appearance of Marcus once again enfolded her. She thought of Kate, the disaster catalyst. The rest of them running behind with dustpans and brushes, cleaning up her messes. In her heart, she felt growing resentment. A new feeling, that one. It was joined by certainty that Marcus's request for a holiday was a useless poultice on a serious wound.

Back in bed, a warm hand searched blindly for hers, swept anguish aside. Their hands were still firmly clasped when they woke. Another metaphor, Ettie thought, rolling towards him to give and seek comfort. A cry came from the nursery. Her hand was released. Ettie sighed. 'I get it, Marcus. Truly I do. There will be a solution. There always is. Please. Give me time.'

'That word, my darling. So small and yet so heavy.'

CHAPTER FIFTEEN

AFTER A WEEK OF INTENSE discussions and detailed planning, it was agreed Lizzie would drive Daisy and Rob to the shack each day in her Land Rover—but only after she was satisfied the walkers had become so familiar with the tricky pathway through the bush that they could find their way blindfolded. They packed a picnic, hoisted on backpacks and clambered inelegantly into their commuter boat for the voyage to Oyster Bay. Ignoring Lizzie's warnings, each insisted he or she was fit enough to tramp the trail to the old shack.

'We'll call it an initial recce,' Sheila said, lifting a foot to inspect her new walking boots, recently ordered online. They were elegant little things, made from soft blue suede and highlighted with dashing red laces. Lizzie gave them two outings before they split at the seams. The others wore sturdy, elastic-sided hiking boots and long, thick socks to discourage leeches and ticks, although they'd sprayed a precautionary amount of insect repellent on their clothes before leaving the house. Sheila skipped dousing her boots, fearing the velvety leather might fade and blotch.

No one said much over the noise of the outboard motor but there was a tangible sense of excitement, of an adventure about to begin and previously undreamed of experiences on the horizon.

Mike Melrose brought the boat alongside the pontoon with a snazzy little turn that made a peacock tail of the wake. Lizzie stepped around her fellow passengers and disembarked with a steadying hand from Gavin. She tied the stern, the bow, with a couple of casual half-hitch knots.

'Enough to hold?' Gavin asked, uneasy.

'More than enough,' Lizzie reassured him.

'One more loop can't hurt, can it?' Gavin asked, bending to the task.

Lizzie held him back. 'They will tighten as the boat moves with the tides. They're easier to loosen this way.'

Mike raised the engine. Frankie wandered across from the boatshed, touched the brim of his cap half-heartedly. 'Booked up for anti-fouls for the next four weeks, if that's what you're after,' he said. 'And you're tethered to a private pontoon, unless something's changed.'

Lizzie emerged from behind the group. The creases between Frankie's eyes ironed out. 'It's you, Lizzie. My apologies. Didn't see you.'

'Meet my fellow housemates,' Lizzie said. 'You'll be seeing a bit of us for a while.'

Frankie scrutinised the group. The frown returned. He scratched the side of his head below the brim of his cap. 'Taking over the place, are you?' He gave a nod towards Kate's home.

'Nothing like that,' Lizzie responded. 'We're on a mission. Getting my shack up to scratch.'

More head scratching. 'Grapevine had you living for eternity in the posh abode' (he made it sound slightly insulting) 'at the end of Stringy Bark Bay. Got it wrong again, eh?'

'Maintenance, Frankie. Shacks need as much TLC as boats.' Lizzie brushed past him, anxious to end the discussion. One careless word and the community would weave a tale more fiction than fact. 'Things to do,' she added. 'And a work-out to get there. We'll be the fittest geriatrics in Cook's Basin by the time the shack is back in order.'

Frankie, a renowned pessimist, shook his head. 'Dead, more likely.'

Lizzie laughed. 'Hopefully, only a trip to the emergency ward, if it comes to that.'

Sheila insisted on taking a group photo, ignoring rolled eyes and loud harrumphs. 'For posterity,' she insisted. 'You'll thank me when you die and it's shown at the funeral.' She was greeted with blank looks. 'What?' she asked.

Gavin took her elbow. 'Never mind.'

The group set off, single file, Lizzie leading the way along the fore-shore, secateurs in her hand to trim a less lethal course through the bush. She gave a running commentary as entertainment and to distract from the discomfort of being stung by the serrated leaves of banksias, scratched by prickly Moses and lacerated by the vicious thorns of cabbage palm fronds. 'Known locally as Roman candles for their ability to burn inside the trunk for days,' she explained. 'Over there? That concrete slab? A fisherman's hut. All that's left of it. Illegal now. Water used to heave with fish. Sharks, too. Legend has it they were thick enough to act as stepping stones to cross to the other side of the bay without getting your feet wet. A shark bounty culled them almost to extinction. How perspectives change.'

She'd planned rest stops. Carried biscuits in her pack, a thermos of coffee that weighed heavily and made her think of calling a halt earlier than planned; but she pushed on, spurred by yelps and groans from her followers, Sheila the loudest. They needed to reach a point of no return to avoid drop-outs.

'Are you sure we're going the right way?' Sheila called from next to last in the line.

'Of course she is,' Gavin, behind her, said testily.

'It's just . . . there's a track there and there.' She pointed left and even further left. 'Are you sure we're on the right one?'

Lizzie called a break and made her way to the rear. 'They're wallaby tracks, Sheila. We're following clear markers left by early settlers. In a minute, you'll see steps chipped into rocks. Like a signpost. In any case, I could do this walk blindfolded.' (God, how often had she said that?) 'Ten more minutes and we'll stop for smoko. You okay to keep going?'

'Get your skates on, love,' Gavin said, giving his wife a not very gentle shove in the small of her back. She turned and poked out her tongue. 'Very grown-up,' he said, shaking his head in disbelief. A palm frond whacked him the face.

'Sorry, dear, thought you were further behind me.'

As promised, a set of steps chiselled out of the rocky hillside appeared. A little beyond it was a passageway through two boulders. 'Smoko,' Lizzie called, stripping off her backpack with relief. 'Biscuits. Coffee. No sugar. Two mugs. We'll have to share.' The others withdrew water bottles. 'Not much of a view from here. Bush thins out closer to the escarpment. Look out for Christmas bells. Still might be a few around at this time of the year. Pretty little things. Soon, you'll be able to see the ocean. Takes your breath away,' Lizzie said, pouring a small amount of coffee as the mugs were passed around.

Mike picked a shellback tick off his trouser leg. Squished it on a rock with his fingernail. In an instant, the others stood and furiously brushed their clothes.

'Bastards,' Gavin said.

'Check my neck, would you?' Sheila asked, sounding tense.

'My wife has a vivid imagination. Oh shit. Hang on. Did anyone bring tweezers?'

Sally fossicked in her backpack. Held up ointment and tweezers.

'Easy does it,' Gavin said, sliding the prongs under the tick's belly and removing the beast with a pop. Sally rubbed ointment on the swelling and wiped away the excess on the hem of her shirt. Sheila looked ready to cry.

'You'll be right,' Lizzie said, soothingly. 'I've had hundreds in my time. Right. All set? Onwards and upwards. Pace yourselves on this stretch. The rocks aren't always stable.'

They reached the shack an hour later, walking past a pile of building materials neatly stacked under a makeshift shelter that Gavin thought might give way in a stiff breeze. Kate, alerted by Cliffy (after a phone call from Lizzie) to their arrival, met them at the gate and led the way to the house, where she'd prepared egg and mayonnaise sandwiches for lunch. 'Chooks are going gangbusters,' she said, a hint of pride in her tone.

'We brought a picnic, just in case,' said Sally, who'd come up with the idea to take supplies to make their arrival easier for Kate to deal with. 'Six extras. Not easy to accommodate without a shop to run to.' She withdrew a hunk of cheddar from her backpack and grimaced at the sight of a soft camembert that hadn't travelled well. Gavin produced a salami made of duck. David held up 'a passable Veneto, although I've had much better in Italy'.

Sheila asked Kate to check her tick bite. 'You were a nurse, weren't you?'

'Not quite,' Kate said. 'A journalist. But it looks fine. Barely a lump.'

'Removed with the skill of a surgeon,' Gavin said.

'Butcher, more likely,' Sheila muttered but with affection.

Lizzie began to assemble lunch. Mike, David and Gavin went outside to scout around. Kate set the kettle on the hob. The kitchen hummed with purpose; the fire too warm until their bodies cooled from the strenuous hike. Soon, the aroma of brewed tea mingled with garlic from the salamis. Kate offered to make a pot of coffee, but she was met with a chorus of nos.

'One a day at our age,' Lizzie explained. 'Makes our hearts work too hard.'

Sally went to call the men and returned with Cliffy. 'Found him on the veranda. Says he could smell lunch a kilometre away and thought he'd wander over to see what was on offer.'

'Call me Cliffy,' he said, nodding around the room.

Lizzie used a teaspoon to point out *Sally, Sheila, Kate you already know*. She reached into her backpack and withdrew a jar of apricot jam. The old man did a little jig and planted a dry-lipped kiss on her downy cheek. 'A girl after me own heart,' he said, almost tearful with appreciation.

The other men stomped down the hallway, filled the room to bursting point. Cliffy made a dash for a chair. Lizzie told Mike to bring in a couple of footstools from the parlour to set near the fire. 'Long time since there was a party in this house,' Cliffy said.

Lizzie put a cuppa in front of him. 'Working bee, Cliffy. Not a party.'

'Feels festive to me, luv.'

Hear, hear. They raised teacups in a toast, warmed the bread over flames then placed it on the table. 'Break off hunks,' Lizzie said. 'There's no bread knife.' Sally made a mental note to bring one on their next visit. Hands clashed over the end bits. Lizzie looked happy. Cliffy thought he'd better dive in or it would all be gone. Kate slipped a plate of dainty egg sandwiches into the melee and handed around paper napkins. 'Throw them in the fire when you've finished with them,' she said, casually.

'Or the compost,' Lizzie added. Kate looked stricken and slipped out of the kitchen. Lizzie reminded herself she was now a visitor and, in future, she should keep her advice to herself.

'She's so thin,' Sheila whispered to Sally, who held a finger to her lips, a stern look in her eye. 'Well, she is!'

'We're here to work,' Mike said, overloud to cover Sheila's gaffe.

'Plenty of it to go round,' Cliffy said. He held up a half-eaten slice of duck salami. 'Never tasted anythin' better.' Then he hastily added, 'Barrin' your apricot jam, Lizzie.'

'What keeps you way up here on the escarpment?' Mike asked Cliffy, genuinely curious.

'Cows. Jersey. Loveliest natures and creamiest milk in the world.'

Sally and David locked eyes across the kitchen table. 'You're a dairy farmer?' Sally asked. 'We were cheesemakers,' she said.

You could've heard a pin drop.

Kate reappeared in the doorway with a basket of eggs. 'Everything alright?' she asked, silence ringing loudly in her ears.

'Oh yeah,' Sally and David replied in unison.

Cliffy didn't quite know what to make of it all.

'The girls are still laying, Cliffy, despite the cold,' Kate said, placing the basket on the counter.

'Won't last. Cold makes them crankier than a blue . . .'

'Arsed fly!' chimed in the cheesemakers, who had somehow dragged their chairs closer to Cliffy, their attention firmly focused on the dairy farmer, who continued to cut the salami, oblivious.

'Where'd you say you could buy this stuff?' Cliffy asked.

After lunch, Cliffy took the men to the ruins of the shed and opened boxes where he'd stored tools salvaged after the big storm tore off the roof and ripped away the walls. Mike admitted hammering a nail straight was beyond his expertise. He understood project management, if that suited. David paced out the footings of the shed, counting under his breath, working out the square metres. Like a tourist in a bric-a-brac shop, Gavin fossicked through piles that Cliffy had deemed junk. He held up one or two items, inspecting them closely, before chucking them back and choosing another, announcing, every now and again, that he'd found treasure. He took a small notebook and a shortened pencil from his shirt pocket and began a list.

David asked, 'How far to your farm from here, Cliffy?'

'Far enough,' Cliffy replied, worried they might want to call in.

'And the milk? There's a market for it?'

'Boutique, they call it.'

'What else?' murmured David, his tone silky with desire.

'Clarabelle and her calf live here, if you're lookin' for somethin' to do, you being a cheesemaker, you'd know how to squeeze a teat, eh? Kate's givin' it a go but her heart's with the chooks. Holstein, mind you, so lacks the cream of a Jersey.'

David threw his arm across Cliffy's shoulders. 'Care to point me in the direction of, er . . . ?'

'Clarabelle,' Cliffy repeated. 'Bein' a Holstein, she can get a bit bossy if you approach her the wrong way. I'll make the introductions, then leave you to get acquainted.'

The two men set off towards the nearest paddock where the last of the summer grass had browned off in the cold weather. 'A biscuit of lucerne hay every now and again and she'll follow you around like a puppy dog for the rest of your life.' He turned at the sound of grinding gears. 'That'll be the blokes to fix the roof. You lot are barred from ladders. Orders. Kate and Lizzie ganged up.'

'Thank God,' David said, with feeling. 'Never had a head for heights.'

Cliffy buried his hands deep in his pockets. 'Cheesemakers, you say. What flavour?'

'Mostly soft. Blues. Ashed. Washed rind.'

Cliffy nodded thoughtfully, gazed deep into the countryside, hearing the promise and potential, and took a moment to frame his reply. 'So you'll be needin' a Jersey's help, occasionally, eh?'

David smiled, pleased the old man had cut straight to the chase. 'You're pretty quick off the mark, mate.'

'Saves time in the long run.' Cliffy was silent for a moment. Standing still, feet planted firmly on the ground, his brain ticking over almost audibly. 'Much profit in cheese?' he asked.

David smiled inwardly. 'How about boutique milk?'

'Pays the bills. Not a lot left over.'

'Let's start small. See how it goes.'

'I've always been partial to a smelly soft cheese,' Cliffy said, dreamy-eyed and almost drooling.

In the distance, Clarabelle raised her head curiously. The calf, fat and glossy, almost as big as her mother, came trotting over, bumped hard against Cliffy. 'You need a name, little miss,' Cliffy said, rubbing the broad expanse of soft skin between her eyes. 'She's half Jersey. We'll see how she goes in a couple of years.'

'There's a sparkle about her,' David said, inhaling a soft bovine scent he hadn't realised he'd missed, scratching behind ears that stuck straight out from her head like handles.

'Sparkler she is then. I'll let Lizzie know. Favoured Daisy meself, but Lizzie said the name was taken. One of your mob, apparently.' Cliffy called Clarabelle, who was hanging back, 'C'mon, c'mon.' Singsong. Held out his hand. Empty, much to Clarabelle's disgust when she investigated with a thick purple tongue slick with saliva and flecks of grass. 'This here's David,' Cliffy told the cow. 'He's your new boss.' Clarabelle let loose with a torrent of stinking, steaming yellow piddle. 'Sign of acceptance,' Cliffy said, grinning.

'If you say so,' David replied, laughing. They turned away. 'Big shed Lizzie had there. Half the area would do to set up a cheesemaking corner.'

'Expensive.'

'Not saving for my old age, mate, I'm well and truly in it.'

'Mind over matter anyway. Meself? Old age seems to run fifteen years ahead of the current number on my personal clock.'

'Can't fault you there.'

⁓

It was late afternoon when Kate and Cliffy waved farewell to the visitors from the front veranda then went inside and, exhausted, collapsed in front of the fire. 'Socialisin' is hard work,' Cliffy muttered, beadily eyeing the kitchen counter to see if there might be a leftover slice of the duck salami lurking.

Kate took the hint and put on the kettle. Alert for judgemental undercurrents, she had been relieved to find only childish enthusiasm for the tasks ahead. Except for Sheila, who'd quickly dropped her gaze each time Kate caught her staring.

'Hope they make it back okay. Thought they might have left a bit earlier. The light fades earlier at this time of the year,' Kate said, assembling the scraps from lunch, along with some crackers she hoped were fresh. She stuck the board on a stool within Cliffy's reach.

'That lot are tougher than a paddock full of scrub bulls,' Cliffy said, piling a biscuit with so much cheese it crumbled and dropped between his overalls and flannel shirt. He fossicked around, popping bits in his mouth as he found them. 'You wouldn't have a drop of that highly commendable grape juice hangin' around, would you? Eases the pain in an old fella's joints as I discovered the other night.'

Kate smiled. 'A tonic, for sure.' She scrabbled in the cupboard of the old dresser and emerged with a bottle of red wine, holding it high in victory. 'Stocked up for the GeriEcstasies.' Grabbing two wine glasses, she set them on the chair with the cheese board, unscrewed the cap and poured a decent slug into both their glasses. 'Cheers!'

The old man acknowledged the toast with a cheeky wink Kate never would have expected of him, took a sip and smacked his lips in appreciation.

'Wine. It loosens the tongue if you've a mind to hear more of me life story,' Cliffy said.

'I'm listening,' Kate replied, raising her glass to him slightly, watching light play on its surface, and grateful for the diversion Cliffy offered. Though the GeriEcstasies had been warm and generous, she was painfully aware that abandoning her child would have shocked and distressed them. She was grateful no one had raised the issue and guessed Lizzie had given them their orders for the day.

Cliffy settled back into the red velvet armchair he'd delivered according to Lizzie's explicit instructions, and stretched his legs towards the fire, casting back to where he'd left off last time. 'They were hard times, after the Second World War. Me father, as I understood it from the little I was told, buggered off quick as a flash when me mum died. Never found out where he ended up. But I'm leapin' ahead here. You see, Mrs Porter, who'd taken me in to raise as her own, took a turn for the worse and found her own way to the pearly gates where I'm sure she was granted immediate entrance, good woman that she was. I became a ward of the state. Packed off to a cattle yard for orphans to be placed in foster care as soon as possible. In those days, there were lists of people willin' to look after kids like me, 'cause we came with a pay cheque from the government. One day, I was called into the office and asked if I wanted to go and live in the country. I jumped at the chance.'

'How old were you?' Kate asked.

'Couldn't rightly say. I put me age up to get out of the home and kept adjustin' it to suit circumstances until I clean forgot the truth.'

'When you married Agnes, though . . .'

'I just made up a year and stuck to it. The chaplain, decent bloke, knew my background and filled in all the blanks on the weddin' certificate to his own satisfaction.'

'But a guess, Cliffy, how old were you when you left the home?'

'Somewhere between eight and eleven. Maybe twelve. Does it matter all that much?'

'Old journalistic habits, Cliffy. Always check your facts. What was the home like?'

Cliffy looked at the toes of his shoes. 'We kids worked in the laundry, earnin' money for the good of the orphanage, they told us. Not a penny ended up in our pockets. Never saw any sign of it on our dinin' table, either. One day, one of the older boys got his arm caught in the wringer. Ripped it off at the shoulder, crushed bones and blood all over the clean sheets, the floor.' He glanced quickly at Kate, then away again. 'All over us. Never saw him again. Later, I heard his arm was gone for good. Farm work, y'see, it was all about daylight and fresh air. No more scrubbin' and me arms would remain anchored in their rightful place.'

Kate shuddered a little, drew her legs under her on the armchair, thinking that Cliffy's mother had died, which was sad, yes, but she couldn't be held responsible for her own death and therefore there could be no recriminations. But how would Claire feel when she was old enough to understand her mother had simply walked out for no apparent reason? Even more worrying was the possibility that Claire might blame herself. Hadn't Kate herself wondered if she'd been smarter, kinder, prettier, would her mother have stayed? She felt herself spiralling down and made an effort to snap back to the present. 'Was farming everything you dreamed it would be?' she asked.

Cliffy gazed into the fire for a moment. 'Let's just say I learned to fight for my rights from the beginnin'. The first family lot treated me like a slave. Up at five, make breakfast, do the milkin', clean the shed, get to school by half past eight. Walked there, naturally. A mile or two, although distances are bigger when you're a kid so I can't be dead certain. Back to work in the dairy until dinner. I was cook. And cleaner. Then it started all over again the next day. Weekends were worst. Come Monday, school seemed like a holiday.'

'Oh Cliffy . . .'

'Nothing to cry about, love. Didn't much matter anyway. After I met Agnes, me heart was full to the brim, each day a steady course. Would've been foolish to ask for more. Mind you, Mrs Porter had been big on teachin' me my rights so I didn't lack the courage to report conditions to the foster home. Quick as a flash I landed up here with a family that treated me like a son. Bought my first pair of shoes with the wages for my first week's work. Imagine how it felt to a kid like me: scones, jam and cream every mornin' for smoko. Cake in the afternoon before headin' to the milkin' shed and a young girl called Agnes with such kindness and warmth in her heart, she melted mine. All of it attached to a pay cheque. I'd found heaven on earth.' Cliffy lapsed into quiet contemplation and for a while, there was only the sound of the fire crackling, an owl hooting. Kate felt warm drowsiness seep into her bones. Cliffy saw Kate fighting off sleep, placed his hands on his knees, and pushed to his feet. 'That's your quota for tonight. Couldn't give you the whole story in one go. It would spoil the suspense.'

Kate nodded drowsily and escorted him to the veranda where he took a minute to stretch his back before he pulled on his boots. He fumbled for a torch in the bugger-it basket near the door and tested the battery. 'Best get to bed young lady. You'll need your beauty sleep before that lot descends on you in the mornin'. A word of advice, if you don't mind?'

Kate shrugged. 'Of course not.'

'Those retirees mean business. Might be best to stay out of their way.'

He patted Kate's shoulder fondly and set off. Kate closed the door. Leaned against it for a moment. Omission, she thought, the details Cliffy couldn't bring himself to utter out loud: the real pain stayed under lock and key.

Quickly, she reopened the door and called out, 'Go carefully, Cliffy.'

'As always,' he called, disappearing into the bush where only the faint glow of the torch gave any indication he existed.

Later, as she lay sleepless, Kate confronted the awful truth that she was virtually condemning Claire to the same emotional merry-go-round of her own childhood and—if she was being strictly accurate—adulthood.

CHAPTER SIXTEEN

ETTIE PACED THE JETTY, AS she had every day for the past week, Claire heavy in her arms, hoping to be struck by a solution to Marcus's plea for respite from the café, her loyalties torn between the pressures of business; the promise she made to a dying man to keep running the café, the essential hub of the offshore community; and her open-ended commitment to Claire's wellbeing. Lost in her thoughts, she didn't pay full attention to the noise of the helicopter until it was almost overhead, the wind from the blades making whirlpools on the water, whipping Ettie's full skirt into furious tangles.

Her hand protecting Claire's head, she ran inside to watch from the open window in the sitting room. The police boat swept past. Richard Baines, new water-police boss, stood tall at the helm. He was a man with a perfect palate, whom she would defend against

Tyrannosaurus rex (if necessary) after his delicate handling of the murder investigation at GeriEcstasy. His offsider, unknown to Ettie, scoured the thick bush on the other side of the bay through binoculars. Her phone pinged. She put Claire on the floor and checked the alert. Missing person. Young woman. French. From Paris. Ettie snorted. As if Paris made a difference.

A moment later, three young men from the house at the end of the bay trotted along the sandy shoreline in front of Ettie's house, heads down, pace steady, like Zulus carrying a message to a distant tribe. The fireboat cruised closer to the boys. 'She's a cracker,' yelled a firey. The boys gave a wave, increased their pace to a comfortable jog. Ettie smiled. Pretty young woman in need of rescuing. What young man could resist the call? She put Claire in her crib. Made a coffee and carried it outside, then took a ringside seat at a drama in progress. Before long, the boys sauntered back, shoulders slumped, dejected and disappointed.

'Find her?' Ettie shouted.

'Turns out she was three metres from the path and two bushwalkers almost tripped over her.'

'No damsel in distress then?'

'From Paris, Ettie. What more is there to say?'

Paris, Ettie thought, her head filling with dreamy images of cobbled streets glistening in the rain; tucked away bistros selling exquisite confections; history embedded on every street corner. Paris with Marcus. She felt almost sick with yearning.

Out of the blue, Ettie was struck by the awful thought that her kindness to Kate had been used and abused and she was like the little boy who put his finger in the dyke to stop Holland from disappearing under floodwaters. 'Plug holes, that's all I ever do,' she said out loud. 'Plug holes in Kate's slipstream. That girl needs a shake-up. Wake-up. Whatever.' Ettie felt a rising sense that she'd let herself be fiercely taken for granted and even badly treated. She pictured Claire in her crib. 'Well, not entirely used and abused,' she conceded. Kate had a good head for business. She was efficient, tough with suppliers and customers trying to skip paying the bill. She'd built a beautiful penthouse above the café. She was a tea connoisseur. Liked old jazz. Open fires. Good wine or none at all. Strove for perfection, even if it was only to keep the salt and pepper shakers clean and filled on the tables. Ensured profits escalated, aware that she, Ettie, suffered from severe numerical dyslexia (she was an artist, a creative person, after all), which meant the bank balance could tilt alarmingly in the wrong direction in no time and without the sharp eye of a vigilant overseer, lead to the ruin that Ettie suspected lay in constant wait.

Then there was the baby. A small, inarticulate, squirmy little bundle around which all decisions revolved. Ettie visualised those sea-green eyes, recalled talking to her about passing seabirds, the light on the water. There was trust in those eyes. Entitlement, too. The art of charm and manipulation deeply embedded from the first breath because how else would babies survive?

Paris, though. In the rain. Or sunshine. Or snow. With Marcus. Over dinner, she would ask him if he was fluent in the language. Perhaps not. To give him hope, when circumstances offered none, would be a cruelty. Anyway, he dreamed of tropical islands, as different from Paris as light and dark.

～

As business was slow, the chef took an early mark, leaving Jenny and Jane to tidy up and lock up. The two women were surprised but didn't question him closely. In a way, it was a relief to have him out of the café. His attention to the finest details, such as removing an untidy crumb from a cake displayed on a plate, tested their patience when all they wanted to do was wipe the benches, mop the floor, and skedaddle.

To hide her worry at Marcus's early arrival, Ettie immediately launched into an account of the day's adventures at the same time as she guided him to his favourite armchair. She described the lost young woman from the streets of Paris ('Surely this woman was not a sex worker, which your statement implies?')—well, from Paris but who knows what street—and the humming testosterone of the local lads from the end of the bay. Despite his tiredness, the chef smiled. 'This city of food and fashion, it never ceases to inspire. Have you ever travelled to Europe, Ettie?'

'Only to Venice on my honeymoon. I blame the city for falling in love with offshore living.' She kissed him on the top of his head, and added, 'I've prepared dinner, so there is nothing for you to do but soak in the view.'

Ettie had half expected the big man to insist his role as chief cook in the house was inviolable, but instead he conceded at once. There was not a skerrick of bravado or faked dismay at being usurped from his staunchly defended role.

'Shall I bring you a small glass of something to fill the time?'

'Nothing. I am content,' he said, gazing out at the way the wind swept the water and listening to the song it let loose in the trees.

Ettie adjusted the position of his footstool and, after removing the chef's shoes, lifted his feet so they rested comfortably. His face pale, eyes closed, he sighed heavily and let his head with its mane of thick white hair fall against the back of the chair.

I don't know how long I will have this wonderful man for, she thought, and with the clenched fist of mortality landing heavily in the region of her stomach, she felt her anger rise against Kate once more. Unable, this time, to force it into submission by focusing on her kindnesses and fiscal nous, 'What kind of a woman dumps her baby?' she muttered, heading for the kitchen but detouring to the nursery to check her charge was still sleeping. She was greeted with a smile so joyous, Claire's thrill of whacking toys strung across her crib so boundless, that nearly all angst dissolved. But a small, rock-hard kernel remained lodged next to her heart.

She popped a new toy and some baby board books into the crib, hoping it would be enough to keep Claire entertained for a little longer, thinking she should keep the living room quiet while

Marcus rested briefly. She went into the kitchen to pull together a meal she'd decided to refer to as a 'family dinner'. Nothing fancy or cheffy. Plain grilled lamb loin chops (yes, macerated with olive oil, garlic and rosemary, a cook has her pride, after all); potatoes parboiled then sautéed with garlic, red capsicum and sprinkled with parsley; a simple green salad doused in a dressing her mother once made: dry mustard, sugar, olive oil and vinegar. How many memories were tied up in food? She recalled her first taste of an orange and almond cake when she and her mother had afternoon tea in a posh café during a shopping trip. It was the moment she understood too sweet could be sickly and a little bitterness could lift flavours. Her thoughts drifted like smoke around the recollection of a pair of red, patent leather shoes with a strap across the instep. Worn with turned down white socks. The style had a name. Mary Janes. Yes! How she loved those shoes, even though they crammed her little toe and every outing resulted in a blister or two.

She spun the greens to dry the leaves and wondered what Parisian shoe shops looked like. As she set a skillet on the stove top for the potatoes, she heard Sam's boat engine, so she hurried along the hallway to the jetty, holding a finger to her lips in a shushing signal. 'Marcus is asleep,' she whispered as Sam came alongside the pontoon.

'Is he crook?' Sam, alarmed, leaped from the boat and tied up, before facing Ettie, frowning.

Ettie shook her head. 'Dog tired and feeling his age.'

'The holiday will do him good.'

'What holiday?'

'Pretend I never said a word.' He set off briskly.

'What holiday?' Ettie asked again, hurrying to keep up with Sam's long strides, feeling the night cold seep through the sleeves of her shirt. By the time they reached the house, Marcus, sleep tousled and with the confused, slightly vacant look of the recently awakened, waited in the doorway. 'Ah, it is good to see you, my friend.'

As if on cue, a wail came from the nursery. Sam covered the distance swiftly. 'Let the cat out of the bag, mate. Sorry,' he called over his shoulder.

'What holiday?' Ettie asked, fixing the chef with a firm look.

'Follow me, my love,' he said, reaching for her hand. 'There are plans wafting in the air and much to discuss, but Sam is essential to this conversation between companions and cohorts.' He continued to burble in his customary way, and Ettie felt the tension ease from her shoulders, as fear for his wellbeing loosened its grip. She promised to reappear by his side with a refreshing glass of honey mead—or would he prefer a big shiraz to rebuild the red blood cells in his tired but much-loved body? A comment that put a twinkle in the chef's eye, a lighthearted skip in his feet, raised the corners of his mouth. Ettie gave him a little punch on the arm and told him to *settle petal*, as she fought the urge to interrogate him: Holiday? What holiday? And if so, what about the baby?

⌒

Said baby, for now, was fed by Sam, played with and bathed, and then carried off to bed: tuckered out after the vigorous rolling, bouncing, tickling and pretend dancing with her dad. Dinner for the adults was a historic event. For the first time ever, they ate in the kitchen. Ettie had thrown a red gingham cloth over the stainless-steel bench, placed a vase of gum leaves in the centre. The cleansing smell of eucalyptus wafted refreshingly over the thick aroma of lamb chops and mingled with the scent of mint squished into a little sugar and stirred into malt vinegar. In this atmosphere of intimacy and informality, Marcus and Sam outlined their plan.

'We will begin with the business of how to run the café when you and I are both absent,' Marcus announced, spearing a chunk of potato, chewing it thoughtfully, nodding his approval towards Ettie.

'But . . .' Ettie began.

'Let me explain before you interject, Ettie, my darling. Please.'

'Marcus, I . . .'

'Ettie!'

The force of the chef's response silenced Ettie in a way that left both Sam and Marcus wide-eyed with amazement. Quickly recovering, Marcus began again.

'The Three Js—by this I mean Jenny, Judy and Jane—have agreed to shoulder the responsibility for the café. Of course, Jane is already in residence under the stairs and is showing an ability with numbers that I wish was not quite so precise . . . but I concede, a business must be aware where the profits and losses lie.'

Sam cleared his throat. Ettie tapped her fingers on the benchtop. The chef, noting their impatience, tried to reign in his tendency to overelaborate. 'Jenny is also already experienced in the ways of the café. Which means I have only to describe the role that Judy will play. Yes! Judy! A good home cook—without your flair, Ettie, and naturally, with none of a chef's flourishes—but a woman whose creations will not disappoint, and who will always be honest. Patrons of the Briny Café can ask for no more when we explain that their beloved Ettie is in need of a holiday.'

'But . . .'

'This holiday, at first, will take no more than three days. This is a test, a trial run. I believe this is the correct description. A period so that we may feel confident if we are ever to attempt a more prolonged departure . . . Paris, I am guessing, holds more promise for you than the tropics.'

Ettie, struggling to follow the chef's meaning, said, 'The baby, Marcus . . .'

'Ah, yes, do you think I have forgotten this wondrous addition to our lives? Of course not. But now I must hand over to my partner in this campaign.' He made a hand signal towards Sam, who straightened on his stool.

'It seems to me, Ettie, that while I have taken a day off here and there as required by current events, and while I have recently made sure to keep all weekends free to care for Claire, I have never had three whole days in a row to do as I please. At least not since the days my mum and dad were alive. So honestly, I'm really looking forward to spending an uninterrupted three days with my daughter, while you and the chef go off to a winery. Ah jeez, sorry, Chef, you were keeping that part a secret and I've blown it.'

'A winery?' Ettie asked, eyes sparkling, face aglow.

'If this is your wish, my love. Naturally, anything can be negotiated that falls within the time limit, but I must tell you in all earnestness and with much regret that Paris or a tropical island is unlikely.'

'A winery,' Ettie breathed. 'To wander among the vines. Eat cheese—not too much, of course. Dine in splendour watching the sun drop behind blue hills. Oh Marcus, what a wonderful idea. Not so far away, either, that we can't rush back if there's a crisis.'

Marcus visibly slumped. He pushed away his plate, a man defeated by Ettie's concern for a baby, a concern that he could not, truthfully, fault.

Ettie saw it, felt it, wished she could grab back her words. She did the next best thing. 'By crisis, I mean raging storms or catastrophic bushfires that threaten the whole community. Anything less, people can sort out for themselves.'

But his joyousness had been curtailed. He pushed back from the kitchen counter, wearing an air of exhaustion and discouragement. Ettie and her responsibilities. He wondered where he was positioned in a long line of them. Not at the head of the queue, of that he was certain. He declined dessert and made his way back to his favourite chair. Ettie's eyes filled with tears. She looked to Sam for support.

'Bloody Kate,' Sam muttered. 'Put out one fire and another sparks. Her bloody legacy. Goes on and on.'

After a quick clean-up, Ettie sat on the arm of Marcus's chair. 'Do you have a preferred destination? A winery you've desired to visit above all others?' Marcus patted her knee without opening his eyes. 'You will always have one eye on the phone and this does not make a holiday. Merely a situation where we are both waiting for one calamity or another to reel us back to Cook's Basin. Where our presence—if you want my honest opinion—will not change whatever has befallen in our absence. So let us put this idea aside, Ettie, until you are ready to let go of the waifs and strays that are tied to your apron strings.'

Sam, desperate to lift the mood, said, 'Just so you know. Doesn't matter what you two decide, Claire is with me for three days straight. Need to square it with Jimmy and slide a few barge jobs around, so it'll probably happen next week. Wednesday, Thursday, Friday. Leading into the weekend, which means you'll have a five-day break from baby duties. What you do with the time is your business. My advice? Make the most of it. And Ettie? Don't even try calling to check on things. I won't pick up. On that note, my two great and good friends, I will collect my sleeping child and head home with her wrapped in my arms for a weekend of fun and games.' He paused in the doorway. 'Jeez guys, go away for a few days. Enjoy. You've earned it. And nothing, I swear nothing, will fall apart the moment your backs are turned.'

'Tempting fate, Sam,' Ettie said, without a hint of humour and reaching for the wine table to tap wood. Marcus lifted a tired hand in farewell. Ettie saw the oven burns striping his skin and swallowed rising tears. If Kate had been within reach, she would cheerfully have strangled the woman. She went to fetch the first-aid kit. Returned to the sitting room to dab Betadine on the chef's wounds. He barely stirred. In the kitchen, she looked at the dessert she'd prepared and sighed. Reached for a bowl. Gave herself a double helping of apple crumble and a triple helping of vanilla ice-cream. Then fiercely regretted the impulse.

∽

By habit, Ettie woke early on Saturday morning even though there was no baby to tend. A brisk breeze from the south sailed in the window and crisped the air, blowing away the fog of sleep. On the bay, a few whitecaps looked like harbingers of hard weather, the kind that meant shutting the windows, lighting the fire, grabbing a blanket and settling on the sofa with a good book and a cup of hot chocolate. If only, she thought, swinging her legs out of bed, slipping her feet into slippers, grabbing a dressing gown and making her way to the kitchen. She found a neatly folded note tucked under the kettle, her name written elegantly on the front in handwriting she instantly recognised.

Apprehensive, she delayed reaching for it. The formality was unsettling. They weren't the note-leaving types. They talked:

Marcus to a fault, sometimes. An endearing fault, she reminded herself.

What if he had decided to spell out his demands, or worse, written in precise lettering and the kind of firm language that left no wriggle room, that he wished their relationship to end? Had she always asked too much of the men she invited into her bed? Is that why she had a past littered with the ghosts of lovers who casually straggled off, occasionally without even a polite farewell glass of wine to mark the moment? Before the arrival of the chef, Ettie's confidence had been rock bottom. She'd been fearful of relationships that seemed to inevitably lead to hurt. Buying the café, making it a success, enjoying the daily banter with the people who wandered in and out, had saved her from falling for the easy, transient charm of practised womanisers. Marcus had been different from the very start. He made her feel valued and safe. But every man had his limits, and it was entirely possible she'd tipped the balance of give and take beyond even his capacities. She pushed the note aside with her index finger, as though it might bite, filled the kettle and hoped a strong cup of tea would give her strength. Wiped a tear from her cheek, unaware till then that one had broken loose.

A fresh brew in her hand, she reached for the note and made her way onto the back deck to shelter from the wind. She sat on the bottom step of a pathway chipped into the hillside, felt the cold and damp seep through her night clothes, and sipped two or three times before placing the mug on the ground.

She took a deep breath. She was a woman, after all, who had coped after her husband had walked out without a backward glance. To survive the pain, she'd ditched the myth of the happy suburban housewife for food and art. After moving to Cutter Island, where she embraced a community she considered to be family but without the hassles, she became the self-appointed welcome committee and educator for dreamy newcomers who were frighteningly ignorant of the subtle ways offshore life could make or break them. It staved off loneliness and filled a void. When she became co-proprietor of the Briny Café, she was certain she'd found that endlessly desired but rarely achieved phenomenon known as fulfilment. Then Marcus, bear-like, open-hearted and unafraid to plunge into what might have turned out to be a risky and even unwise liaison, had appeared and thrown himself into a court-ship that had threatened every hard-won emotional defence she'd erected. The moment she realised he was seeking nothing but ready to give everything, it felt like she'd been touched on the shoulder by a gilt-edged wand. She stared at the creamy, thick paper that she suspected might define her future. her shoulders sagged, her spirit waned. She swallowed a sob. The wind picked up. Above her, treetops swayed, leaves falling like teardrops into her lap, her hair.

'Get on with it, Ettie,' she said out loud. With the tip of her fingers, like the paper might be red hot, she unfolded the note and read through blurred eyes.

A moment later, she squashed the note against her chest with both hands and cried until her tears ran out, the tea was stone cold and her bottom had become numb. She looked down at the chef's neat writing to be sure she hadn't misunderstood. '*We will find a solution. I, Marcus Allenby, make this promise to Ettie, the love of my life.*'

She stood, turned in a shaky circle once or twice, her eyes wet, and declared to the trees, 'Thank God.' She rubbed her damp face with the cuff of a sleeve, and saw below, in point form, that he had written that the winery had been booked. The date set. Together, under the influence of great wine and good food, surrounded by bare and twisted vines, under a (hopefully) sunny blue sky, the solution to their mutual happiness would make itself apparent.

Ettie's emotions somersaulted between euphoria and fury: any last niggle of concern for Kate's mental state consigned to the rubbish bin. She totted up the escalating peripheral damage and decided the time for compassion and understanding was over. She considered her options. One overrode all others. She would confront Kate and to hell with the consequences. Someone must know her whereabouts. People didn't dissolve into thin air. She tapped her fingers on her thigh. Who would know? She had a flash of intuition, the same sort that convinced her a baby was being born high on the escarpment during a killer storm. She dragged her mobile phone from her pocket to dial Lizzie.

'If you don't tell me exactly where to find her right this minute, I will come after you on my broomstick,' Ettie said before Lizzie had a chance to say hello. 'We're talking life and death, Lizzie, so don't beat around the bush.'

Ettie heard a long sigh, the sound of sipping. 'We're just finishing breakfast. I'll call you in an hour.'

Ettie, who'd worked herself into an incandescent rage, shouted, 'Now, Lizzie, or I'll jump in the boat and come around to beat down your door.'

'Life or death, you say?' Lizzie calmly responded.

'Marcus . . .'

Ettie heard the sound of chair legs scraping the timber. Lizzie told her to hang on, she was heading for a more secluded spot. Moments later, explaining she was now in her suite, Lizzie asked, 'What's really going on, Ettie?'

'The café is killing him,' Ettie said, her voice breaking with emotion. 'The baby is sucking the life out of both of us. In a good way, it goes without saying. But I'm trying to keep everything on an even keel and not doing a great job of it. I have asked too much of Marcus. He is bone weary. He wants—needs—a break and the only way is for Kate to shoulder at least some of her responsibilities. But you see, Lizzie, I have no idea where to find her. Do you?'

The pause at the other end of the conversation told Ettie everything she needed to know. 'I suppose you've been sworn to secrecy,' Ettie added, as the silence stretched unbearably.

'You're putting me in a difficult position,' Lizzie said.

'Quite frankly, Lizzie dear, I don't give a damn,' Ettie said.

'I cannot break a trust,' Lizzie said.

Ettie responded bluntly by killing the call.

Ettie showered, dressed, pulled on her walking boots and, filled with righteous zeal, set off for Lizzie's shack where she was sure, beyond doubt, that Kate was hiding out. Call it infallible women's intuition, based on the fact that Lizzie neither confirmed nor denied knowing Kate's whereabouts. She resolved to return with a plan to restore a work-life balance or bust in the attempt. To risk damaging Marcus's health and their relationship perhaps beyond repair was a sacrifice she was not prepared to make. For a giddy second, she imagined their wedding: considered the menu for a celebration feast. Ditched it. To join in the eyes of the law felt tawdry and mercenary, somehow. What she and Marcus had was enough: too valuable to reduce to convention.

As always, once she'd decided on a course of action, Ettie's equilibrium returned and she dared to dream of visiting Paris. Maybe Nathalie on Cutter Island might teach her a few carefully chosen phrases. To whisper words of love across candlelit dinners in a language universally famous for the greatest love stories ever told (to be fair, the Russians weren't slouches, either): nothing could equal the thrill. Some of those love stories ended quite tragically, it was true, but she would not allow that to happen to her and Marcus. With her mind focused firmly on *happily ever after,* Ettie sprayed her clothes to ward off ticks and set off with what she later thought of as fire and brimstone in her belly. *Carpe diem.* Hadn't that been a lifelong mantra?

Way off on the horizon, storm clouds gathered. She paused, undecided about whether to continue or return home. Chided herself for lacking courage and kept on. In her pocket, she felt the reassuring bulk of her mobile phone. Seize the day but live to seize another. Common sense, really. Kate had plenty of that, too. When she burned bridges, she made sure there was a safety net.

At the thought of Kate, Ettie picked up her pace. Those long daily walks with Claire strapped to her back had improved her fitness. With luck, she'd outpace the rain.

She noted the track beyond Kate's house had been recently cleared, which confirmed her belief that Kate was holed up in Lizzie's shack, and she made good time. When she reached the plateau, she scanned the bush for landmarks—a couple of old car doors; a scribbly gum with a carved arrow to point the way; entrance gateposts threaded by hungry white ants and held together by a toothpick of timber—afraid of getting lost. She didn't have a hope of noticing the red-bellied black snake coiled in a patch of weak sunlight until she almost stepped on it.

'Shit,' she shrieked, leaping away. The snake raised an eyelid but stayed still. She saw, then, that its back was broken, and it was dying. Pity welled. 'You're meant to sleep in cold weather,' she murmured, keeping her distance. 'A bird get you? Sea eagle? Or one of the wedgetails?' She whispered a few rough sacred words she knew were incorrect but they were said with goodwill, so that had to mean something. With a sigh of apology, she picked up a stick and gently pushed the snake off the track and out of danger from the double indignity of her heavily booted foot on the return trip. Although it would be thoroughly dead by then, and probably hauled off by a hungry critter.

A walk in the bush, she thought. Who knew what it might throw at you? She noticed, then, a hessian sack tossed off to the side of the track and almost hidden under a thatch of prickly Moses. A sign of movement within. Another snake? Dumped by poachers if rangers were about? Then she heard a pitiful whimper. Without thinking, but careful of the thorns, she dragged the bag free. Holding it close to the ground and grabbing the corners, she tipped out the contents, ready to leap to safety. A small tan and white bundle toppled to the ground and hunched tightly at the sight of her, snout tucked into pink paws, liquid brown eyes rimmed with black like carefully applied eyeliner, overflowing with mute pleading.

'Oh God,' Ettie murmured, scooping up a handful of skin and bones. The puppy snuggled into her neck, clung on ferociously. Cold wet nose. Strength in the limbs. Not long in the bag, then. 'Who did this to you?' she asked. 'Who would do such an awful thing?' A rough pink tongue licked Ettie's nose. With a good feed and a warm bed, it would survive, she thought. The ends of her mouth curved upwards as she formed a plan that would tip Kate's current existence into chaos. Karma, she told herself without a shred of guilt.

A short distance further on, with the puppy firmly tucked against her chest, she saw the first car door. Soon after, the second.

And then there it was, the arrow carved into the silver white trunk of the scribbly gum.

'Nearly there,' she said soothingly, stroking a furry head with her index finger. The feel of a little beating heart next to hers was oddly comforting in the eerie loneliness of the bush, where she could easily have walked straight past the elusive, narrow, chalk-white track and found herself spinning in circles.

Further on, she ducked under the post and rail fence, hand pressed lightly against the warm little body that had crawled higher to rest at her throat, the sound of contented snuffling tugging at her heartstrings. 'Poor baby,' she said softly. At the sight of the house, she yelled, 'Cooee! Cooee!'

She was met with silence when she knocked on the back door. She turned and scanned the grounds, keeping an eye out for movement, a human form. Nothing. She heard footsteps down the hallway, the back door opened and Kate stood there wearing gardening gloves, carrying a trowel, her face streaked with dirt and perspiration, knees of her overalls stiff with ingrained soil.

'Ettie?' As if she couldn't believe her eyes.

'In the flesh. Could kill for a cup of tea. If you have the time.' The last said with a trace of acid irony.

Kate gave herself a little shake, put down the trowel and pulled off her gardening gloves, throwing them in a basket near the door. She stepped aside. Ettie squeezed past, the pup tucked inside the collar of her jacket and invisible, held against her chest as though swearing an oath, when it was in fact to support the little animal. Kate looked well, she noted, colour in her cheeks and alert, with a sharp light in her eyes.

'Some cereal, too, mushed with milk. In a small bowl. I've brought you a new lodger.'

Kate, not listening—perhaps scrambling to figure out how Ettie had found her—failed to pick up on the request. 'Cereal. Of course. I'll put the kettle on.'

Inside the warmth of the kitchen, Ettie looked around before removing her jacket, throwing it over the back of a chair. 'Always loved this shack,' she said. 'A home to be lived in instead of looked at or admired. Not that I've been here very often. Once or twice. Lizzie has always been very private.' Ettie quickly took in the sight of a plate that showed the trail ends of a sandwich, apple core, muesli bar wrapper, and what looked like cake crumbs. So she was eating, it seemed. She took a shallow bowl from a shelf, searched along a row of storage jars before grabbing one.

'Make yourself at home,' Kate said drily.

Ettie spun around, feeling the fire in her own eyes. 'Don't mind if I do. Warm some milk, would you? Or have you forgotten how?'

'I could fix some toast, if you'd rather,' Kate said, ignoring the knife thrust, or perhaps unprepared. Ettie was not a woman who ordinarily meant to wound.

'It's not for me. I picked up a hitchhiker.' She gently withdrew the puppy from her clothing and held it out to Kate, who quickly stepped away. The pup, suspended in the air, legs scrabbling for a foothold, whimpered. 'Dumped on the track,' Ettie said, drawing the pup close again. 'It's going to need a home and you're closest.'

'Oh no. Not here. Sam . . .'

'Is already busy running a business and looking after a motherless child.'

Kate turned away, a tide of red rising from her chest. 'How did you know I was here?' she asked.

'Cook's Basin. No secret lasts beyond the sun going down. But in case you're wondering, Lizzie never betrayed you. I could fib and say I'd noticed the GeriAncients suddenly get busy and with Lizzie leading the charge, the shack had to be their focus. But truthfully, it was a guess based on my intuition, which as you know is infallible.' Ettie risked a smile, which went unnoticed.

Kate put a small amount of milk in a saucepan and warmed it on the hob. Ettie set the puppy on the floor where it instantly squatted and piddled. 'Paper towels, please,' she said, reverting to brisk business again. 'She'll need to be house-trained. And given a name, too, so she knows she's joined the family.'

'Ettie, I really can't take on a puppy.'

'You can. And you will. Not negotiable. How about Foxy? She has the look of a fox terrier about her.' Ettie wiped up the mess. Kate sprayed detergent. The pup looked small and insignificant on the timber floor. Lost but with a spark of hope in her eyes. 'Here, hold her while I ditch the paper towels.' The pup thrust quickly into Kate's hands.

'Chuck the stuff in the fire,' Kate said. 'It'll stink out the bin.' She held the pup away from her body like a filthy object. Ettie fixed the food, placed the bowl on the floor and pointed. Kate set the pup down. She sniffed, buried her snout in the mush and gobbled, licking the bowl clean. An upward look of what Ettie swore was thanks.

'What is it about rescued animals? They give you gratitude and unflinching loyalty for life if you let them. Treat her right, Kate, and she'll be a soul mate. No. Don't say a word. She's staying. End of story. In a day or two, you'll miss her if she's not getting under your feet. Like babies, if I'm not mistaken.'

Kate ignored the barb and opted for neutral ground. 'Foxy is a terrible name,' she said, and Ettie knew she'd won.

'How about Lucky?'

'Or Spot for the tan dot on her back. Or Tigger . . .'

'Tigger. That sounds about right.' Ettie bent low and held out a finger dipped in milk. 'Come, Tigger, come.' The pup looked confused. 'Come, Tigger.' Slow steps, a pink tongue reaching out. 'She's a smart pup,' Ettie said, lifting her once again to nestle against her neck. 'A quick learner. Word of advice. Soon as she starts to sniff around, take her outside. Means she's looking for somewhere to pee or poo.'

'I'll find a basket, make a bed on the back deck.'

Ettie's eyes widened. 'She's one mouthful for a python, Kate, and too young to find her way home if she wanders off. Beside the fireplace will work nicely to keep her warm. Or let her sleep next to your bed for a few days until she learns this is home.'

Kate looked trapped. Ettie, feeling smug, made herself comfortable by the fire. Ticked off the wins on the fingers of her left hand. Two so far, and she'd barely begun. The pup snored lightly, exhaling damp warm air on Ettie's skin. The heat made Ettie sleepy, and she was lulled by the serenity of Lizzie's shack. Clean and tidy beat new and shiny every time. She felt a pang when she thought about her own passion for arranging and styling right down to the angle of a napkin set on a plate.

She woke sometime later, slightly confused and wondering what she was doing in Lizzie's shack, and what exactly had finally made her break her vow to stay away from Kate until the young woman had dealt with her own demons. *Ah yes. Vineyards. Paris.*

Satisfied she was back on track, she saw the fire had been stoked, the kitchen tidied and Tigger was cheerfully chewing the rim of her new basket. She reached for the puppy, the comfort of warm fur, the delight of being needed. 'And therein lies my downfall,' she told the pup, wondering whether the compulsion to feel needed by others was selfish or genuine altruism. Probably a bit of both, she decided.

Hearing footsteps in the hallway, she straightened, returned the pup to her basket only to see it leap out, start sniffing around. 'Kate! The pup needs a piddle. Outside now or double the order for paper towels.'

The young woman flew in, gathered the dog and bolted outside. Ettie smiled, her thoughts more coherent now.

'How often do I feed her?' Kate asked, when she returned with the pup following on her heels and already committed.

'Four times a day. Small helpings.' Ettie looked around the room. 'How do you get supplies?' she asked.

'Cliffy does the shopping,' Kate responded. 'I reimburse him, of course.'

'Well, put some specialised puppy food on the list; or even better, make her food from scratch. There are recipes all over the internet. Like all living things, the pup will thrive with love and care.' As soon as the words were out, Ettie felt mean, but she resisted softening the statement. Kate looked healthy. If depression of some kind had driven her to the shack, she could see no visible sign of it now.

Kate blushed and picked up the puppy, placing her back in the basket. She stoked the fire. Put on the kettle. While the room throbbed with unspoken words, she washed her hands at the kitchen sink and prepared another bowl of mush, leaving it on the counter.

'You'll have guessed I've tracked you down for a reason,' Ettie said, breaking the silence.

Kate nodded; sat heavily by the fire. She avoided looking directly at Ettie, focused instead on Tigger.

'I'll be brief,' Ettie said, standing with her back to the flames, hands clasped tightly behind her.

'Babies, as you know, are a full-time job so, while I am caring for Claire, Marcus is being leached dry by the café. He's exhausted. Overwhelmed. He feels trapped at a time of life when he thought he'd be ticking off his bucket list. Also, his feet hurt.'

The corners of Kate's mouth lifted slightly.

'He wants to travel and, Kate, I want to go with him.'

'Is this a build-up to saying you want to sell . . .'

'No! Bertie trusted me to keep the café as a hallowed institution for offshorers. He'd send down a lightning strike if I sold it to the highest bidder, which—if you'll forgive me—is what I know you would insist on doing, regardless of the impact of an unsympathetic new owner on the community. The café services its people with tact, kindness and, mostly, a blind eye.'

The kettle boiled noisily. Kate got up, removed it from the hob, fussed with tea leaves, the teapot, cups and saucers. She remained silent.

'The thing is, we're trialling a three-day excursion to a winery. Sam will take a few days off and look after Claire until we return. He has her every weekend anyway. If all goes well, the next stop for me and Marcus might be Paris for three weeks. Maybe four. Oh, don't worry about the café. We've locked in a good team. Jenny, of course, Judy as back-up cook, Jane in accounts. The extra staff means the salary we've continued to pay you will be reduced to a stipend calculated by Jane. Don't expect too much. She makes Scrooge look generous but it's the best we can do. The food will be honest although understandably lacking Marcus's inspiration.

Which leaves the problem of caring for Claire through the week. You're unemployed. You live close by. And she's your daughter. Time to re-engage with your child, Kate.'

Ettie watched the colour drain from Kate's face, her sudden breathlessness. Ettie recognised fear and flight responses but Kate had nowhere to run. Kate's hand, as she poured the tea, shook. Not entirely back on track mentally, then, Ettie thought and took pity. 'We've made the bookings but there's enough time to prepare. Sam will continue with his weekend shifts, but you will both have to work out a system that is in Claire's best interests. You'll need a cot, of course, and all the other stuff that goes with babies. I'll leave you to sort all that.'

Kate pulled out a chair from the table. Dipped her head so her dark hair fell over her face, making it unreadable. Wrapped both hands around her mug as though it might shatter if she let go. Ettie, now filled with remorse for being tough, almost pleaded, 'This—the shack, living like a hermit—it has to be temporary. You must have understood that from the start.'

Kate gave an almost imperceptible nod, which Ettie took as agreement.

A great maw of silence opened in the room. Ettie's phone pinged with a text from Lizzie that she ignored. Finally, she stood, picked up the puppy, kissed its head, handed it to Kate, who held it a little closer this time, then left via the front door.

Out of hearing, she called Lizzie's mobile phone. 'I've just left Kate. I gave her a robust talking to. I'm on my way back to

Kingfish Bay.' She checked the sky and saw the storm clouds had melted away or gone out to sea. A woman who shamelessly believed in omens, she saw it as a positive sign.

As Ettie headed in the direction of home, Lizzie stayed on the line to explain how the GeriEcstasies and Cliffy had shepherded the young woman through the earliest dark days. Then she asked what else had been discussed in the shack in a way that made Ettie's ears tingle, though she couldn't put her finger on the reason why. 'Arrangements for child care when Marcus and I take a holiday that could be as long as a month if Paris is our destination. Paris, Lizzie, just imagine!'

❧

Later, when Ettie told the chef about her visit, she described Kate as a woman ready to faint. 'But I didn't weaken. Nor even wobble for a tiny moment. You are my life and that child is Kate's responsibility,' she told him.

His eyes filled with relief and she kneeled beside him, her hands on his thighs.

'The pup?' Marcus asked.

'Tucked under her chin. Nose nuzzled into that lovely little hollow at the tip of the sternum. There's a name for it. I'd have to watch *The English Patient* again to find it, though. Quite touching, the two of them.'

Marcus nodded and reached for Ettie's hand, enfolding it in his warm and calloused paws. 'My understanding—correct me if I am wrong—is that Paris is not too far away for an old man like me to dare to create little dreams and plans.'

'I forgot to ask. Do you speak French?'

'It is the city of love and romance. We will not need words.'

Ettie sighed. Turned her thoughts from the wrench of leaving Claire to visiting the city of romance with a man she loved beyond measure. In bed later, she read him a response she'd written to his note and watched the furrow in his brow, the tightness in his lips, disappear and he reached for her and she laid her head where she could hear the steady thump of his beautiful heart. It was only later that she wondered why Lizzie had asked if anything else had been discussed, as though something no one had the courage to confront lurked under the surface. She shrugged the idea aside. Blamed her vivid imagination.

cం

Sam sat wordless at the dinner table while Ettie told him where Kate was living. She recounted her phone conversation with Lizzie in more detail, explaining how Lizzie (sworn to secrecy) and the GeriAncients had joined forces to rebuild the shack, pretending they needed a project and Kate just happened to be in the line of fire. Cliffy, she added, had nursed Kate through the worst times, teaching her self-sufficiency and self-reliance that left no time for any unhealthy navel-gazing and ensured she fell into bed exhausted. For the chef's peace of mind, she skipped any mention of a snake that should have had more sense than to be out and about in the cold weather but spent a great wadge of time recounting her close encounter with a hessian bag that contained a gorgeous little puppy that was now in Kate's care.

'How did she look, Ettie?' he asked, when Ettie had run out of steam.

'Thin. But clear-eyed and her skin was a good colour. From the gardening, I expect. Definitely coming good. I'd say that's an accurate interpretation of her wellbeing. Actually, I reckon the outdoor life suits her.'

'Did you discuss the holiday plans?' Sam asked, aware Ettie tended to skirt around difficult topics.

Ettie's face turned pink. 'Naturally, Sam.'

'In detail?' Sam asked, his suspicions aroused by the colour of Ettie's cheeks.

'Well, as much detail as there is at the moment.'

Watching the by-play, Marcus delicately pushed back his chair from the table so not even the rug under his feet wrinkled. 'I will clear the way for dessert,' he said.

Sam watched him leave the room, the old-man shuffle of his feet, shoulders rounded with tiredness.

'This holiday can't come fast enough,' Ettie murmured.

'I feel responsible,' Sam said. 'It was too much to ask, to have you looking after Claire when you had a café to run.'

'You didn't ask,' Ettie said. 'I insisted and, to be fair, looking after Claire has been wonderful. But now I need to care for Marcus.'

'Did she say anything about me?' Sam asked.

'Who? Kate?'

Sam nodded.

'We didn't have a conversation, Sam. I gave Kate an ultimatum, non-negotiable and imminent. I didn't leave her room to move.'

'But Ettie,' Marcus said, entering the room with a large cake on a stand, 'this woman who talks in ultimatums, this is not like the woman of whom I am so fond.' He set the stand on the table and went to a drawer in the dresser to get a knife. 'If I am not mistaken, I smell almonds and blueberries, perhaps a hint of orange peel. I am right?' He passed Ettie a slice on a plate with flowers festooning the edge.

'When have you ever been wrong?' Ettie asked, humour adding a shine to her eyes.

'Well, there was a time . . .' Marcus guffawed. 'But in truth, although I thought I was wrong, I was right!' His laughter thundered and bounced, filling the dining room with his old energy. 'Which means, if I am not mistaken, that I was still wrong.' He passed Sam his dessert, tears of laughter running down his cheeks until, noting Sam and Ettie's puzzlement, he added, 'Must I explain this to you?' He wiped the moisture from his eyes.

'Oh right. I get it, Chef,' Sam said. 'Two wrongs make a right. Or maybe they don't!'

'Yes, yes, my friend. Exactly. And this is something we must remember when we address the issue of who will care for baby Claire in our absence. All must be right from the start, with no room for error.'

'If Kate fails to fulfil her side of the bargain,' Sam said seriously, 'I will take a month's holiday with great pleasure. It will give me time to train Jimmy in the rewarding career of a nanny.'

∽

Two days later, feeling lighthearted, Ettie and Marcus set off for their romantic three-day break.

CHAPTER SEVENTEEN

HIGH ON THE ESCARPMENT, DELIVERY day for the cheesemaking equipment came with the myriad complications of living on a property accessible only across National Park land. To circumvent the need to get permission for a delivery truck to enter the grounds, the GeriEcstasies decided to use Cliffy's tractor to transport shelving, benchtops, tables and all the large paraphernalia required to produce delicious cheese. (Artisanal, of course.) Lizzie's ancient Land Rover would manage the smaller items, such as sinks, strainers and tubs. Arrangements were made to meet the truck at the entrance gate before the ten a.m. opening time to create as little disruption to park visitors as possible. With luck, the sun would shine and the handover proceed quickly and efficiently. To be on hand to help with logistics, the team set off from Stringy Bark Bay in the pre-dawn light, pausing only to watch the ocean turn from red to vivid pink as the sun broached the horizon. 'Glorious,' Sheila breathed. A remark that had everyone looking at her in surprise. 'What?' she said, annoyed by the reaction. 'I appreciate nature as much as anyone else.'

Sally, eager to cut off what could escalate into a marital spat, went to Sheila's side. 'Of course you do, dear. Look how successful you were in the fashion business.'

Mollified, Sheila dug a finger into Gavin's ribs. 'What did I do?' he asked.

'Nothing, that's my point,' said his wife.

Lizzie clapped her hands. 'Time to get moving again,' she said firmly.

⌒

At home, Cliffy attached the trailer to his ancient tractor and set off at the speed of a browsing tortoise, to meet the crew at Lizzie's shack. He arrived to cheers of encouragement and swept the hat from his head to bow to his audience. 'A genuine antique machine,' Mike said, running his hands over the big wheels, then standing back a little to get a better view of the whole machine.

'Want to have a drive?' Cliffy asked, grinning and aware sports cars were more to Mike's taste.

'Another time, perhaps,' Mike quickly replied.

David, to less applause but much encouragement, climbed into Lizzie's equally antique Land Rover. After a couple of false starts that had the assembly either praying or crossing their fingers according to individual beliefs, the engine kicked over with a blurt of black exhaust and the motorcade set off at royal tour speed along the rutted tracks of farmland and National Park.

Cliffy and David found the truck with the driver holding a map and looking confused at the park gates. Cliffy waved from his high seat in the faded green tractor and called out a greeting. The driver, relieved, folded away the map then watched with a combination of alarm and amusement as the old dairy farmer manoeuvred the dented, scratched and patched trailer as close as possible for an easy off-load. When he was satisfied he could do no better, Cliffy clambered slowly to the ground and went to shake hands with the truckie. 'Left your engine running, mate,' the truckie said, nodding in the direction of the ancient beast.

'Haven't lost me marbles, if that's what you're thinkin'. It's one start-up a day or Betsy goes on strike. Safer to keep her nicely tickin' over.'

The truckie wandered over to inspect the tractor more closely. 'She belongs in a junkyard,' he said, patting a giant scabby wheel that he thought might be one of the originals. Before Cliffy could respond, he shook his head in disbelief and walked to the Land Rover where David was dropping the back seat to make more storage space. 'But this old girl is a different kettle of fish,' he added, 'a collector would pay a fortune for her.' He peered inside, sussing out the internal condition of the vehicle. 'If you ever wanted to sell . . .'

'Not mine to sell,' David said, a little tersely. He'd become quite fond of a machine that had handled the rough and tumble of bush tracks for more than forty years without much more than a grease and oil change and new tyres.

'Woman who owns it, name of Lizzie, treats the car like a member of the family,' Cliffy chipped in.

'Still, I could give you my phone number. You never know.'

'Oh, yes we do,' Cliffy and David said in unison.

By silent agreement, the three men marched to the truck to start unloading. The truckie threw open the rear doors and jumped into the cargo area easily. Cliffy and David looked at each other and shrugged. Not a leap for them today but *back* in the day . . .

'Got me flummoxed but,' the truckie said, pulling the first flat pack off a pile and sliding it towards the old fellas.

'What?'

'All this stuff heading into a National Park. What's it for?'

Cliffy, still rankling a little from the truckie's unfeeling comment about his beloved tractor, was tempted to suggest he mind his own business but pointed towards the boxes instead. 'Let's get this show on the road, eh?'

David stepped forwards to help.

'Outta me way, mate,' Cliffy said, nudging him aside.

'Deny me the excitement of unloading the goodies. Wouldn't have picked you as a man with a mean streak, Cliffy.'

'Lookin' after your old man's back, is all,' Cliffy responded benignly. 'Me being the youngest—bar Kate and the pup—in a collection of interferin' old fusspots.'

'You're the youngest!' the truckie said, visibly appalled. 'Jeez, boys, I don't like your chances with this stuff from here.'

Cliffy gave him a look that killed the conversation stone dead. He told David to fetch ropes from the back of the Land Rover. 'Tie the boxes up tight on the trailer. If one falls off, I'll remind you of it for the rest of your days. However many that may be, heh, heh.'

The truckie shook his head and did his best to help balance a stack of assorted shapes and sizes in the least precarious way. When the job was finished, he stood back while Cliffy revved the idling tractor and crunched the gearstick with a noise that shocked a flock of white cockatoos into hysterical flight. David turned the key for the Land Rover. The ancient engine coughed once or twice, blurted noisily from the exhaust, then muscled up with a guttural roar. The truckie watched the museum-quality GeriEcstasy fleet set off slowly along the bumpy track, the boxes on the tractor trailer swaying a little but holding firm. He wondered if he should alert the rangers to a couple of old fellas with grey hair and bent backs who might be building a dope refinery in the bush. Decided against it. Live and let live.

⌒

As they pulled up at the shack, the smell of scones emerging from the wood-fired oven almost assaulted Cliffy and David. They exchanged a quick look that spoke volumes, ditched the idea of unloading and followed their noses towards the food. In the kitchen, Lizzie, flushed from the heat, raised her eyebrows. 'How did it go?' she asked.

'Sweet as a nut,' Cliffy replied, kissing the tips of his fingers.

A large pot of lamb and barley soup, hanging from a hook above the fire, simmered lazily. Cliffy went over and lifted the lid, inhaling the aroma. David automatically set out plates and spoons, and the others, who'd gone outside to check out the loads, filed back into the kitchen, everyone talking at once. Cliffy pulled on a heat-resistant glove, lifted the soup pot off the hook and placed it on a thick chopping board in the middle of the kitchen table. Kate stacked warmed soup bowls in front of Lizzie's usual seat so she could serve. Sally took the tray of scones from the oven and tipped them onto a plate, gingerly pushing one or two that had stuck. The fire crackled, soup was slurped, cutlery clinked, and every so often a groan of contentment came from one end of the table or the other. Cliffy patted his stomach and announced he would soon have to go on a diet or start jogging. Gavin burped. Mike glanced at Lizzie as if to apologise for his friend. Sheila caught the eye contact and grinned inwardly.

One minute before one o'clock, Mike clapped his hands and stood. 'Time's up. It's back to work.' Kate cleared the table. Lizzie did the washing up. Daisy wiped dishes and put them away. Sheila offered to peel and chop vegetables for tomorrow's lunch, (another broth that would slow cook over the fire all night) but Lizzie took her elbow and steered her towards the hallway.

'Kate and I have some private business to discuss, and if I'm not mistaken, Gavin has his eye on the sofa. You'll need to cut him off at the pass,' she said. Sheila sprinted into action. Gavin, about to step into the parlour, was caught in the act. 'No time for afternoon naps, my darling. Many hands, etcetera, and the new shed equipment needs the kind of organising only you can do,' she said. She winked at Lizzie—who'd waited in the hallway to be sure Sheila wasn't tempted to listen at the door—and added, 'Never hurts to boost a man's ego.'

Outside, Cliffy and David had begun unloading the tractor. Mike, overseer and storeman, ticked off the purchases against an invoice on a clipboard and declared the freight was in order.

Kate, who'd caught Lizzie's words, tried to slither past the old woman, muttering about weeds and compost, but Lizzie was too quick and grabbed her wrist and pulled her back into the kitchen.

'Denial is dangerous enough,' Lizzie said, getting straight to the point. 'But cowardice is worse. Which, if you don't mind me saying, you are showing a strong tendency towards, if not embracing fully.' Kate, white-faced and trapped, busied herself sorting cutlery. Lizzie straightened the chairs around the table then took a seat in front of the fire and patted the chair nearest to her.

'Sit down, Kate. And don't try to escape because I will follow you like a bad smell.' Kate sighed, placed the last spoon into the drawer and turned around, leaning her backside against the dresser. Lizzie patted the chair again and, reluctantly, Kate sat down, her back ramrod straight, hands folded neatly in her lap. Only a faint flush rising from her throat gave away her discomfort.

Lizzie said, 'I've been putting off this discussion for a while.'

'What discussion?' Kate looked away, and then back.

'About you, Sam and the baby.'

'It's not a subject I'm keen to revisit.'

'Nevertheless, with Ettie and Marcus planning a holiday, and Claire coming to live here for a few weeks, for my own peace of mind, I need a few answers.'

Kate made a dismissive gesture with one hand, suggesting Lizzie was out of order.

'You must know by now that I have only your best interests at heart or you wouldn't be living here. I believe I have earned the right to ask questions, Kate, whether you like it or not. It goes without saying that you are entitled to refuse to answer.'

Kate flopped back into the chair, aware she had nothing to gain and much to lose. 'What do you want to know, Lizzie?' Her tone was icy; granite shone coldly from her eyes.

'Are you well enough to care for Claire?'

'Do you mean mentally? I'm okay, Lizzie, if that's what's worrying you. Always have been. Well, perhaps not always, but despite my anxiety about Claire's safety once she started to crawl, I figured I'd learn ways to cope.'

'Then why did you leave the baby with Sam? Given the paternity issue, wouldn't it have been more honest to keep Claire with you?'

Outside, there were shouts of laughter like noise from a kid's playground. A high-pitched squeal from Sheila. Cliffy yelling in mock anger. 'Not there, here!' Somewhere, a cockatoo screeched, which set off his mates. Noisy miners joined the hullaballoo and jolted kookaburras out of their afternoon somnolence, so for a few minutes, the bush roared. Inside the kitchen, the silence was deafening.

Kate picked at the skin around her fingernails, then hurriedly clenched her fists against further assault. Lizzie waited, her mouth set firm, and her eyes never left Kate's face. Finally she said, 'It is not a frivolous question, Kate.'

Words spilled quietly. Lizzie leaned closer to better hear.

'I'd already done enough to hurt Sam. Taking Claire would have snuffed out the last of his good-hearted innocence. It would have left him bitter and twisted. I couldn't do that.'

'Do you love the child?'

Kate stood to throw a small piece of kindling on the fire, avoiding Lizzie's scrutiny. 'Love? Oh yes, Lizzie, I love Claire. But I can't look at her without feeling guilty. As if I'm not good enough to be her mother. So it's complicated.' She coughed away the huskiness that conjoined with the word 'love' and now the words came faster and louder: 'I see Claire and I see Sam. Then I feel the betrayal and I have no idea how to make it right.'

Lizzie held out her hands to the flames. 'You're a smart young woman, Kate. You know the solution but lack the courage. Am I right?'

'What's the solution, Lizzie? God, if you know it, you tell me.'

'Tell Sam the truth. If you don't, it will dog you forever and impact every single day of your life until you die.'

'And if I do that, it will impact every single day of three lives instead of just one,' Kate responded fiercely.

'Can't you see that there's no alternative? The damage has been done. It's time to fix it.' Like a distant echo, travelling from a time when she sat crying and broken on a rock in the bush, her mentor's words returned to her. She repeated them to Kate. 'You're a young woman. You've got a life to live. I remember Dorothy saying those words to me when I thought my future was over.'

Kate's eyes flew to the framed sketch of Dorothy returned to the mantelpiece by Lizzie when Kate became a tenant of the shack. 'She must have been amazing.'

'She was. And so is Sam.' Lizzie paused, choosing her words carefully. 'He doesn't strike me as a man who'd let the arrangement of Claire's DNA get in the way of his love for her . . . or you, if it comes to that.' Lizzie stood and brushed non-existent fluff from her jeans. 'I'll ask Sam to join us here at the weekend. He can bring Claire and the Ancient gals will babysit while the Ancient blokes fiddle with the details of construction and cheese-making. Then the two of you can discuss the finer points of child care during Ettie and Marcus's holiday. And Kate?' She made a sweeping gesture taking in the four corners of the shabby old room still drenched with the floury smell of baked scones. 'You can't hide here forever.'

∽

When they learned that Ettie had virtually forced Kate to reunite with her child, the GeriEcstasies threw themselves into the restoration of the shack with a frenzy they'd thought impossible at their age, overriding Kate's objections with a casual wave of a hand, shrug of shoulders, warm smiles. 'The baby, Kate. The house must be airtight and warm for the baby.'

David and Cliffy retreated to the shed, where they did a trial run of the new equipment and discussed the benefits of fresh, raw, unrefrigerated milk for creating a cheese that seduced and enticed. Cliffy had a bounce in his step. David dropped ten years from his calendar age.

'They're like a couple of schoolboys building a cubbyhouse,' Sally said, watching them from the veranda, where she held a cup of tea and contemplated the wisdom of a second scone smothered in Lizzie's jam. 'I haven't seen him this fired up since we sold the business.'

Sheila, who'd quickly traded her wrecked glamorous boots for a pair of tough, elastic-sided Redbacks, stuck her feet on a stool and grinned. 'They were always getting in the way in Stringy Bark Bay. Lost little boys without a project beyond brushing spider webs, chopping wood and stoking the fire. This is so much better . . . for all of us.'

Sally nodded. 'Men without a project are aimless. Whereas we women . . .'

'Know how to relax!' Sheila said, laughing.

The sound of a lawn-mower came closer. Gavin rounded the corner in a cloud of dust and waved. 'Didn't he cut the few blades of grass left last week?' Sally asked, puzzled.

'Yep. He hated the job when we lived in suburbia. Go figure.'

Sheila succumbed to the temptation of another scone, licked the overflow of melted butter and jam from her fingers. 'Lizzie and Mike. What do you think?'

'What do you mean?'

'Come on Sally, look at them. Never far from each other. Grinning for no reason. Next, they'll be finishing each other's sentences.'

'Lizzie's nearly eighty, for God's sake. And Mike's not far behind.'

'The desire to love and be loved never dies, I'm reliably informed.'

'By whom?' Sally asked.

Sheila tapped a finger to her nose. 'My lips are sealed.'

'Lizzie said something?'

'Don't be ridiculous. I'm not sure she even realises what's going on.'

'Nothing's going on. I'd stake my life on it! They're old!

'So are we!' Sheila said, as though age was irrelevant.

'Yes, but we have history with our partners. If anything happened to David, I couldn't think of anything worse than going back on the market, as we said in our youth.'

Sally visualised cows in a saleyard; farmers checking legs, hips, the roundness of backsides before putting up a hand to bid at auction. Up popped an image of Sheila, back on the market, defiantly perched in the middle of the herd in her stilettos, fending off the competition. She laughed.

'What's so funny?' Sheila asked, frowning.

'Nothing.' She swallowed more laughter. 'Nothing at all.'

'It's about loneliness, isn't it?' Sheila continued, warming to her theme. 'Companionship. Talking to someone at the end of the day. Even to Gavin, who occasionally cares enough to listen.'

'The thing is . . . we've all heard each other's stories a thousand times, over what sometimes feels like a thousand years, and we're all too polite to say, "Enough! No more. Tis not so sweet now, as it was before . . ." Apologies to Shakespeare and all that. Lizzie is fresh blood. A new audience. Mike will run out of puff soon and the same old stories will be resuscitated, revamped and retold. Like all of us, Lizzie will roll her eyes and invent an excuse to leave the room. Let's clear up. Time to get back to work.'

Sheila shook her head. 'Not sure about all that. They're either smitten or hatching a top-secret plan.'

'When's the baby arriving?' Sally asked, changing the subject.

'I'd stake my life something's going on they're not telling us about,' Sheila said, ignoring the question and scooping Tigger, who was looking for a playmate, into her arms.

'That puppy redefines cuteness. Kate will have her hands full when two mouths are wide open and demanding food.'

'Anyway, for what it's worth, I'd put my money on smitten,' Sheila said firmly.

'Now that you've mentioned it, I'd vote for top-secret plans. Neither of them has what I would call the soppy look of love. More like joined in practical endeavour. But what?'

⁓

The cheesemaking business was underway by the end of the week. Cliffy pointed out that cow's milk was lacklustre over the ungenerous winter, and suggested they'd be better off waiting for the lush nourishment of spring.

David overrode his doubts. 'Early days and lots of trial and error ahead,' he said. 'No products are allowed off the property anyway, until all the permits are in place and health department inspections carried out.' Cliffy visibly blanched at the thought of government bureaucracy—a phenomenon he had long distrusted and considered devoid of common-sense—finding its way onto the hallowed ground of the two last freeholds on the escarpment. David laid a consoling hand on his shoulder. 'Modern life, Cliffy. There's no escape in this digital age. Blink and someone records it.'

'Or charges a bloomin' fee to allow us the privilege of workin' our backsides off,' he retorted, grumpily.

David laughed. 'You're sounding like a Luddite, mate, but you've got it in a nutshell.'

Cliffy was proud of the rich cream that rose to the top of his non-homogenised milk, which could liven up a dull dessert for no extra cost to the consumer. His mother-in-law, and later his wife, he told David, also made clotted cream when the milk was at its peak, slow cooking it overnight in the residual heat of a wood-burning stove. No permission required. Scones and strawberry jam elevated to a standard just short of holy, in his (unbiased) opinion.

'Strawberry?' David questioned, shocked to hear the word fall from the lips of a man who revered those blushing golden explosions of flavour that translated into apricot jam so exquisitely.

'Agnes's mum favoured strawberry, but when she tasted a batch made from Lizzie's apricot tree, the jury was hung. After Agnes died, Lizzie continued the tradition. About the permits . . .'

Seeing rebelliousness build in Cliffy's faded blue eyes, David quickly made his point: 'Health department regulations, follow them or pay a price if someone gets a wobbly tummy.'

Cliffy almost reeled. 'You're makin' me wonder why we're doin' this, mate. At your age—which is considerably ahead of mine, if you don't mind me repeatin' meself—takin' risks is one of the first signs of encroachin' doolally-ness. As for me, I'm comfy with me life, right down to the soles of me shoes. I'm beginnin' to think tryin' to give Kate a future and you blokes somethin' to do might be settin' us on the path to endin' our present.'

'Have faith, my friend,' David said, slapping Cliffy on the back and causing the not-as-old man to cough.

'Trust me, I'm tryin', but from where I'm standin' right now, I'm feelin' more thorns cuttin' through me flesh than me nose twitchin' from smellin' the roses.'

'Another thing I've been thinking. Our products are going to need a name. Lizzie reckoned something with *Agnes* sounded about right,' David said, playing his trump card. 'What do you reckon about Agnes's Farm House Cheese? Or Agnes's Sweet Grass Dairy Cheese?'

Cliffy's objections melted away at the memory of his wife, whom he thought about at least once a day and occasionally spoke to in the dead of night, when there was no work to take his mind off the loss, and the loneliness was unbearable. 'Wish she'd lived to see it. She was partial to a good soft cheese,' he said, pleased her name would live on after he joined her on the other side of the great divide.

CHAPTER EIGHTEEN

AT HOME IN STRINGY BARK Bay, Lizzie made one last attempt to persuade Sheila against throwing a party to celebrate Claire's return to the arms of her mother. 'It has all the hallmarks of a disaster in the making,' Lizzie warned. Sally, who was also against the plan, carefully tried to explain Kate and the baby would need tranquillity and privacy to re-establish their relationship. Daisy nodded her agreement but refused to be drawn any further into the debate. 'Of course we'll give them their privacy,' Sheila said dismissively. 'But there are bound to be awkward moments. A festive atmosphere will take the pressure off the couple.' Lizzie turned to Sally for help.

'It's going to be difficult whether we turn up or not,' Sally said, avoiding a direct answer. 'Perhaps if we agree to stay out of their way—in the cheese room or seeing to the cattle . . .'

'Why should *we* stay out of the way? We're the ones doing all the hard work around the place. Can't Kate, Sam and the baby go off together to bond or do whatever they need to do?' Sheila continued to argue. 'And what if everything goes pear-shaped? Kate will need our support more than ever.'

Lizzie, torn between frustration and fury, glanced at Sally and Daisy for support. Both of them looked down at what they were doing without a word. Boxed into a corner, Lizzie capitulated reluctantly. 'Okay, but let's keep it casual. We don't want to make this any harder for them than it already is.'

'Maybe we can hand out a little relationship advice,' Sheila said, happily triumphant. 'We're all veterans of long-term marriages— well, not you, Lizzie—so we've learned a thing or two about focusing on the good and ignoring the unpleasant.'

Lizzie looked at Sheila in disbelief, Sally almost choked. Daisy covered a cough with her hand. The appearance of Mike ended the discussion.

'How's it going, ladies?' he asked. 'Any more thoughts on whether we should go ahead with the plan or back off?'

Lizzie looked at him helplessly and indicated the frenzied preparations going on around them, raising her shoulders in defeat. 'A party it is,' she said. She'd already voiced her concerns to him about the wisdom of bombarding the shack during a delicate reunion. Mike understood her position but warned that the group motto of *one all for one and all for one* meant everyone would try to avoid any conflict in the decision-making process.

'How about we call it a picnic instead?' Mike suggested diplomatically. 'Sounds more impromptu than planned.'

'But . . .' Sheila began.

'Great idea,' chorused Lizzie, Daisy and Sally.

As the thrill of total victory waned, Sheila, in charge of making pastry for a tomato tart that included a little cornmeal for crunch, grumped, 'Why do I have to make the bloody pastry? Anything that doesn't come from a deli is above my pay grade.'

Daisy, thinly slicing the tomatoes, said, 'Never too late to learn, dear.'

'The bloody butter will not rub in. Look, there are lumps everywhere.'

'Pass me the bowl and here's the knife. You slice, I'll rub.'

'Thank God,' Sheila said, rolling her eyes and dumping the mixing bowl in Daisy's lap with relief.

'It's an unusual pastry,' Daisy explained. 'Doesn't need resting. Very crisp. Holds the moisture of the tomatoes without going soggy.'

'Ouch!' Sheila held up a bleeding finger.

'Get a bandaid. You're not escaping that easily. And get a move on. We're detouring to the Square to load the food and wine into Lizzie's Land Rover.'

'Are we all getting a lift?' Sheila asked, thrilled.

'No dear, just Lizzie, Rob and me, as usual.'

'Sometimes, I think you're lucky to be in a wheelchair. Oh God, sorry. What a thing to say!'

'Not your best effort,' Daisy replied equably.

⁓

While the GeriEcstasies prepared the picnic, Sam packed a bag with Claire's essentials and dressed her in a nifty little outfit of washed blue denim that Ettie swore was the latest in baby fashion. He slipped her feet into matching shoes that resulted in such outrage he removed them. The kid wouldn't be walking anyway, he rationalised. He checked the time. Figured the trip would take an hour. Made an instant coffee and called to let Kate know he'd be leaving shortly. Then, fired by nerves and caffeine, he set off.

He sped across the waterway from Cutter Island to Kate's pontoon. Removed Claire's lifejacket and slipped her into the baby carrier. Frankie wandered over holding a dripping paintbrush. 'Kid's sprouting like greens in a glass container on a windowsill,' he said.

'Can't hang around, we're on a mission. We're meeting up with Kate at Lizzie's shack,' Sam replied.

'You going to carry her all the way?' He pointed the paint-brush at Claire.

'Easy as, mate.' Sam pulled a beanie onto the baby's head. Checked her socks were still on her feet and not floating in the bay, considered having another go at putting on her shoes and then decided against the idea. Strapped her to his chest.

Frankie put down his paint brush and gave the kid—fist in her mouth, eyes unsure of Frankie—a little hoist, testing her weight with his hand. 'Reckon the chef's been cooking for her, eh? She's a solid little thing.' He turned back to the boatshed. 'Got your phone, mate? In case you need to call triple 0?'

'Very funny,' Sam said. He picked up the carry-all with a spare hand, the other lightly protecting Claire's head, and set off, applauding the clearing work the GeriEcstasies had consistently carried out on the once horribly overgrown track. 'Better than a walk in the botanical gardens,' he told his daughter, who looked up at him with sea-green eyes almost the same colour as her mother's, but with far more openness and trust. He whistled a tune, hoping to distract from his upcoming meeting with Kate, but the ruse failed. By the time he took a break on the flat rock outside the cave, he couldn't sort one stream of thought from another. He pulled a picnic blanket from the carry bag, extracted a snack and a drink, disengaged Claire from his chest and sat her on his lap. She wriggled and squirmed and he lay her on the blanket, glad to be free from her weight. He looked away for a moment, scrabbling to find his water bottle, looked back and almost keeled over. The kid was crawling. It felt like he'd been handed the world.

'Who's a clever girl then?' he murmured, following closely, ready to scoop her to safety. The kid, proud, turned her head towards her father. Later, Sam told everyone it was as though she wanted to make sure he'd seen this historic moment. Then she felt flat on her face and let out an unholy yell. A little scratched on her chin, hands filthy, an historic moment gone haywire, Claire was inconsolable. 'Every worthwhile endeavour is attached to pain,' he said, rubbing her vulnerable little back until the sobs subsided into hiccups and then wet-cheeked silence. He checked her injuries, wiped away the blood with a spit-moistened finger and decided the astonishing miracle of Claire crawling would deflect from the hoary questions of whether he had neglected his responsibilities on a bushwalk. Blame would dissolve in the rightful celebration of her monumental achievement. He strapped her to his chest once more. 'Onwards and upwards,' he said, but the kid was asleep, knocked out by the effort of her historic moment.

❧

Sam, feeling his muscles screaming with fatigue after trekking with a load on his chest and another carried in one hand, arrived on the edge of a scene of intense activity. People scurrying. Tablecloth being flung. Fire burning in an old washing machine drum in the middle of the lawn. Chairs carried two by two and placed around the picnic table. Sally swept the veranda. The puppy pounced on the broom and refused to let go. Sally laughed, played toreador. Tigger growled happily. In the midst of this, Cliffy arrived on his tractor with three large stainless steel milk cans tied in the bucket. The blokes dropped their rakes and rushed over to grab a handle each and carried them to the cool room attached to the cheesemaking area. Lizzie appeared on the veranda carrying plates. Tigger abandoned the broom and went for her ankles. Sally scooped the pup safely out of range. Lizzie noticed Sam hovering on the perimeter of the lawn, dumped the plates on a chair, and rushed over to take the carry bag from him. 'You look exhausted,' she said. 'And what on earth has happened to Claire?' The child woke and whimpered. Sam opened his mouth to explain but was assaulted by a team of GeriEcstasies determined to give him a rock-star welcome. David took the bag from Lizzie. Gavin unclipped the baby carrier and scooped the child into his arms.

Cliffy switched off the tractor engine and climbed down from his seat with a few grunts and groans. He walked over to Gavin and held out his arms. 'First rights are mine, mate, always will be, barrin' the dad, of course.' Gavin acquiesced with relief. The rippling stench from Claire's nappy had brought on a dizzy spell. Cliffy shook his head and gave Sam a hard look. 'Smell's fit to fell a church congregation.'

'Immune to it, mate,' Sam said.

Cliffy grinned and handed Claire back to her father. 'Over to you,' he said.

Sam fossicked in the carry bag for a clean nappy. Sally grabbed it from him and whisked into action. 'You need a few minutes to recover. I'll take her into Kate's bedroom to do the deed.

After she'd gone, Sam scanned the bustling scene for Kate. Lizzie, seeing the yearning on his face, explained, 'She's project managing lunch, which means making sure we old women stay out of each other's way in the kitchen but the job gets done.'

Sam nodded and pointed at the shed. 'What's with the milk delivery?'

'Long story. We'll tell you during lunch. A private word, Sam?' He followed Lizzie around the winding pathway to where her dendrobiums were hoarding their resources for their extravagant, creamy, cascading blooms of spring. Sam looked at her uneasily. His seaman's instincts on full alert.

'Everything alright, Lizzie? Nothing to worry about, is there?'

'Suggest a walk, or something, so you and Kate can go off alone to sort out your childcare arrangements without the well-meaning but inevitably confusing input of seven very bossy individuals.'

'Ah,' Sam said, relieved there wasn't more to the conversation. 'Gotcha.'

'Allow a bit of time. Kate is apprehensive. Not about the child. About how you feel towards her.' Lizzie closed her eyes and struggled to think of a way to indicate Sam should probe deeply if Kate shone even a weak light into her motives for abandoning her family. Sam waited patiently, catching the whiff of innuendo but at a loss as to its source.

'Something on your mind, Lizzie? Kate's okay, isn't she? She's coming good, isn't she?'

Lizzie sighed, torn between her instinct to help and her conviction that to interfere could end in catastrophe. In the end, she settled for the least contentious response she could muster. 'There's a lot for you two to discuss. Try not to rush through the details.' She smiled reassuringly. 'Listen to me, will you? Warning against being smothered by the GeriEcstasies' good intentions and being guilty of the same crime.'

Sam fell into step behind her and returned to the garden, trying but failing to suppress a growing desire to set eyes on Kate, afraid, too, that he might be unable to hold back the kick to his heart, the twinge in his gut, when he clapped eyes on her slim silhouette, recognised the lightly perfumed scent of her a few seconds before she came into view. And there she was, her back to him, hands on hips, directing operations. 'I made that pastry myself,' he heard Sheila boast.

'Bit of a stretch, don't you think?' Daisy retorted.

'Let's not go into details, Daisy dear. The tart looks quite spectacular, though. Remember when the only tomato you could buy was red? Now look at them. All the colours of the rainbow. I had a pair of shoes in those colours once. It was in the seventies, of course.'

Sally appeared with the baby, scrubbed and restored. Sam hesitated on the fringe of the group to give himself time to settle his emotions. He watched as Kate opened her arms. She loves the child, he thought, and wondered for the thousandth time what drove Kate in her decision-making. Claire, wary, held back for a moment, her fist in her mouth as though considering her options. 'Hey, baby,' Kate said. Claire leaned towards her mother. The crowd let out a collective sigh of relief. Everyone began talking at once. Sheila muttered something about babies recognising a mother's unique smell. Sally looked longingly at the child, remembering the glorious feel of a baby in her arms. She sighed. She and David had decided long ago that the greatest gift they could give their own two children and their now almost adult grandchildren was their independence in old age.

Kate rocked the baby and did a little turn, caught sight of Sam and smiled. He felt the old fillip that he feared no other woman would ever spark, gave a small wave and came over.

'Come inside. You look like you could do with a long drink of water. And you can tell me how her face got decorated?' Kate said. She headed back into the house. Sam followed. In the kitchen, she asked him to hold Claire while she checked the bread was warm enough. Instead of taking the child, he told her to put her on the floor.

Kate, puzzled, did as she was told. Claire gave a little cry, unsure of her surroundings. Sam leaned forwards, showing her his familiar face. Satisfied, she rolled forwards and stabilised on all fours, then she made a beeline for the bottom shelf of the dresser where a row of small baskets held tea towels, washcloths, napkins and the miscellaneous detritus the GeriEcstasies brought with them on every visit *just in case*. Kate laughed in a way she'd managed all too rarely when they co-habited and turned towards him with sparkling eyes.

'Everyone has to see this.' She scooped the child into her arms and while Sam grabbed the breadbasket, he wondered at the invisible connection between a mother and child that allowed Claire to quickly feel safe and relaxed in the arms of a woman she hadn't seen for months. Chemistry, he thought, almost keeling over with the memory of it.

Outside, the GeriEcstasies were gathered in a circle around the fire drum, hands out to the flames, the chitchat animated in a way that never ceased to amaze Kate, who wondered what they had to talk about when they spent almost every waking hour in each other's company. She called for attention. Curious eyes turned in her direction. 'Watch this!' She lowered the baby to the ground and kneeled next to her. Claire looked around with the enchantment of a child who might have landed on the moon, then took off at a pace Sam later called Olympic material.

It ended badly, of course. Tigger, all tangly legs and floppy ears, jumped on the kid, ready to play. Claire began to howl. Sally dived on the pup. A dew claw dug into the thin skin of her arm and blood spurted like an open tap. Kate pulled the baby out of the way. David grabbed the overexcited pup and held her high in the air. Cliffy extracted a clean handkerchief from his pocket and used it to apply pressure to Sally's gash. A smiling Mike appeared on the veranda carrying a bucket filled with ice and a bottle of champagne. Alarmed by the chaos, at a critical moment he looked up from the steps leading from the veranda to the grass, lost his balance and toppled. Gavin caught the bottle mid-air like a test cricketer. Lizzie hurried to help Mike to his feet. Sheila stepped back from the mayhem and set fire to her jeans. Sally grabbed a water jug and tipped the contents over her legs.

Daisy said drily, 'Our lot don't seem to be too good at events.' A pause. Then raucous laughter.

Cliffy, who'd witnessed the knock-on effect of a small baby making her first independent moves, tried to wipe the grin from his face and cleared his throat. 'The kid knows how to make an entrance, and the little mite not even a year old. What a star already.'

Lizzie led a lame Mike to a chair. Sheila caught Sally's eye with a look that spoke volumes. There were shouts for champagne to toast the kid's achievement. Sheila said, 'I hope you remember how to put child locks on cupboards, Gavin, because this baby has her skates on already.' Kate blanched and ran inside to remove the cleaning products from under the sink.

Gavin asked Lizzie if her doorways were standard widths. Lizzie looked at him blankly. 'For the gates, so Claire can't escape the house when no one's looking.'

'Ah.'

Kate returned to the group in time for a toast to Claire's new skill. She added, 'To the people who have given me more than I can ever repay. Thank you.'

Lunch began with a vengeance, Claire passed briefly from one lap to another like a living toy, stuffing titbits into her mouth at every stop, until Kate, seeing the first flush of exhaustion reach her eyes, took her away to be put down for an afternoon nap. Daisy tapped her cutlery against her glass for silence and said, 'A small taste of dessert wine, please Mike, to go alongside our first sampling of an Agnes creation.' A collective *ah* rose from the table. Sam looked confused. Lizzie filled him in. David went off to fetch the small round cheese from the kitchen where it had been brought to room temperature. Lizzie said Mike should rest his knee and she would get the wine. Sheila rolled her eyes. Sally pretended she hadn't noticed.

David gently placed the cheese in the centre of the table as though it represented the holy grail. He delicately cut small wedges and placed a piece on individual plates, which he passed around. 'A taste without the confusion of crackers or pastes and an honest opinion,' he instructed.

Lizzie asked Mike to open the wine but insisted she would do the honours with the pouring. Sally glared at Sheila to pre-empt any knowing looks in her direction. Instead of leaping into the cheese tasting, everyone waited patiently, unhurriedly, in the thinning afternoon light for Kate to return from settling Claire: their bellies too full to make much of an attempt at conversation. Gavin rose once or twice, to throw more wood on the campfire, the sun's warmth weakening as the afternoon wore on.

After a while, Sam said he would relieve Kate from baby duty. Lizzie caught his arm as he went past. 'An opportunity for that chat, perhaps?' Sam felt a return of his uneasiness and went off without replying. A moment later, Kate reappeared.

Lizzie sighed. No chat then.

Daisy leaned towards Lizzie and said, 'Such a privilege to be allowed to be useful at our age. We are all in your debt.'

'Works both ways,' Lizzie responded.

David rubbed his hands together and dipped his head to signify the moment of truth had arrived. Rich, yellow, gooey strings of flavour, reeking of pasture and age and something reminiscent of the earth's raw fecundity, drizzled and looped on the way to their mouths.

After several moments of savouring his own portion, Cliffy said, 'Agnes would be proud and honoured.'

Without a word, Kate went back inside to bring out a plain manila folder. She handed around individual copies of a marketing plan. Mike raised his glass of dessert wine to a sky turning slate grey as clouds rolled in from the coast. 'Looks like we're in business,' he said. *Hear, hear.*

In the house, Claire finally gave up her grip on wakefulness and succumbed to the coma-like sleep of the exhausted. Sam returned to grey heads bent over paperwork, giving it the same concentration as sorting out a last will and testament. 'The cheese is quite magnificent,' Kate told him, her face glowing and happy. Sam tried to look thrilled. Deep down, he sensed it signalled the possibility that Kate might never return to her Oyster Bay home. Any vague hope of reconciliation was sucked out of a heart he'd thought was beyond any further damage.

CHAPTER NINETEEN

LIZZIE WAS INEXPLICABLY QUIET AND withdrawn on the return trek to Stringy Bark Bay. Back at the house, where everyone groaned at the thought of more food, they skipped dinner and retired to their rooms, mentally and physically drained. As Lizzie reached her door, Mike touched her arm lightly. 'Everything alright, Lizzie?'

'Just tired, Mike. It was a good day, though, don't you think? And the cheese is a hit.'

'I wish I had as much faith in the project as everyone else. I feel as though we're messing with Cliffy's life and livelihood and that the whole project could explode in our faces.'

'Cliffy's resilient and he wouldn't have agreed to the idea if he didn't believe in it. It's Kate I'm more worried about.'

Mike looked puzzled. 'Why? She has the shack, the cheese project and a heap of geriatrics keeping an eye on her wellbeing.

Her absence at the café is no longer an issue and if the look on her face was any indication, she seems to be very happy to accept Claire back into her life.'

'It's slightly more complicated than that.'

Mike was about to speak. Lizzie cut him off with a hand to his chest. Sheila emerged from her suite and caught the gesture. 'Sorry,' she said, almost smirking. 'Didn't mean to interrupt.'

'You're not interrupting,' Lizzie said. She stepped away from Mike and closed the door gently behind her. Mike went to his suite. Sheila stood in the hallway for a moment, trying to remember why she'd left her room in the first place. Sighed heavily and went back inside, hoping that retracing her footsteps would jog her memory. Romance was in the air, though, or she'd eat her best pair of shoes. One of them, anyway. And perhaps not her best.

ဢ

After the GeriEcstasies had gone home and Sam had taken Claire back to Kingfish Bay to be reunited with Ettie and Marcus, Kate and Cliffy sat companionably in front of the fire, their feet stretched towards the flames. Kate murmured something about dinner but Cliffy shook his head.

'You look dog-tired,' she said, concerned.

Cliffy got to his feet with a few creaks and groans. He rattled the embers and threw on another log. 'That little girl of yours is a heartbreaker already,' he said, resuming his seat. 'You can tell an old fella to mind his own business, but you reckon you can manage five days a week alone up here on the escarpment with a bub?'

'Less hazardous here than Oyster Bay, Cliffy.'

'I can be here in minutes if the pressure starts to get you down. Never forget that.'

Kate reached for his hand. 'Thank you, my friend.'

'Honorary godfather and grandparent, after all.'

'Getting dark, Cliffy, and we're both about ready to drop with tiredness. There's Lizzie's bed here, if you'd prefer.'

Cliffy got to his feet and shook his head. 'Me girls would only worry if I wasn't there at the crack of dawn to see them into the milkin' shed,' he said.

Kate smiled and went to find a torch. When she tried to hand it to him, he waved it away. 'Full moon to guide me,' he said, pulling on his boots. Kate kissed his scratchy cheek, which gave the old man a start before he broke into a grin, executed a one-fingered salute and hobbled off.

She watched him disappear into the gloom, taking her time to absorb the quiet bigness of the ancient, breathing bush, hoping it would settle her misgivings, quell a rising fear that a dire unravelling of all her carefully woven fabrications had been set in motion. She suppressed an urge to run and keep running. Time to face the music, she told herself, wincing at her use of a cliché she would have condemned Sam for. They were catchy little things, clichés.

 ∽

Kate heard the crack, like a gunshot, but thought nothing more about it until her phone rang at a time of night that invoked instant fear.

'A branch, love,' Cliffy said. 'It's pinned me down. Done me best but I can't shift it.' His voice was raspy, breathless.

'On my way and dialling triple 0,' she almost yelled. 'A minute or two, Cliffy. I'll be there.' Her tone meant to soothe now. There was no reply.

She grabbed a torch and, running, gave breathless, sketchy details to the calm voice on the end of the emergency line, trying hard not to scream her fear.

She tried to pin his location by timing his departure. Less than ten minutes ago, she thought. He couldn't have gone too far. She searched the track near the shack and then realised he'd probably taken the short cut through the bush. Aware every second counted, she crashed through the darkness, calling out to the old man whom she loved more than herself. Dialling his phone until the constant refrain from his voicemail sent her to the edge of madness. She rang Sam. Heard him on his way before she'd finished filling him in.

'Claire?' she asked.

'With Ettie,' he replied.

Guided by instinct and blind faith, after several more dread-filled minutes, Kate found Cliffy underneath the canopy of an angophora, the lingering scent of its long-faded summer blooms adrift in the still night air. He lay with his eyes closed, his skin the colour of parchment. She reached down and laid a hand on his forehead. Felt the clammy coldness.

'Sorry to be a nuisance,' he whispered in a small voice that Kate could barely recognise or hear.

'Shh. Have you out of here in a jiffy,' she said, hoping she'd kept the sound of her own terror at bay. She removed her coat with shaking hands, anxiety spreading through her body. She draped it over his legs, one of which was twisted at an unnatural angle. Rested the torch against the smoothness of the trunk so its beam lit up the tree, obscenely decorative but a beacon in the darkness. The spot where the branch had come off looming above was like a botched amputation.

She punched in their coordinates on the phone for the rescue mob. Had a quick discussion with their leader. Felt gut-churning fear that help wouldn't arrive soon enough. Took one of Cliffy's hands in her own and tried to rub some warmth into it, yabbering in a way the oldies sometimes did when it seemed to Kate they were in a rush to get out all the words before they forgot what they were trying to say. She thought about placing her sweater under Cliffy's head but feared his back might be damaged and if she moved him even slightly she might cripple him forever.

Sam found Jimmy and the mutt waiting on the dock. 'Saw the lights go on,' Jimmy said, already wearing his hi-vis gear, his eyes like saucers.

'Can't you sleep, mate?'

'Longfella, he lets off a growl when he reckons I need to pay attention. Added a bark this time so I knew it was big.'

'I'll explain what's going on, but mate, one question and I'll put you out at the side of the road. Every second counts. Give me a nod to show you understand.' The kid climbed in the commuter boat without a word. Longfellow rode lookout on the bow.

Sam left the boat at the commuter dock and the trio ran to the car park where his old ute kicked into life with the first turn of the key. He drove like a maniac, Jimmy gripping the seat's safety handle, Longfellow braced between his legs on the floor. When he reached the turn-off to the National Park, he was confronted with red and blue flashing lights and a fleet of emergency vehicles. Men in yellow uniforms held torches, their heads bent over paper maps. No signal, they told him. 'No idea where to go.'

'Follow me,' Sam ordered, praying he could remember the twisty way he'd driven just once in Lizzie's Land Rover and in broad daylight to deliver a load of firewood in the days before he bought the *Mary Kay*. Another ute pulled up. A guy called Damian, according to the tag on the pocket of the fleece he wore over colourful pyjamas, stuck his head out the window.

'Heard the call. Thought about rolling over and going back to sleep but I couldn't let you fellas trash the park or drive off an escarpment following dodgy digital directions in mostly uncharted territory.' Damian slid his car into first gear, engaging four-wheel drive at the same time. 'Follow me. Not too close. Sometimes, you need to back up to make a turn.'

The first responders climbed into their fire truck, gold fluoro bands on their trousers pulsing in the beam from headlights. The paramedics had a whispered conversation then knocked on the driver's door. 'Sounds like the ambulance might not be able to make it all the way. Two-wheel drive. Room for one more and some gear in there?'

Sam, excused from navigating, moved to the rear of a strobing procession that looked weirdly festive in the dark bush. Jimmy, eyes on stalks by now but honouring his promise to remain silent, mutely begged Sam to fill him in.

'It's Cliffy, mate. He's had an accident. Kate's with him but we're not sure exactly where. That's all I know.'

Jimmy restricted his response to a nod and rubbed Longfellow's ear. Sam heard him praying under his breath.

In the end, Longfellow was instrumental in finding Cliffy and Kate. Blinded by their own flashing lights, the cavalcade drove past Kate's weakening beacon. The mistake launched Longfellow into a frenzy of barking, a frantic scrabbling to be let out of the car, and a dash to the lead vehicle to bring it to a halt. Then he ran into the scrub, leaving the rescuers no alternative but to follow on foot. Five minutes later, they found Kate, tears streaming down her face.

'He's dead,' she cried out. 'He's dead. Where were you? It's taken you hours to get here. And now he's dead and there was nothing I could do to save him.' She lashed out at the paramedic who tried to draw her away, striking him in the face. 'I couldn't even lift the bloody branch off him,' she wailed. 'A stupid branch, not even a tree trunk. A stupid branch.' She was beyond logic: the branch was colossal. This time, the paramedic managed to loosen her grip. He felt Cliffy's wrist for a pulse. Scrambled into action. 'Not dead yet,' he said, his eyes focused on his patient.

❦

Cliffy, sheet white, lay in a hospital bed, where monitors beeped in peaks and falls that took Kate on a roller-coaster of fear and hope as she sat in vigil for hours. Alongside the frightening electronic soundtrack, the curtains screening him rattled like dice in a plastic cup each time a nurse drew them aside to check vital signs. Finally, against her wishes but under doctor's orders, Sam pried her from Cliffy's side. Her face streaked with tears and dirt, she still carried a vague honey and eucalyptus smell of the Australian bush.

'C'mon, Kate,' he said, reaching for her hand. 'It's time to leave.' She let herself be guided stumbling from the room. Sam pressed the button to open the doors into the corridor where lifts took them to the ground floor, his arm around Kate's waist to keep her from falling. 'Where would you like to go? The shack?

Oyster Bay? The Island? I could make up a spare bed. Run you back and forth to the shore. You could be by his side in minutes.'

And there it was, the unspoken possibility that Cliffy might not make it. Broken ribs, they said. A leg that would need a steel rod for him to walk again. Carpentering stuff, Kate told herself. Nuts and bolts. Fixable, like a door hanging on its hinges. She was blindly optimistic, until they talked about a collapsed lung and kidneys that refused to kick into gear. A result of the pressure on them, they explained, and—as it turned out— lucky she'd been unable to lift the bough. If she had, the quick release of pressure might have killed him. The giant angophora, a century old or more: well, the branch weighed more than an average-sized tree.

'He'll be okay, though,' Kate had told them flatly, allowing no room for doubt. The specialists, three or four by the end of the day, had shaken their heads. There was only so much they could mend. They would do their best. Her father, was he? 'My best friend,' she'd replied.

'What was he doing so far off track?' she asked Sam when they reached the ground floor and fluorescent arrows directed them towards the car park. 'He set off to go straight home. That tree was way off course. Why didn't he take a torch? I should have walked him home. He's . . .'

'. . . a tough old bugger who's looked after himself for more years than any of us know. He'll come good, Kate, I can feel it in my bones.'

'You, Artie, Ettie—always optimistic despite the odds.'

'Beats falling down a mine shaft before you have to. But he'll need you, Kate. More than he's ever needed anyone in his life, and it'll rip his guts out to admit it.'

CHAPTER TWENTY

KATE AND THE PUP MOVED into Sam's Island home to be closer to the hospital, lighting a bonfire of rumour. Even the penny pinchers and environmental warriors who deplored throw-away cups ordered a takeaway coffee from the Briny Café (no lid, please, they're not biodegradable) to get the lowdown.

'Seen who's back?' they asked.

'Yup,' Jenny responded.

'Well?'

'Well, what?'

'Well, is she hanging around? Or not?'

'I wouldn't know. Anything to go with the coffee?' A hard, flat look on her face that deterred the most determined gossipmongers from further questions.

Sam ignored every thinly disguised query until the Misses Skettle, nonagenarian twin sisters who lived at Stony Point, arrived on his doorstep with a batch of pickles made in their newly renovated kitchen as a welcome back gift for Kate. 'It's a temporary arrangement,' Sam explained gently, aware their arrival was triggered by kindness, not nosiness. 'She has a friend gravely ill in hospital. Needs to be close by.'

The two women, neat in pink as always, apologised, left the pickles, said they could be called upon to help if needed and returned home by ferry (turning down Sam's offer of a lift).

When Ettie continued to care for Claire while Kate kept up long bedside visits to Cliffy, the situation was clear enough and the subject was dropped in favour of discussing the uncharacteristically freezing weather so early in the season. Climate change, chorused the young ones. Weather, muttered the oldies.

Sam dossed in the cramped spare room where a single bed from his childhood barely contained his frame and where he'd placed a cot for Claire's weekend stayovers.

For the first couple of days, Kate and Sam tiptoed around each other in the sparse, shabby rooms of the weatherboard house Sam had called home ever since he'd scraped together enough cash to buy it outright, two decades before the current real estate boom. Overly polite, like strangers, they were both painfully aware an ill-chosen word, a thoughtless gesture, might knock the footings from their new-found companionship and send it hurtling back into the bitterness and hurt of a confused and failed relationship. Underlying every spoken word were their fears for Cliffy, their hopes for his survival, and Kate's belief she should be held accountable for letting a tired old man walk home on his own. Sam's constant reassurance that Cliffy made his own decisions—and always would—was no consolation.

A week after the accident, Cliffy's hold on life was still gossamer thin. He hadn't opened his eyes or mumbled even a barely coherent word. Kate carefully declined invitations—delivered via Sam—to dine with Ettie and the chef. By the time she returned from the hospital, she explained, it would be way past Claire's bedtime and she'd end up disrupting the whole household for no apparent gain. Ettie made an effort to understand, but Kate's absence rankled, sparking another slow fizz of fury deep in Ettie's heart, even as she reminded herself Cliffy was in dire need of support while Claire was surrounded by it. Bloody Kate.

While Cliffy hovered between life and death, the GeriEcstasies mustered daily around the kitchen table in Lizzie's old shack.

David, the authority on milk, and Rob and Daisy, legendary cattle farmers, outlined the new jobs for each of them, to ensure Cliffy came home to a herd in prime condition. Daisy suggested Lizzie and Mike assume responsibility for the chooks—whose egg output continued to remain steady, despite the cold. Something to do with the hours of daylight instead of the mercury reading apparently. Sally, she said, could help David with the milking. Gavin and Sheila were the post milking clean-up team. Lizzie interrupted Daisy's flow to say she was undaunted by the massive and casual bodily expulsions of healthy and relaxed cows, so she'd be happy to join the clean-up team. Beside her, Mike raised his hand. He wasn't bad with a hose.

'You can be an extra pair of hands to wash the udders before the teat cups are latched on,' Sally said, her face wreathed in gleeful innocence.

'Great,' he croaked, pale at the gills.

'And sometimes teats need to be stimulated with a little massage,' she added for good measure. Mike, beyond words, could only nod.

Sheila volunteered to tidy up Cliffy's old weatherboard house with its lean that echoed the direction of the winter winds, but Lizzie leaped to her feet in horror. 'No!' she shouted. 'Leave the personal stuff alone,' she added, more calmly. 'An old man had his pride.'

'But just a dust and a vacuum so he returns to a clean home wouldn't hurt,' Sheila insisted.

'The house is a shrine to Agnes. Move one item an inch and it would be the same as taking a hammer to his soul.'

Sheila began to argue with her husband about letting go of the dead and moving on with life. 'You'd have a replacement lined up in no time if I dropped off the perch,' she muttered. 'Someone thirty years younger with strong ankles who could wear stilettos without a break for twelve hours.'

'Statistically, women outlive men. I'll die long before you.'

With escalating intensity, they bickered over who'd be laid in the ground first (or rehoused in an antique porcelain urn, colour to blend with their suite), until Mike quietly took Gavin aside. 'Mate, trust me, this is one argument with Sheila you don't want to win.'

Two weeks after the accident, Cliffy's prognosis remained tilted more in the direction of hope than certainty, but not a splinter of doubt entered the conversation. His death was unthinkable. A man like Cliffy, well as soon as he regained consciousness, he'd just tell the docs he'd be right, and he would. *Hear, hear.*

⌒

Each morning, Sam ferried Kate ashore. She went straight to the hospital to sit by Cliffy's bedside and hold his hand, willing her warmth and the strength of her grip to transmute into life-saving energy. So far, not even a quiver signalled he was aware of her presence.

On the sixteenth day after the accident, Kate arrived to find the ICU swarming with police. Before she was allowed to enter, she was frisked, her ID checked and her bona fides double-checked with hospital staff. 'What's going on?' she whispered to the nurse who led her to her customary spot beside Cliffy's bed.

'Gang wars. A bloke's been shot through the gut. Another bullet's been dug out of his back. Don't worry, he'll be gone in a day or two.'

'Miracles of modern medicine,' Kate said, impressed.

The nurse, her name tag obscured by a pocket stuffed with surgical gloves, rolled her eyes. 'Miracle if he survives, you mean.'

'Oh.'

'From what the cops have said, only his mother will miss him. But you didn't hear that from me.'

Kate, realising she'd found someone unafraid to speak her mind, asked, 'What about my old boy? Cliffy?'

But the nurse refused to be drawn. Kate felt more fearful than ever. For perhaps the hundredth time in her life she thought: it's the not knowing that does such awful damage.

⟡

Later in the day, an icy blast of cold air straight off the icefloes pummelled the south-facing side of the Island. It found its way through every crack in Sam's house until the temperature reached a level that would give the fridge a run for its money. While he waited for a pick-up call from Kate, he checked his old wood-burning stove hadn't succumbed to rust before setting a fire. Then he considered his dinner options: the chef's Louisiana pork and beans, Ettie's veal meatballs (*serve with pasta or mashed potatoes, and a salad,* according to the note that was stuck to the lid of the casserole dish), or Amelia's curried sausages. He took a moment to thank the mysterious forces that had led him to be a child of Cook's Basin and a member of a community that would keep your fridge full until there was no longer any need.

The scent of curry leaked from the container. His tastebuds tilted him in that direction (his mum's mince curry—powder pre-blended—with sultanas and shredded coconut was a child-hood favourite), but he figured Kate was more an Italian meatball girl. He found a few potatoes and started peeling. A quick inspection of the blackening salad greens lying dead in the bottom of the fridge meant that option was a no-go. He dug out some peas from the freezer instead. By the time Kate called, the sweet aroma of oregano hung lightly in the warm air and the pup was sound asleep in front of the fire, so close Sam was surprised he hadn't picked up the smell of singed fur.

He set off across the water, one of his warmest jackets ready to throw around Kate's shoulders for the return journey. The pup was already riding lookout on the bow and finding boat life to her taste.

In the murky twilight that coated the bay with an oily sheen, he sped towards the ferry wharf. Its green light etched Kate's dark silhouette with a ghostly glow. Her shoulders were rounded, a slight stoop, as though she was wilting and could founder at any moment.

⌒

At the dinner table, having given Kate time to settle after a spending the day at Cliffy's bedside, Sam asked, 'How's Cliffy?'

'No change,' she told him, staring into a plate loaded with more food than she'd eat in a week. She picked up a fork. Sam placed a glass of red wine in front of her, the bottle close by.

'It's full of antioxidants and you look like you need a hit.'

Kate nodded, pushed a meatball around the plate. 'I just wish someone would tell me what his chances are,' she said, dropping any attempt to eat. 'Every day I go in hoping for some sign he's getting better, and every day it's the same.'

'He's still alive, Kate, and that means there's hope.' Sam got up to fetch a second wine glass and poured a drink for himself.

Kate's eyes widened. 'Never thought I'd see you ditch the grain for the grape,' she said.

'Weather's too cold for a beer.' He took a sip, surprised at how delicious both the wine's flavour and texture felt as he swallowed. He took another sip. Attacked his food. 'Bloody tasty. Have a go, luv. Ettie will ask for a report tomorrow. If I tell her you didn't touch it, she'll be here with chicken soup and a list of orders as long as my arm.'

'I don't know where she finds the energy.'

'From an overwhelming desire to be kind no matter the cost to herself.'

'Or the chef. They have both been so . . .'

'Ah, Kate, if Ettie is happy, then so is Marcus.'

The wine seemed to evaporate. The warmth from the fire made them drowsy. Sam turned off the overhead lights after he cleared the table, leaving the orange glow of the fire to fill the room. Kate scooped the pup onto her lap and stretched out her legs until her feet were close enough to the heat to roast. Sam set a small table near her chair and refilled her glass. Pulled another chair close by. Kate mentally scrolled through his long history of kindnesses and felt her betrayal rise like bile. She sculled the last of her wine and wiped her lips, aware she was moderately drunk. Sam held up the almost empty wine bottle, raising his eyebrow in a question. She nodded. He tipped the last drops into her glass. Returned his gaze to the flames. Kate swigged in a way that drew his attention. He locked eyes with her. Watched a tear gather in a corner, spill and trickle past the freckles that dusted her cheek.

'Cliffy will be okay . . .'

She shook her head, swallowed. 'You know what they say?'

'No,' Sam said, not sure where she was going.

She held up her empty glass, stared through the dusty dregs. '*In vino veritas*.'

'Not sure where you're going with this, luv.'

'Do you know the saying?'

He damped down a shiver of irritation. 'In wine, truth. There's not a drinker on the Island who hasn't learned that lesson without a shitload of regret tied to it.'

'I've done a terrible thing, Sam . . .'

'Cliffy's accident had nothing . . .'

'I'm not talking about Cliffy. You, Sam, I've done a terrible thing to you.'

'Relationships break up all the time . . .'

Her voice cracked and the words came out clumsily. 'Something so terrible I don't know where to begin.' She held the pup close to her face, hiding behind the warm little body. The sleepy pup nuzzled into the hollow of her neck, barely awake.

Sam felt his gut churn, tried to guess where the conversation was going.

'I'm a big boy, Kate,' he said after a while. 'There's not much that I can think of that might shock the socks off me.'

'It's about Claire . . .'

She put the pup on the floor and asked if there was any more wine. There was a tone to her request and a rigidity to her face that made his heart lurch. It ignited a fear he'd suppressed, unravelled something he'd always known but refused to confront.

'I know she's not mine, Kate, if that's where you're headed,' he said, wanting to get in first, dull the shock of what he knew was coming.

Kate looked as if she'd been slapped. 'How . . .'

'A million small things that all added up. Moments between us that suddenly went skew-whiff. A voice tone slightly off. Ear tips bright red. All bundled around the word "father". Couldn't see any point in asking. Far as I was concerned, she was mine.' He stood and walked to the door leading to the deck, gazed out to the sea. 'Jimmy saw it. Or sensed it. "When's she gonna start looking like you, Sam?" Kid's got instincts even I don't under-stand. Could drill the truth out of a block of wood, that boy, with just a gaze from his innocent blue eyes.'

'Do you want to know who?'

'Not really. Claire will need to know one day. But that day's a long way off.' Sam added another log to the fire and sat down with the heaviness of an old man. Like his heart had become too weighty for the rest of him.

'I'll make plans. Go away. Once Cliffy is better, I'll take Claire, move cities. Start again.'

Sam, a concrete slab lying somewhere between his head and his gut, tried to envisage a life without Claire. All those empty spaces Kate and the child would leave, he thought. For Ettie. Marcus. Jimmy. Artie. Amelia. The GeriEcstasies and the cheese project. Cliffy . . . if he survived. And Sam's own loss would be a bottomless chasm. Even the interfering, good-hearted, motley herd of mismatched characters who propped each other up in dire times would be left to wonder what they'd done wrong, because the truth was nobody's else's business, and exposing it would be a crime and serve no real purpose. A child might sink without all that support. And where would he be if he let that happen on his watch? Unable to use a mirror to shave, if he had to make a guess.

'The father. He knows about Claire?'

Kate shook her head. 'No.'

'You going to tell him?'

'No.'

'He has a right to know, Kate.'

'He's married. Already has other children.'

'Ah,' Sam said, understanding. He searched for the right words, a way to frame them so they wouldn't land a killer blow to a woman already bent double with guilt, but still give him an answer. 'The father . . .'

'If you're wondering if he means anything to me, the answer is no.'

Sam felt the concrete slab lift a little. 'You didn't have to tell me, Kate. Could have bumbled along the way we were.'

'Secrets, Sam. They hollow you out.'

'Lizzie knows, doesn't she? Kept pushing me to have a quiet word that day at the shack.'

'She knows. Nobody else. Told me if there was ever to be any future for you and me, it had to be said.'

And there it was, a weak sliver of light now, shining under the slab.

Sam shifted in his chair, leaned forwards, resting his elbows on his knees, his face reflected the dancing flames from the fire. After a while, he said, 'Paternity, not sure it matters all that much. An arrangement of cells when you boil it down. Claire, well, I'm her father in every sense of the word that counts.' He heard Kate exhale heavily, as though she'd been holding her breath, waiting to see how he would react.

'Lizzie said you'd say that. I didn't believe her.'

'Then you don't know me very well.'

'The world never quite turns out the way you think it will, does it?'

'It'll keep turning, Kate, with zigs and zags that can knock you off your perch if you're not careful. You just have to hang on.'

He reached for her hand across the great divide of their chairs. They locked eyes. Looked away. But it was all there, the closing of one chapter and the beginning of something new, with no deceit trailing along, waiting to trip them up and bring them crashing to their knees.

CHAPTER TWENTY-ONE

THE FOLLOWING DAY, KATE AND Sam were told that Cliffy had opened his eyes. Yes, he'd turned a corner, according to the doctors, but there was a long way to go yet. Best not to get too hopeful.

A few days later, Kate took Claire to visit him. Claire tried to grab the clear thin lines of plastic pumping life-giving fluid and drugs into a broken body; the old man reached a hand festooned with purple and yellow bruises, needles, tubes and adhesive tape, to touch the feathery softness of the baby's cheek. Kate wept out loud. She swung the child in a dance of delight, dipping and swinging, humming nonsense under the breath. Cliffy coughed a laugh, which made him grimace with the pain that shot from his cracked ribs to his scrawny neck.

Kate stopped mid-dance and went quickly to his side. He lifted a hand and whispered, 'Best tonic in the world, you two.' His first words. Another marker on the road to recovery.

The next day, after almost three weeks in the ominous quiet of intensive care, Cliffy, with his high-tech paraphernalia clattering alongside him like a noisy acolyte, was moved into the general chaos of a ward for people who would survive.

When more visitors were permitted, Kate held up her hand to ward off a stampede. Even so, he was swamped by so many well-wishers, the bloke from the room next door poked his head in to ask if he was famous or something. Cliffy, his sense of humour on the mend although more than a word or two was still painful, nodded: *Yes*. It'd give the bloke something to gnaw away at, he thought, grinning to himself.

In the quietness of scaled down action in the ward and evenings closing in earlier, he drifted off to sleep. He dreamed of Agnes as a young girl and not so different from a young lady called Kate who'd arrived and turned his life upside down. They reckoned he'd saved her. None of them could see it was the other way round. Except for Lizzie, who'd twisted the words of the covenant on the property because she'd seen a way to save not just one, but two souls. Lizzie, he thought. One in a million. He wondered if being a writer gave her the knack of seeing beyond the surface of people and discarded the thought. Lizzie cared, that's what made her so special. His mind drifted as the nightly painkillers kicked in and he fell into what he imagined death might be. Which, when he thought about it, he'd already given a test run.

⁓

The GeriEcstasies changed their routine to include an illegal morning visit to the hospital before heading to the shack to roll up their sleeves to attack the daily chores. They received a job list from the cracked lips of the old man, which Sheila diligently wrote in a small spiral notebook before swapping it for a larger size before the week was up. The new routine presented a problem. Instead of the whole group, barring Daisy and Rob who travelled in Lizzie's old Land Rover, trekking from Oyster Bay, it would save time and effort if everyone went straight from the hospital to the farm. Transport was needed for eight people and one wheelchair. Lizzie's tough old Land Rover couldn't handle that kind of pressure.

A meeting was held over a dinner of an old-fashioned beef stew made with brisket, carrots, swedes and celery, followed by an equally old-fashioned apple pie, dotted with cloves and topped with a pastry decorated with cut-outs of leaves, to decide how to handle this new challenge.

Without consulting his fellow residents, Mike took a day off from farming duties and went off on his own to buy a new, shiny white LandCruiser 4WD. It was a serious break with the communal covenant that all purchases over a hundred dollars should be discussed before taking action but Mike felt he didn't have the right to ask the group to chip in for such a large item expense. He would wear the entire cost himself. He wasn't even certain whether it was legal for a vehicle to have eight owners. Reassured by motives he believed to be in the best interests of one and all, he dressed in his smartest clothes, which immediately set off alarm bells in the household, who were, as usual, dressed in scruffy farmhand working clobber. 'Doctor's appointment,' he said, realising too late that it would ring even louder bells. 'Annual skin check,' he hastened to add. There was a collective sigh of relief. The women instinctively checked their arms for spots, ran fingers over faces, and told themselves it would be wise to follow Mike's lead in the not-too-distant future.

At the hospital, Mike said a brief hello to Cliffy and made his excuses. Everyone else found chairs and Sheila waited with her pen poised over a notebook for the rundown of farm duties to spill from Cliffy's dry and cracked lips in his still-hoarse voice.

~

When the car salesman asked to see his driver's licence before he test-drove the car out of the showroom, Mike was outraged. 'I've been driving cars since before your grandparents even knew you were a glimmer in the distant future.'

The salesman, who looked twelve years old, held the keys out of reach until Mike whipped out his wallet and waved the card in front of his face.

'Almost eighty, mate,' said the salesman (*call me Stevie*), doubtful. 'It's a beast of a vehicle. Reckon you're up to it?'

Mike smiled in a way that would have sent the other GeriEcstasies running for cover. 'Let's see, shall we?' he asked, all sugar with the spice to come.

'Sure. A cruise around the block suit you?' Stevie oozing condescension and the fake bonhomie of the young humouring the old.

'I've got a better idea,' Mike said, now intent on revenge.

When they returned to the showroom an hour later, Stevie was white-faced, his sharp blue suit rumpled beyond recognition and the car covered in scratches, dust and mud after skidding, slaloming and flying over the ruts and fissures of the tracks leading to the shack.

Stevie fell into a sleekly modern chair at a coffee table strewn with tantalising magazines glamorising Outback Australia, and said, 'If you don't buy it, mate, I'll be looking for another job as soon as I finish with the chiropractor.'

'I'll take it,' Mike said, smiling, giving Stevie a thump on the back that almost sent him flying. They set off to fill in the paperwork, a spring in Mike's step, Stevie still a bit shaky in the legs but feeling steadier by the minute.

'I'll pick it up tomorrow.' Mike paused, an evil glint in his eye. 'And clean her up a bit, would you? Dirty cars create a sloppy impression. Doesn't look good on an eighty-year-old, eh? I'll need a lift back to the Square, too. No rush.'

Stevie held out his hand to shake Mike's. 'I'll drive this time, if you don't mind.'

'Good on you.'

⁓

That night, over a quickly cobbled together dinner, Mike skipped the finer details of his day when he informed the team a new chariot would join the fleet and he'd pick it up the following day. A communal vehicle, he said before apologising for buying it without consultation. It was his choice alone, he explained, and therefore his responsibility. He hoped there would be no hard feelings.

He was greeted with a shocked silence. Before he could ask their forgiveness, Rob responded sheepishly, 'Let my driver's licence lapse. Didn't think I'd be needing it.'

There were nods around the table, followed by a *me, too*, from Sally and Gavin.

'No worries,' Mike said. 'I'm still legal and so is Lizzie.'

Lizzie coughed into her fist and bowed her head. 'I'm not quite legal,' she confessed. 'And I'm afraid the Land Rover hasn't been registered for about ten years.'

There was a stunned silence, followed by everyone talking at once. Gavin said he would organise a licence test immediately. Sally said she'd join him. Sheila, the official chauffeur on shopping expeditions, offered to become lead driver of the new vehicle.

Mike scrabbled for a polite way to say no. Sheila's bingles (minor and consistently blamed on her stilettos sticking in the rubber floor mat at the wrong time) had been dinner-party conversation for more than two decades. Finally, Mike tapped his wine glass for attention. 'These are all technical details that can be addressed quite easily. Lizzie, if you give me the paperwork for the Land Rover, I'll book it in for a roadworthy certificate. Rob, how long do you reckon it will take to renew your licence?'

'Not Rob,' Daisy said quickly. 'He has enough to do looking after me.' A response that triggered a few curious stares.

'No matter,' Mike said. 'I'll do most of the driving anyway and one or two of you as back-up is enough.'

Later, as Lizzie and Daisy cleared the kitchen while the others retired to the sitting room to discuss repairs that needed attention and to go over the schedule for the following day, Lizzie broached the subject.

'His eyesight isn't what it used to be,' Daisy said abruptly.

'Did he fail the clock test or the word association when he went for his medical?' Lizzie asked.

Daisy sighed. 'The nurse, barely out of primary school, wanted to know if he wet his pants at night or even during the day. When she handed him the clock to fill in a time of ten past eleven, he was still so furious, he got it wrong. He tried to have a second go but the paper was snatched away before he had a chance. Then the doc asked him for a list of all the animals he knew. So, of course, he told him about Tess and Mac.'

'Tess and Mac?'

'Our working dogs.'

'Sounds reasonable.'

'He mentioned Topsy and Tansy, our two milking cows, Sinbad, the ginger shed cat. When the doc kept asking for more, he went through just about every animal he'd ever known, and if they didn't have names, he gave the location where they lived. You know, wallabies at Rocky Point, dingoes at Dusty Corner.'

'Misunderstood the question, eh?'

'There are other little signs. Invisible to anyone who doesn't look for them. I cover moments that are off-kilter, insist I was the one at fault when he gets confused.'

Her voice soft, Lizzie said, 'There are two of us now, to look out for him. Just so you know.'

'He's on medication. It slows the condition.'

They finished tidying in silence, then Daisy said, 'Coming here has helped. I was terrified of the obvious pitfalls for someone with Rob's condition. Maybe I'm biased or blinded by familiarity, but being constantly engaged and challenged seems to have slowed the decline.' Daisy shrugged, pragmatic as always. 'For the time being, anyway.'

Lizzie put a hand on Daisy's shoulder, Daisy placed her own— mottled with brown spots, and rough with the residue of hard work—on top. Lizzie said, 'I saw an apron once, printed with the words *Adventure Prevents Dementia*. On that basis, he'll be right for another century.'

Together they returned to the others, all bright smiles and overloud chat. An outsider would have seen through the charade immediately.

లం

After that night of unholy confessions, when hope—that dastardly emotion that drove the human race beyond reason—surged throat-high, Kate withdrew into her shell once again. Every attempt Sam made to draw her out had resulted in a litany of weak excuses. A headache. Desire for a hot bath. Exhaustion after a day at the hospital. After a while, he took the hint, but muzzling the topic of how to handle Claire's paternity for her future benefit was almost as bad as failing to address it.

One Sunday evening, her thin-lipped silence a growing flame in his belly, he'd taken his life in his hands and said, 'We need to have a conversation about Claire, Kate. The birth certificate for a start . . .' She turned on him.

'We'll never be able to wipe the slate clean, Sam. You and Lizzie, you're dreamers, full of good intentions but trust me, they wither and die over time. Best we quit any idea of getting back together before we end up loathing each other.'

He'd backed away as though she'd physically struck him, removed himself to the deck and waited until he heard the bedroom door close before re-entering the house. The next day, she packed her bags. Cliffy was due to come home and he needed her, she'd told him flatly, avoiding eye contact. It wasn't exactly a lie, but with the date for Cliffy's welcome-home party still unscheduled, her meaning was clear: whatever you're thinking, there is no future for us.

Back in the bedroom he'd vacated for Kate, which she'd left clean and tidy, with the dusty corners gleaming as though she planned her escape days before, the lingering scent of her threatened to unravel his heart and mind. He felt himself descending into a mood as dark as night, tinged at it was with fury at Kate's injustice, her misreading of his motives that were, and always would be, to protect the child. His child. DNA be damned.

ᢍ

One morning, when the blue sky made a lie of the temperature and people referred to it as a three-layer day, Jimmy had finally had enough. 'You're me best mate, Sam, but I've gotta tell ya, me patience is wearin' thin and you're not the only barge in Cook's Basin.'

Sam, who'd been steering the *Mary Kay* on an erratic course to service a mooring in Blue Swimmer Bay, looked at him in astonishment. 'Eh?'

'Ya head's gone AWOL! You couldn't find your way out of a paper bag. For your information, Blue Swimmer's that way.' He flung his arm out to the left. 'Same place it's always been. Ten more minutes and we'll be counting penguins on Cat Island.'

'Eh? Glenn offer you a berth, did he, the sneaky bugger?'

Jimmy's shoulders slumped and he let out a long sigh. 'Just tryin' to get your attention, which if you don't mind me sayin', has been seriously lacking since Kate walked out your front door.'

'What about Glenn?' Sam asked, flicking lovelorn pain overboard to give fury a stronger toehold.

'Course he didn't offer me a berth, you bunny. Punts don't have berths. The tinnie does all the work. I'm tryin' to get you to focus, Sam. You're all over the shop like a . . .'

'Did you just call me a . . . a bunny?'

And in it came like a rising tide, a slow pressure that erupted into gut-busting laughter. The worry on the kid's face cleared, Sam spun the helm till the faithful *Mary Kay* was back on a true course and they both felt it when the low-hanging black fug that had taken up permanent residence in the cabin was pushed out the door.

'Back on an even keel, then?' Jimmy asked, beaming.

'Bunny?'

Anyone passing would have thought the pair in the cabin were doubled over with pain. But it was raw hilarity. The kind that had tears running down their faces and turned any attempted speech into nonsensical hiccups. Then Sam swung into Blue Swimmer Bay, the kid squared his scrawny shoulders, the dog ran to the bow.

The sun goes down. The sun comes up. Sam's age-old mantra restored to settle his heart and mind. Long as that goes on, anything's possible, he thought: believing it, this time.

'I'm all ears, if you need to unload,' Jimmy said.

'Jeez, mate, where'd you pick up a line like that?'

The kid blushed. 'Becky says I'm a good listener.'

Oh ker-rist, thought Sam, the kid's in love again. As if he didn't have enough to worry about. He considered Ettie and the chef's upcoming jaunt to the fleshpots of Paris, opening the possibility of full-time care for Claire, given that Kate and the GeriEcstasies would have their hands full with Cliffy, looking after the farm and launching the cheesemaking business. He gave Jimmy a long, calculating appraisal. 'You ever seen a movie called *Mrs Doubtfire?*' he asked.

'Where the bloke turns into a nanny to be near his kids?' Jimmy looked pleased with himself.

'Yup. Well, you my friend will have the immeasurable pleasure of looking after Claire for a day here and there when Ettie and the chef take off for Paris. Great training, mate, for when you have a family of your own.' And if that didn't cure him of young love, Sam thought, nothing would.

⌒

The next morning, Sam showered and dressed before dawn, planning to do a clean-up on the *Mary Kay* before he and Jimmy began wearing away a tight schedule of jobs. The kid had turned into an eco-warrior and every time Sam tried to chuck away an old rag or a frayed piece of rope, it turned into an environmental argument about the pros and cons of repurposing or discarding. He couldn't fault the kid's ethics but the barge had limited space and junk cluttered both the deck and the mind.

Outside, fish, seagulls and birds were still sensibly asleep, and not even the throaty mumble from a slow commuter boat disturbed the peace. Frisky winds were predicted but at this hour, with the day readying to shake off the night, the bay slept. He took a moment to breathe in the brine of low tide, wet sand and the soupy residue of a heavy sea mist. He sighed when the smell of Jimmy's pungent hair gel reached him seconds before the kid landed next to him, almost knocking him flat, followed by Longfellow, who had the slightly disapproving and forlorn look of a dog cruelly interrupted from his rest.

'How do you do it, Jimmy? How do you know the second I walk out the door? You got a camera rigged up somewhere with an alarm that goes off every time I move? Or what?'

The kid shuffled, not sure if he was in trouble. Sam slung an arm around his shoulder, to reassure him. 'Give me a hint, mate. Your timing is eerily uncanny.'

'We got business this mornin'?' Jimmy asked, dodging the question.

Artie, Sam thought, a man who slept with his binoculars by his side and one eye open. Legacy of his days as a live-aboard, after a stroke ended his mobility and he threatened to do the same to any Island do-gooder who suggested a nursing home might be more appropriate than a yacht held together by barnacles and hope. It couldn't be anyone else.

'Had your brekky?' Sam asked, giving up the idea of a clean-up.

'Nah.'

'Longfellow had his brekky?'

'Nah.'

'You make the tea. I'll cook toast to get us through to ten o'clock, when we'll hit the back deck of the Briny Café and put in an order that stretches Marcus to the limit. What do you say?'

'Got any peanut butter?'

'Vegemite.'

'You want me to break the news to Longfella or will you?'

The man and the boy went inside as the first lights appeared on Cutter Island.

⌀

Kate walked down the hallway of the shack and into the kitchen. She stoked the fire, filled the kettle, warmed the teapot. Settled into one of Lizzie's red velvet armchairs, steam rising from a mug held in both hands. Blew to cool the brew and sipped.

She'd gently quizzed the old man, who was still in hospital, about the reason he'd veered so far off the track that terrible night when he'd nearly died, but was still no wiser. He thought he'd heard a call for help, he told her. A bushwalker lost and hurt, had heard his footsteps, he'd thought.

'Must've been a bird call,' he said.

'Did you hear it more than once?'

'Just the once at first. Loud and clear as day. *Over here! Over here!* Like a mudlark. Then fainter and fainter. Must've been a lyrebird. Great mimics, lyrebirds.'

'Seen many of them in the area?' Kate asked. They were common around Oyster Bay, their calls uncannily realistic—sirens, computer ca-chinks, the full-throated song of magpies, whistles of king parrots, soaring notes of butcher birds, all wrapped in a symphony that signalled a copyist, not a singular species. But she'd not heard nor seen any so high on the escarpment.

'Can't say as I have,' he replied.

'Can you remember anything else at all, Cliffy?'

'A ghost. Not Agnes, or I'd have given up and followed in the space of a heartbeat.' He paused sheepishly. 'Like I said, I was out of me mind once the pain set in.'

Kate held his hand soothingly and switched the subject to give him an update on Claire's progress. The kid could now open cupboards, which was causing havoc in the chef's kitchen, and yet every new disaster was applauded as a sign of progress instead of being chastised. Marcus even coped when he found her sitting on the floor chewing a set of measuring spoons and ripping up the baking paper she managed to get out of the box. '"*Such advances, Kate,*" he insisted, when I tried to apologise. "*We must be proud of this, no?*"'

Kate mimicked Marcus's voice, his gestures, getting a smile out of Cliffy. 'Then he hands her a wooden spoon and a saucepan and tells me the house reverberates with drumbeats until they're all ready to run screaming to the end of the jetty to throw themselves into the water to escape.'

'She's doing okay, then,' Cliffy said, his eyes closing as he could no longer fight the call to sleep.

'More than okay,' Kate said, even though he couldn't hear her.

Kate finished her tea, rinsed the mug and left it to dry on the rack, explaining Cliffy's ghost as either a hallucination or an image induced by painkillers after the accident. She followed the sound of voices to the cheese room, Sally and David, wearing hairnets, looked up when she entered and smiled. They returned to tapping, sniffing and turning rounds of cheese as they discussed adding fresh ricotta to the product list, and maybe a semi-hard cheese with a short maturing time. It would require a different culture to Agnes's Farm House Cheese, but it was worth a try. There had always been a strong market for the product. It sounded like Swahili to Kate's ears and she quickly left them to it.

Kate followed the pathway through what would always be known as Lizzie's garden, paused to pull a few weeds from the vegetable patch, threw them to the scavenging chooks as she passed. She ducked under the ant-ravaged post and rail fence, a short cut that bypassed the gateway, and took a moment to get her bearings.

Winter had altered the landscape, leaching colour from the grass and thinning tree foliage so it drooped in what looked like exhaustion after the effort demanded to battle the heat of summer.

She walked the familiar route towards Cliffy's house, searching for the point where the emergency vehicles had veered off, ploughing through scrub until they could go no further. The sickening fear of that awful night stuck in her throat, making her nervous and anxious for no real reason. She told herself to get a grip and kept going.

When she reached the angophora, it's trunk smooth as skin, its branches rising majestically, she swore she could still smell the scent of long-gone flowers, lingering like perfume in a discarded scarf. She hesitated, the horrific memories of that dreadful night rising to the surface. She pressed down an urge to run back to the warmth and safety of the shack, the reassuring presence of other people, normality.

She saw that the branch that nearly killed Cliffy was already camouflaged by new growth and squatted at the end where it had been severed, running her fingers over the break. She felt the dusty residue left by white ants—such tiny creatures, with the power to fell a forest. Nothing suspicious, she thought, and yet she couldn't shake a nagging worry. The lyrebird hypothesis felt wrong to her. What could possibly have lured Cliffy so far off his familiar trail?

On the trek back to the shack, as always, she considered the money angle and asked herself who had the most to gain from Cliffy's death? But killing a man whose fresh milk tapped into a small market and barely paid the bills seemed ludicrous. Without his expertise, anyway, the herd was virtually worthless. It had to be about the land, she thought, it was always about land. She pulled out her mobile phone and dialled Lizzie. The call went to voicemail but was returned instantly. 'Are you okay?' Lizzie asked, unable to keep the concern out of her voice.

'Fine. Just walking. Clearing my head. But I wondered, Lizzie, if you had any idea what Cliffy's property might be worth?'

'He'll never sell, if that's what you're thinking.'

'No, nothing like that.'

'What's this about, Kate?'

'I'm on my way back. We need to talk.'

⟳

The smell of lunch filled the house. Pumpkin soup with the aroma of ginger, chilli and garlic rising from pot. In the kitchen, the GeriEcstasies were busy warming bread, setting the table. While most of the crew had dirty patches on their knees and elbows, Mike and Lizzie somehow managed to look immaculate. Sally held up a bottle of iodine and demanded anyone with cuts line up for attention. Sheila was first to obey. The others surreptitiously licked their fingers and rubbed away any blood spots. Kate sidled up to Lizzie and asked if she had a moment to chat.

Lizzie spun the young woman to face the group. 'All for one and one for all,' she said. *Hear, hear.*

'But . . .'

'Spit it out, dear,' Daisy said, ladling soup into bowls. 'And let's get started on lunch before the food gets cold.'

'It's just . . . I still can't make sense of why Cliffy wandered off in the night unless he was lured there by someone who wanted to harm him.'

Sheila gave a little scream. 'Are we all in danger?'

'Don't be ridiculous, Sheila,' Gavin said. 'Who would want to hurt Cliffy? Maybe he got confused? A dark night? A few too many glasses of wine, which he's not used to?'

Daisy passed Kate a bowl of soup. Spoons clinked against crockery.

'So you went back to the tree,' Lizzie said matter-of-factly. 'As did Mike and I. Like you, we were certain Cliffy would never have wandered so far off the track without a reason. But there was nothing to find, Kate. An old man's confusion . . .'

'He's younger than you lot,' Kate said defensively.

'Ah yes, but we are accustomed to wine. Cliffy probably hasn't had more than a couple of glasses in a couple of decades.'

Everyone began to talk at once. Mike called for quiet.

Kate broke in. 'Who stands to gain if Cliffy dies, Lizzie? It's freehold land. A developer's dream.'

Lizzie sighed. 'You're not going to leave this alone, are you?'

Kate shook her head. 'I care for Cliffy . . .'

'We all do!'

Hear, hear.

Lizzie said, 'The land is zoned rural and the only access is through a national park, which means it can't be developed without a long and costly legal battle with no guaranteed outcome. Accept what happened, Kate. A freak accident. That's all. Believe me, if there was more, I'd have the entire police force looking for evidence.'

The group grew silent. At some point, Kate put on the kettle and made more tea. Sally cleared the table and brought out chocolate brownies cut into bite-sized squares and dusted with cocoa. Hands automatically reached out. Rob, who'd been unnaturally quiet throughout, said, 'The cow that got Daisy and put her in a wheelchair. An accident, Kate. Nothing more.'

Rob seemed to drift into his own world for a moment or two. Daisy placed her hand on his leg and said, 'There was nothing to be done. I lost concentration for a moment. That's all it takes.'

Rob seemed to come back to the present with a jolt. 'I blame myself. Always will.'

'Yes, I know,' Daisy said. 'But let it go now. It was an accident, like Cliffy.'

Rob beamed and spooned salt into his cup of tea.

Without a fuss, Lizzie muttered something about how easy it was to confuse salt and sugar when they both came in a bowl. Daisy swapped teacups with Rob, who sipped, oblivious to the concern that drifted around the table.

Kate, unaware of the by-play and reluctant to let go of her theory, said, 'It wouldn't hurt to find out who stands to benefit from his death.'

'It's me,' Lizzie said. Everyone in the room stared at her, speechless. 'I'm the one who inherits the property if Cliffy dies before me.'

'But what if you die first, Lizzie? Which you're bound to, given the difference in your ages,' Sheila said, fingers tapping the table nervously, her eyes darting to the four corners of the room. 'There could be a murderer out there right now.'

'Unlikely,' Lizzie said, unruffled. 'And if—as you suggested—I die first, Cliffy inherits from me.'

Rob looked thoughtful. 'Accidents happen. Fact of life. Best we're careful around the cattle, though. Ask Daisy. She knows what can happen.'

'No argument there,' Daisy said, leaning to place a kiss on his cheek.

❧

At the hospital the next day, Kate learned that Cliffy was being transferred to a rehab facility for the final stages of his treatment. 'They're talkin' a wheelchair,' he said, his voice catching on the word, his eyes wide with distress.

'You need physiotherapy, Cliffy, exercises to strengthen your muscles,' Kate explained. 'It's not forever. Only until you're back to being a hundred per cent.'

'Walkin' the paddock every day would do just as well.'

'Give it a go, my friend. There's nothing to lose and much to gain.'

He reached for Kate's hand and held it sandwiched between his own, gave an embarrassed grin and asked, 'How's that motley crew of cheesemakers farin' without my steady hand on the helm?'

Kate laughed. 'Pretty good. Although lunches are getting longer and longer and the time between the washing up and going home is getting shorter and shorter.'

CHAPTER TWENTY-TWO

AFTER THREE WEEKS IN REHAB, Cliffy, with the putty-like pallor of a man who'd been enclosed within four walls for too long, emerged wearing a flannel shirt under denim overalls, work boots on his feet. All delivered by Lizzie, who was the only person Cliffy would allow to look in his wardrobe. Only the wheelchair gave him away as a bloke with a journey ahead. He raised his face to the sun, sniffed the air with closed eyes, an expression on his face that was close to holy, and gave a small yip of joy. Kate walked up to him and saw the pink return to his cheeks, the sparkle to his eyes, a smile—genuine and the first for a very long time—mask the suffering on his face.

Mike stepped out of a car in the pick-up and drop-off zone and opened the passenger door with a smile and a flourish. 'Your chariot awaits,' he said.

Cliffy took a moment to enjoy his new-found freedom. 'New car?' he asked. Mike nodded, trying to keep his expression neutral as he absorbed the sight of this frail version of Cliffy, although why he'd expected anything different, he couldn't say.

'Lizzie's old Land Rover?' Cliffy asked.

'Still going strong. And so is Lizzie. She's here, waiting inside the car for you.'

He held out a hand to help Cliffy out of the wheelchair, which the old man ignored. He struggled to his feet in clothes that hung loosely off his bones and took a seat beside his dearest friend. 'Almost apricot season,' he said, by way of a safe and time-honoured opener that was guaranteed to kill any maudlin emotion, and fell into his seat with a grunt.

'You're jumping the gun a bit, aren't you?'

'S'pose you lot finished every jar in my absence.'

Lizzie reached into a cardboard box on the floor between her feet and withdrew a fat, round and fancy glass tub of golden jam. 'Welcome back, and please don't do anything like this to us again,' she said, placing the jar in his hands. Ambushed by kindness, Cliffy's bottom lip trembled. Lizzie looked away to give him his privacy. Kate wondered at the power of a small act of love when weeks of crushing pain had failed to draw a single howl.

Mike folded the wheelchair to fit in the rear. 'You can leave that behind,' Cliffy told him. 'Some other poor bastard is goin' to need it more than me.'

Mike looked at Lizzie for guidance. 'Agnes's old chair still works. That'll do in a pinch.'

Mike pushed the wheelchair back inside the building and left it with a few others that had been haphazardly abandoned inside the entrance. He returned to the car, a spring in his step, and climbed into the driver's seat.

'*Andiamo,*' Cliffy roared from the rear, tapping him on the shoulder.

'Been studying languages in your spare time?' Lizzie asked wryly.

'Italian physio,' Cliffy replied smugly.

'Know any other words?'

'None that I would repeat in front of a woman.'

They laughed and Lizzie told him the cows would be ecstatic to see his return. 'David doesn't have your charisma.'

'The chooks?'

'Sally does her best but draws the line at backrubs.'

'The house?'

'Untouched beyond cleaning out the fridge.' She heard the hiss of relief. 'Mind you, the cobwebs have taken over and the dust is an inch thick.'

Beside her, Cliffy nestled into the soft leather comfort of the seat, while the car slid smoothly forwards. 'Forgive an old man for sayin' but never had a comfier ride in me life.'

'Lucky your old Vauxhall can't hear you. She'd backfire on the spot . . .' And they slid into the easy chatter of friends with a long and common history.

༄

The crew decided that Cliffy should reside with Kate in Lizzie's shack, just until he felt confident enough to go it alone. He protested, of course, but no one took any notice.

His first tentative forays into the fresh air were short: a walk as far as the cheese room where he inspected the trays with a critical eye. Unable to find fault, he ran a finger over benchtops. 'Clean as a whistle,' he declared approvingly.

After a day or two, with the help of a walking stick, he shuffled as far as Lizzie's dendrobiums. Then progressed to the chook pen and the vegetable garden where he noted the spinach crop was huge and needed eating and the cabbages were coming along nicely.

Before the week ended, to the assembled mob sitting at the kitchen table after a long lunch, he declared himself ready to go home.

David told him to take it easy for a while longer: 'To be on the safe side, mate.'

Mike said he needed Cliffy's experience with a small carpentry job.

Sally said with the coming of new spring growth, the taste and texture of the milk would change and his expertise would be sought in the cheese room.

Sheila opened her mouth but, fearing she might say something inappropriate, everyone spoke at once. Kate had the final word. 'I need you here for a while longer, Cliffy. The nights are lonely when everyone goes home.'

Unable to deny Kate, he gave in.

The following day, Cliffy was sprung carrying an armful of firewood into the kitchen. The oldies set up a roster to keep him under close observation and assigned Rob to take charge of the wood supply. *No more accidents. Never mind you Cliffy, we can't handle the stress.* Cliffy promised to behave. No one believed a word. Rob delivered the wood to the cheese room. Daisy asked for a small trailer to be hooked to her wheelchair where Rob could load the logs. They'd make all future deliveries together.

In the meantime, Cliffy was shown photos of his beloved cows on the oldies' phones until the longing in the old man's eyes brought David undone and he moved the whole herd to Lizzie's best paddock. Cliffy almost cried with joy as one by one his girls came up, sniffed and nuzzled, and satisfied, ambled off. Rip, chew, rip, chew.

'Hypnotic,' Mike admitted.

'Better than meditation if you care to spend time with them,' David agreed. They carried over a sawn log so Cliffy could sit nearby for as long as he needed to. Later in the afternoon, Cliffy insisted on helping to walk the cows home for the afternoon milking session.

'Good for me overall fitness program,' he said, with a touch of pleading in his voice. David didn't have the heart to deny him, and the pattern was set for the foreseeable future.

The ancient wheelchair used by Cliffy's wife and later by Lizzie, when she broke her ankle, remained stored on the back veranda, with a family of redback spiders residing under the seat. Each evening, Kate cooked dinner and when the clearing up was done, she and Cliffy sat in front of the fire and talked about the finer points of cheesemaking; the progress in the vegetable garden; the day the bull—a gonad-swinging beast with the gentleness of a lamb—would be walked in from the main road to service the herd; the leak in the bathroom tap. Small things that constituted daily life.

One night, the two of them sitting in front of the fire after a robust dinner made from a recipe in a cookbook written to nourish the weak, Cliffy moaned that pretty soon he'd be forced to let out a notch in his belt.

⁓

A few days later, when Lizzie's phone rang amid the mayhem of getting lunch on the table, no one paid much attention. Except Mike.

'Good call?' he asked, when she returned to the kitchen to quietly slip into her place at the table. He got a nod, nothing more, which had the same effect as running up a distress flag on a ship.

'Oh goodness,' Sheila said, picking up the vibe. 'Nobody's died, have they?'

Lizzie laughed. A group exhalation of relief at the table. 'It was a producer. He wants to revive one of my plays.'

'Really,' Sheila said. 'Thought they'd be way out of date by now.' Gavin kicked her under the table.

'Me, too,' Lizzie said.

Mike raised his glass. 'This may be the age of snap chats and abbreviated text communication, but human nature doesn't change and Lizzie nails what drives us all with acuity but also compassion. Your work is timeless, Lizzie.'

'You've read my plays?' she asked, amazed.

'Of course.'

Sheila smirked and, this time, she kicked Sally under the table. Cliffy reached to pat Lizzie's arm in gentle congratulations. David, always keen to find an excuse to celebrate, suggested a bottle of wine should be opened to toast the moment. Daisy said a dinner in Stringy Bark Bay might be a better option, given Mike had to drive them by car and then boat to get home and would have to abstain. Her tone was firm enough to dissuade dissent.

'Which play?' asked Mike, curious.

'How many have you written?' Sheila asked, butting in. 'I never realised you were famous . . .'

'I'm not,' Lizzie said. 'And we have work to do. Let's save the discussion for tonight.'

'Oh,' Sheila said, deflated. 'Did you ever get around to writing that play for Donna? Remember . . . ?'

Mike pushed back his chair with a noise like scratching a blackboard with a fingernail. Daisy directed a terse, 'Not now, dear,' to Sheila, then asked everyone to pass empty plates to her. Cliffy, not sure about undercurrents he couldn't name, declared he'd done enough housework for the day. Perhaps Sheila might like to do the dishes. The look on her face sent the table into hysterics.

༄

Back at the house in Stringy Bark Bay, as the last light struck the lagoon and turned the water a deep turquoise, Mike took Lizzie aside and apologised for Sheila's lack of sensitivity.

Lizzie shrugged. 'If anyone should apologise, it's me. I should never have agreed to Donna's request.'

Mike dropped his head in what might have been a small bow. 'Gracious as always, Lizzie. Thank you.' He straightened and grinned. 'If you need an agent . . . ?'

She slipped her arm through his and together they walked into the kitchen where Sally was cooking up a storm, Sheila was getting in the way and Daisy was gathering cutlery to set the table. 'Where are the boys?' Mike asked as Lizzie withdrew her arm and moved to help with the preparations.

'Discussing the choice of wine in the pantry. They're not sure if champagne should be drunk tonight or saved for the opening night.'

'That's easy,' Mike responded. 'Let's do both.'

Hear, hear.

Over a dinner of shoulder of lamb cooked in a cast-iron pot with a drizzle of balsamic, heaps of garlic cloves and a frond of rosemary, Daisy asked, 'So how many plays *have* you written?'

'Four. Television scripts turned out to be far more lucrative.'

'And which one is back in the limelight?' Mike asked.

'*Family Matters*.'

Rob looked up from his plate. 'Daisy and I are planning to have children one day.' Frowns around the table. Anxious looks thrown in Daisy's direction.

'Yes, dear,' she responded, ignoring the sudden silence. 'But soon we will have Claire to bring joy to our lives. Such a gift.' Rob nodded and returned to slicing the meat on his plate. Talk fired up but it wasn't the same, the verve leached out by a rising apprehension no one could—or felt inclined—to quite put a finger on. Every so often, people glanced towards Rob, puzzled.

After dinner, Lizzie rugged up and went for a walk on the beach to commune with the spirits residing within the silvery arms of the mangroves and to mull over the phone call. Mike had been kind, but the play was outdated. It would serve no purpose to give the go-ahead. She turned towards the house, saw the shadowy figure of Mike on the jetty. She waved. He raised his hand in return and went inside. He cared for her, she thought, the realisation not quite a surprise nor unwelcome.

She'd chosen to live like a recluse, her career a way to pay the bills. There were moments—not enough in hindsight but enough to keep her going back to the show-business trough at the time— when her adrenalin pumped and it felt like flying. But she was no Shakespeare, nor Chekhov. There lingered in her, though, the hope that like Thornton Wilder, she'd found words to convey the depths hidden in ordinary people.

But all lives were ordinary, weren't they? And every life ended in death. She would decline the offer. Resist the temptation to indulge in the empty hot air of show business. She had nothing more to prove.

CHAPTER TWENTY-THREE

WHEN ETTIE LEARNED THAT CLIFFY was almost back to his old self and Kate's nursing duties were virtually non-existent, she arranged to transfer Claire back into Kate's full-time care, feeling less regret than she'd anticipated and more joy than she'd expected. Babies should stay with their mothers if at all possible. Before the handover, she went over the details with Sam, the GeriEcstasies and Cliffy, ensuring Kate had enough back-up if the pressure started to mount. Before she could ask him what time he'd pick up Claire to make the journey to the shack, Sam casually explained he had a big delivery of urgent building supplies to oversee and the GeriEcstasies had taken on the responsibility. His words struck an off note with Ettie but she was too excited to dwell on it.

The next day, buoyed by the happy knowledge Marcus was almost certainly experiencing similar emotions, she skipped through the flywire door of the café, filled with excitement and inspiration (new recipes for the Paris holiday team with fewer cheffy flourishes), tied on an apron, lifted a wooden spoon and announced to one and all that she was back in business behind the counter of the Briny Café. As she whipped, fried, sautéed, baked and swizzled, her mind teemed with images of wandering hand-in-hand with Marcus along the cobbled streets of Paris with nothing more onerous to contemplate than where to eat dinner.

At home, she felt only brief nostalgia around Claire's bath time—which she quickly dismissed. The child had a mother and a father. There was enormous contentment (and great freedom) to be found in the role of honorary grandparent. One of many, anyway. The GeriEcstasy women remained in full-on surrogate granny mode, eager to have a role in Claire's future, even if it didn't stretch much beyond nappy changing and bootee knitting bees. Cliffy, they told her when they popped into the café for coffee and cake and to welcome her return, jealously insisted on first holding rights *given his role in her birth*. Hadn't they heard that story more times than they could count?

When Ettie diplomatically asked whether Claire would be warm and comfortable during the end stages of what had been a very cold winter, Lizzie reassured her that there wasn't a single loose window frame or dodgy floorboard left in the house. The renovations were so professional, she added, the shack might survive another hundred years. In a rare moment of sentimentality, she added it was a credit to the hard work and tenacity of a bunch of stubborn oldies, who'd be shunted aside in what was known as the real world.

Ettie slid an extra slice of banana bread in Lizzie's direction with a smile. 'She's still so little—I couldn't help worrying.'

'Perfectly natural,' Lizzie responded. 'I'm happy to report she's adjusting beautifully.'

'And Kate?'

Lizzie hesitated. 'She's adjusting, too. She's beginning to understand there's no such thing as a faultless parent and all she can do is her best. A hard lesson for a woman who's always strived for perfection. With so many helping hands, they'll both be fine.'

After Lizzie left, Ettie took a moment to wonder who has the right to decide what constitutes the *real* world? Unable to come up with a suitable answer, she decided to discuss it with Marcus over *moules marinières* in a little street café on the Left Bank. Or any bank, for that matter. Paris. How could a single word evoke so many glorious images?

Meanwhile, Marcus—his fishing rods and reels cleaned and oiled; with a bucket containing a sharp knife, small cutting board and bait at his feet; a cool box filled with ice and stowed away safely—could be seen heading out to sea in his swanky timber runabout, in the pre-dawn light. There was a new spring in his step ('My hoofers are no longer kaput'), his old twinkle was back in his eyes. He caught kingfish, flathead, snapper, leatherjackets ('that require finesse to bring out their finest qualities') and tailor ('best smoked, in my opinion, which is correct, of course').

He returned in the late afternoon, his face burnished by sea, sun and wind, and eyes bright with success, to retire to the kitchen to honour his catch with his customary attention to the smallest detail. 'Even thirty seconds too long in a pan, my darling Ettie, can reduce a dish to ruin, which for me, allows entrance to despair.'

'Despair!' Ettie said. 'Never, Marcus.' She suggested a night of lamb chops and mashed potatoes to give him a break from the pressure, but he pooh-poohed the thought.

'I am a chef. Pressure is my oxygen. This tailor, I will smoke it now. We will enjoy it on a thin slice of toasted baguette with a condiment of your choice, which, of course, I would prefer to be fine slices of preserved lemon.'

'Yes, my love,' she replied, holding back a sigh and feigning enthusiasm. She'd never been a big fish eater. As a country child, the battered fillets came with dubious provenance, and were more torture than treat. 'I'll bring a fresh baguette from the café tomorrow.' But Marcus, smoker and fish in hand, had disappeared out the back. Ettie had recently read that French people love to eat meat, cooked so the blood pooled on a plate and so tender it melted in the mouth. Something to look forward to. She almost swooned.

∞

One Sunday morning, about six weeks after Claire returned to Kate's care, and as the season in the northern hemisphere crept towards mid-autumn, Ettie put up a sign outside the café. It announced that she and Marcus had booked a whirlwind trip to Paris; the Three Js were the new and inspired temporary team; it would be business as usual at the Briny Café—and she and Marcus would send postcards regularly to keep customers up to date with their travels.

Within an hour, someone had scrawled: 'Good on youse.' The following hour, someone else added: 'Bring back some new recipes.' Later: 'Not too Frenchy, though.' Finally: 'Don't ditch the pineapple in the burger.'

With the date of departure settled, Ettie—who'd long had a stand-off relationship with the computer—trawled Parisian websites with the intensity of a stalker and wrote endless lists of organised tours for Marcus to consult. All of which he diligently read before putting aside.

One night, he smiled, crumpled the pile of notes into a ball and chucked it into the fire. 'Let us be free souls and choose, each day, the excursions that would please us most. Is this not better than booking tickets and being tied to a timetable that will only wear us out if a dinner stretches late into the night and our greatest wish the following morning is to stay in bed drinking *café au lait* and nibbling freshly baked croissants?'

Ettie, slightly cross-eyed and rendered barmy by the vast number of options available, grinned with relief.

'But our accommodation, my love. This, we need to book in advance.' Marcus took over the mind-boggling work of trawling the internet, and eventually declared, 'This one. Perhaps not authentically old Paris—but there will be hot water, clean bed linen and room service. This is important, is it not?'

Ettie, round-eyed and disturbed that anything could be less than perfect in the city of her dreams, said, 'Oh yes, my love. At our age, romance is better when conjoined with clean sheets and hot water.'

'Hot water,' murmured Marcus. 'And a bath where we can sip champagne and ease our aching bones after walking to the furthest corners of each exciting arrondissement.'

'Bliss.'

'*Parfait!*'

'*Perfetto*,' Ettie agreed, wondering how soon after their return she could suggest a trip to Italy without sounding impatient or impolite.

⁓

Ettie went into a spin trying to sort out her travel wardrobe. Suddenly, everything she owned looked either faded, worn, out-of-date or as if they'd been scooped out of the dodgy sale section in the budget department. Suddenly, Paris seemed more daunting than exciting. Would the smart women on the swanky boulevards take one look at her and raise their eyebrows disdainfully as they passed by? Would the staff at their hotel treat her and the chef condescendingly—perhaps even dismissively—when Ettie appeared in tie-dyed skirts that made her feel free and adventurous in Cook's Basin but might be hideously unacceptable in the world's most fashionable city? She had earned a solid standing in Cook's Basin, one that filled her with a sense of self-worth. In Paris, she would be just another tourist passing through in strange clothes and comfortable shoes. She felt herself shrinking into the sense of inferiority that had once nailed itself to her persona. The hard-won confidence from making a success of the Briny Café dissolved like fairy floss on the tongue. Her excitement wobbled, fear of the unknown refused to abate. She found herself listing the things she would miss by leaving for so long: the change of the seasons, the daily gains made by Claire, fish jumping in the bay, birdsong at dawn, Jimmy's fluctuating romances, Artie's wit, Sam's benevolence and support.

Feeling tears in her eyes, she told herself to stop being such a ninny and to consider her good fortune. But beads of sweat broke out on her forehead; she felt anxiety pressing down, breathlessness. A bloody hot flush, she diagnosed, brought on by stress of her own making. Well, she'd show those Parisians a thing or two about Cook's Basin chic. And she had three weeks to lose ten kilograms.

Two nights later, the chef heard her wailing as he came through the door. He ran to her side and gathered her in his arms. Suggested a large cocktail to cure what ailed. Ettie laughed through her tears, remembering the chef's lethal blend of overproof spirits with a hint of lime juice that left her unable to find her legs when she tried to stand. 'One of your killer cocktails?' she asked.

'Yes, yes, because this is also a truth drug that will make it easy for you to reveal what is bringing you sadness instead of saying words you know I would prefer to hear.'

Ettie whispered, 'Will I look like a freak in my hippy clothes when I am in Paris and will people wonder what such a beautiful, handsome, brave and glorious man is doing on the arm of a flouncy woman on the wrong side of middle age?'

The chef, relieved Claire was not at the heart of the problem, roared with laughter. 'I will be the envy of every man who lays eyes on you,' he said without a hint of guile. 'You are a rare and wondrous spirit, which is revealed in your clothes like a billboard on the side of a highway. But then, I must be honest.'

Ettie's heart sank. She took a deep breath and drew in her stomach.

'The weather can be cold even though autumn will be holding back winter, so perhaps you will have to shop for warmer clothes than are required in the balmy climate of Cook's Basin. It goes without saying that I will help in this matter as I—a man who was born into the cold winters of Germany before coming to Australia with my parents—am an expert in the intricacies of coats, hats and gloves.' Ettie instantly resolved to lock her insecurities in a tin box before tossing the key in the deep water of Kingfish Bay. Along with the box.

Later, as she lay in the arms of a man she knew to be a genuine hero, she pondered the fragility of ego. Well, to be strictly accurate, *her* ego. A long history of setbacks had been offset by the love, care and support of a good community without whom she would have probably floundered and even sunk, but it could never be erased. A fear of failure constantly lurked, ready to chew through to the bone at the first sign of inadequacy. She told herself she must be vigilant if she was to hold the black dog at bay during her Paris adventure. Remind (reassure?) herself that she was Ettie Brookbank, co-owner of the highly successful Briny Café located on the idyllic shores of Cook's Basin, a paradise that would be the envy of any French person the moment he or she set eyes on it. And she was loved by a man who towered above all others and she loved him in return with a heart that had been zipped shut, until he appeared at her door with a box of chocolates he had made with his own two hands. She'd detected the intoxicating scent of adoration trapped within the oozing boozy strawberry filling, and had been a goner from that day onward. Bloomed and blossomed under the spell of a love she believed to be as close to unconditional as humanly possible.

Winter segued into spring and, high on the escarpment, Kate made Cliffy's bed while he fed Claire boiled egg soldiers in a hit and miss game that had Tigger drooling. She smoothed the cover, fluffed the pillows. Tomorrow, she'd change all the bed linen, which meant an early start if it was to be hung out to dry before the GeriEcstasies descended. She pulled out her mobile phone to check the weather report. Fine and sunny. The solar batteries would cope. All systems go.

Cliffy was wiping egg yolk from his cheeks when she braved the morning battlefield. 'Got the arm of a fast bowler,' Cliffy said, with a patient expression. He's had enough, Kate thought, and she laid odds that in a week or so he'd sneak off to his own home in the dead of night with not a soul awake to stop him.

'Right. How about I finish up with Claire?'

Cliffy threw her a damp cloth. 'You're gunna need it.' Then he was gone in a flash.

Kate finished the job. Set Claire on the floor next to Tigger, which would keep her entertained while she prepped the kitchen for smoko. Solitary by nature, she couldn't find fault with Cliffy yearning for his former serenity. God knows, there were mornings when she almost dreaded the arrival of the white LandCruiser, which spilled out its passengers like noisy retirees on a bus trip. Speaking of which . . .

They filed in like family, which they were in a peculiar way, plonking themselves down at the table—same places every time— to get what Mike referred to as their *riding instructions* for the day.

Kate left them to it. Gathered Claire in her arms and set off for the vegetable garden. Under Cliffy and Lizzie's direction, the early spring planting was well underway. Beetroot, capsicum, beans, lettuce, broccoli, cabbage and so much more. There was a small army to feed now, and any excess produce would be pounced on by Sally who swore she could taste the difference between home-grown and store-bought, daring anyone to call her a liar.

Kate didn't have a minute to herself for the rest of the day until Cliffy declared he was so buggered he was barely fit for a knackery and took himself off to bed. She tiptoed in to check on Claire, asleep in a cot in her bedroom, and returned to the kitchen. An old blanket over her knees, the overhead light knocking back the romance of the fire, she settled down to read Lizzie's play, discreetly delivered by Mike at her request, a few days earlier. At her feet, Tigger curled in her basket, snout under paws, softly snuffling with a twitch every now and then.

When the hands on the kitchen clock pointed to three a.m., she rose, her legs stiff from digging in the garden and sitting for too long. She stoked the fire, which had reduced to glowing embers but still threw out enough heat to keep the chill from the air. She thought about brewing a pot of tea but realised it was far too late. Went outside instead, carrying Tigger, treading softly so as not to wake the household, pleased with the way the newly oiled hinges on the door allowed a noiseless opening.

Outside, a festive kind of night, all sparkle and shine, and over there, a falling star. But she didn't believe in wishes. Luck was all in the way you made your bed. Wisdom according to her mother, Emily, whose lack of bed-making skills had had ramifications way beyond her death. And what about your bed, Kate, she asked herself? She looked up again and swore she saw Sam's kind and craggy face with a smile that had the power to lift her heart, painted in the stars above. How did she always manage to make a mess of things when all she meant to do was protect the people she cared about from hurt? After that night of truth and confession, she'd lain awake for hours, wondering whether she and Sam really could make a go of it. Just before dawn, a sickening thought crept from deep in her subconscious. Would their reconciliation condemn Sam to a lifetime of examining the face of every stranger who entered the café, for a resemblance to Claire? Better to run again, she'd decided, she'd done him enough damage. She looked back at a thousand innocent moments she'd blown out of all proportion to force him to give up on her. Mentioning Claire's birth certificate had presented the opportunity and she'd taken what she now recognised as the gutless way out. What would it take for her to believe they had a future? Faith? His? And hers? She called softly to Tigger, sniffing a blade of grass as though it held the answers to every question tossed high by the universe. If only, she thought. She picked up the pup and went back inside.

In her bedroom, she checked on Claire sleeping peacefully in her cot, resisting the urge to place a finger under her nostril to check she breathed. She'd put those days of high anxiety, when every chore felt like climbing Everest, behind her. The time on the bedside clock showed it was hideously late but she couldn't sleep. To distract from thinking about problems she couldn't resolve, she turned her mind to Cliffy. She was fully aware he'd been cunningly manoeuvred into staying on in the shack after his strength returned, to provide support if she needed it when the GeriEcstasies weren't around. He'd become closer than family to her, a thought that made her wonder whether Cliffy was the orphan he believed himself to be or whether he had siblings strewn randomly around the countryside. If she could find any family, it would be her gift to him for more than she could ever repay. Buried under the gesture was her burning need to prove, once and for all, that nothing more than lapsed concentration on a dark night after a couple of glasses of wine had led to the freak accident that had almost killed a kind old man; one who'd never done anyone any harm in his entire life. It was well past four a.m. when she drifted off to sleep.

❧

Kate was woken by the sound of a car and sat up in shock. She checked the time. Ten o'clock. Claire's cot was empty. The back door crashed shut. Stomp, stomp. Sounds from the kitchen ramped up. Voices bright, Claire banged something. Cliffy—she assumed it was Cliffy—made loud shushing sounds. A sudden, short-lived hush. Kate left her bed, pulled on a dressing gown and pushed her feet into slippers. 'Sorry, folks, overslept,' she announced from the doorway. A sea of anxious faces studied her closely. 'Not sick!' she said, pre-empting a bombardment of concern. 'Sat up late.'

'Ah.' One and all turned back to their chores. Smoko landed on the table with a thump. A cake today, one of Sally's best efforts, according to Sheila, a woman customarily so frugal with compliments everyone stared at her in amazement. 'What? The last one was soggy . . .'

'Serve up, Sheila,' Daisy said, passing her a knife. Rob took his place by Daisy's side, filled his mug with milk and began to drink.

'No tea for you today?' Sally asked, holding the pot in one hand. Rob looked at his mug, confused.

Daisy answered, 'The tannin is upsetting his stomach.' A slight pause around the table.

'A whole glass of milk, though?' Sheila said, with a hint of outrage.

'Well, it's not as if there's a shortage on a dairy farm,' Daisy responded sharply.

⌒

That night, alone in the kitchen with Cliffy, dishes cleared and cleaned, table spotless, the fire crackling nicely, the scrappy night sounds of the bush signalling all was well, Kate suggested a glass of wine that would pair nicely with the remnants of a round of cheese, which was all the better for enjoying the warmth of the kitchen.

'What do you reckon, Cliffy?' she asked, making the question sound as casual as possible. 'Do you think you might have a brother or a sister stashed somewhere? Older siblings that were sent off to different homes after your mum died and your dad scarpered?'

He took a sip of wine and relaxed, his shoulders slackening in the way of tired farmers at the end of the working day. 'Not sure, luv, although I remember snippets Mrs Porter dropped into the conversation every so often—mostly about me father being as spineless as a jellyfish—wonderin' about the *other kids*. Didn't mean much at the time. She raised me till the age of eight like I was her flesh and blood. Lovely woman with a chest you could rest a tea tray on. Good scone baker but Agnes was better if we're gettin' down to tin tacks.' Her name exhaled, like a prayer. 'Not sure how old Mrs Porter was when she died and it felt like me family had been ripped out from under me. She was a stickler for grammar, though you might not think it listenin' to me these days. And pronunciation, now I'm thinkin' back. *It's a picture, Cliff my boy, not a pitcher, which you would use for milk or water. Pic-ture.* Can just about hear her sayin' it, like her voice is comin' down the chimney. Never stern, y'know. In those days, educated speech could mean the difference between gettin' hired or not. It was a form of snobbery now that I think back. Meant you came from folks who had enough money to send you to school instead of to work in the cattle yard.'

'She wasn't married?'

'Nah. Well, he'd buggered off—excuse me language—without even leavin' a note. She'd always wanted kids, said family made sense of what we humans were put on earth for—so when my father was lookin' for a place to park me, she stepped forwards with her arms wide open.'

Kate leaned forwards, resting her elbows on her knees, thinking about the importance of family in a child's life. Her own family had been a train wreck but she'd yearned for her mother to come home, for her father to find happiness, for her childhood to be cocooned by love. Were all children the same? She only had to look at the way Claire reached up to be held by Cliffy every time she set eyes on him, the way she turned to make sure her mother was watching if she did something she thought was pretty clever, to know children craved love. In the end, it was all about love. The rest was just bunting holding together daily life with varying degrees of success.

'Do you realise, Cliffy, that I didn't even know your surname until you went to hospital?' Kate said, returning to the moment.

'For a kid without a family, I ended up with a moniker fit for a king: Clifford John Standish Porter, although the Porter was dropped after I landed in the orphanage.'

Kate left the subject alone. Offered another dribble of wine. Cliffy shook his head.

'I'm ready to go home, love,' he said, every word like withdrawing money from the bank. 'Nothin' for me to do here, what with the oldies runnin' around like headless chooks. Well, Sheila, anyway. The others understand what a day's work entails.'

'Sheila's strength is retail. She's the one who'll help to sell the cheese when the time comes.'

'She's alright. If me antenna's up to scratch, though, reckon Daisy will soon have her hands full with Rob. Ah, don't think we're all blind, luv. I've been seein' the signs for a while. Prompted Lizzie and me to have the conversation.'

'Conversation?'

'The one where we tell each other what we'd want done if we're headed down the same twisty road. No, don't say a word. Nothin' to say anyway. Lap of the gods, that's where it lays.'

Kate raised her glass. 'Let the gods be kind, then,' she said. 'About going home . . .'

'All the chat, Kate, it's doin' me head in. It's like bein' in party mode day after day. A man needs his solitude, no offence intended, to be able to get his thoughts in order.' On cue, Claire let out a wail. 'I'll clean up, luv. You see to the bub.'

৵

The next morning, on her return from buying supplies, the scene that greeted Kate was bucolic: a baby and puppy playing surrounded by elderly women; knitting needles clicking to the rhythm of slow murmurings; Sheila's foot tapping in time to her stitches. That woman could never be still.

Mike rose from his chair on the veranda. David and Gavin emerged from the cheese room wiping their hands on their aprons.

'Where's Cliffy?' Kate asked.

Everyone looked around, as though they'd dropped a handkerchief somewhere.

'Seeing to the cows?' Gavin guessed.

'Nope. All done,' David replied.

'Chooks?'

'Eggs collected, feed bins full,' Sally said.

Lizzie wandered back from the garden, her arms full of clippings destined for the compost bin.

'Have you seen Cliffy?' Kate asked.

'Not for a while. Why?'

Kate sighed. 'He's homesick. He's probably gone back to his farm.'

'Why would he go home when he's got all of us waiting on him hand and foot?' Sheila asked.

Gavin shook his head, ashamed with the way his wife's mind galloped in the direction of criticism instead of understanding. Sally rolled her eyes. Everyone turned to look in the direction of Cliffy's house. A thin spiral of smoke curled upwards. 'That's odd,' Lizzie said, frowning, 'smoke's in the wrong place to be coming from the house.'

Mike went to her side. 'A pile burn?'

'Maybe, although he hasn't had time to do much clearing.'

'Why don't we drive over to take a look?' Mike suggested.

They found Cliffy, with a hose in one hand and a wet hessian bag in the other, beating knee-high flames on the perimeter of his lawn. Lizzie immediately dialled the fire brigade, Mike grabbed the hose. Kate broke off green branches to smother the flames that rippled along lazily without enough energy in the cool weather, before they reached the National Park. By the time the fireys arrived, they'd managed to contain the damage to a small area.

'A spark from the mower set it off,' Cliffy, red-faced with embarrassment, explained.

While the fireys assured him it was nothing short of freakish to happen at this time of year and he couldn't be held to account, the old man wondered how he'd conjured yet another bizarre moment in a life that had been comparatively free of even minor accidents. He pondered whether he might be getting old—and discarded the idea instantly. Mind over matter, he reminded himself with a shake like a wet dog to dislodge any lingering doubts. Still, age crept up on a bloke if he let down his guard, and what choice had there been with all those do-good retirees looking for ways to be helpful? None at all.

༄

At the shack, his confidence still a little shaky, Cliffy took himself to bed long before dark, batting away sympathy, offers of help. The household gathered in the kitchen where a bottle of cognac and a stack of water glasses stood regally on the kitchen table for anyone who felt the need.

'Did you meet Tom?' Sheila asked. Eight pairs of eyes fell on her.

'Who?' asked Lizzie, confused.

'Tom, the firey with eyes as blue as the sea and a six-pack body under his shirt.'

'Jesus, Sheila, I thought you'd lost the capacity to shock, but once again, you've proved me wrong.'

Mike rounded up his team. Lizzie stood, but folded her arms, her expression firm. 'I'm going to stay overnight, to keep an eye on Cliffy. He and I have lots to sort out, and it's best if we do it on our own tomorrow,' she said. Her jaw was set, and her tone made it clear that the GeriEcstasies should also take a day off.

Kate began to say she'd be fine looking after Cliffy herself, but Lizzie pushed on, saying if Kate didn't mind, she and Claire could spend the night with Sam. And perhaps tomorrow, it might be time to check on the condition of her Oyster Bay home. Houses mouldered without attention, especially houses close to water. After all the work and money she'd spent on it, etcetera, etcetera. With no room to negotiate, Kate capitulated with ill-concealed reluctance.

Mike caught Lizzie's drift and nodded. He went to wait on the veranda. Sheila recorked the cognac but Sally wouldn't let her take it with her. 'It'll serve a better purpose here,' she said. 'No. Don't argue. None of us are in the mood.'

Lizzie called Sam to alert him to Kate and Claire's arrival and then called Ettie to say she could expect a visit at the café from the

GeriEcstasies en masse. After a big day, they might need a bit of looking after and perhaps a bucket of hot chippies might do the trick before they headed home.

Meanwhile, news of the bushfire—embellished and exaggerated to the point of absurdity—had spread through the community like a contagious disease. And even though summer was still a distant promise, vows were made to check water pumps, clear rubbish in gutters and yards, and fireproof properties. It paid to be vigilant in an era of erratic and extreme weather events, although God forbid, another big storm would definitely test an offshorer's endurance.

~

When Kate, Claire and the GeriEcstasies arrived at the Point, where Sam, Jimmy, Ettie and Marcus were waiting to help if needed, Ettie instinctively reached for Claire and pleaded to be allowed to have her for a sleepover. She'd been having baby withdrawals, she said, crossing her fingers behind her back and then uncrossing them when she realised it was true.

'We will eat battered flathead,' Marcus announced. 'Caught this very day and so fresh I might smack its face. A joke,' he added, in case anyone had missed the point. Ettie winked at Kate and shook her head. It would never happen. Fish bones and all that.

Sam kissed the top of Claire's head and caught Kate looking at him. 'She gets more beautiful every day, Kate. Like you.'

Ettie wanted to cheer but the chef beat her to it. 'Yes! I feel it! Romance is in the air!' Ettie dragged him away, Claire held firmly in her arms, before the moment between the young couple could be diminished.

Left behind, and unsure how to navigate the electricity he felt crackling all over the place, Jimmy dragged a toe on the pavement, pointed at the *Mary Kay* tied at the end of the café deck and said, 'Your chariot awaits.' So completely out of character, Kate and Sam laughed and any awkwardness passed.

'Cutter Island? Or, if you'd prefer, Oyster Bay,' Sam said, looking across the water to mask the hope in his eyes.

'There's nothing to eat at Oyster Bay. So Cutter Island, if that's okay,' Kate said.

'Not sure there's much for dinner on offer at my place, either,' Sam said, unable to keep the grin from his face. 'A sauso roll or two, at best.'

'Anything but scones,' Kate replied with passion. Then: 'Pork or beef?'

'New recipe. Pork and veal.'

Kate laughed. Sam decided to trust that love conquered all if it was given enough time.

Kate slipped her hand into his, and stood close to him on the deck of the *Mary Kay* while Jimmy steered a steady course for home.

'Can we do this, Sam?' she asked.

'Nothing to it,' he replied, smiling and enfolding her in his arms.

CHAPTER TWENTY-FOUR

CHANGE SWEPT IN LIKE A tornado along with the voluptuously erratic spring tides. Cliffy asked if Lizzie would mind if he cut the work schedule for the oldies to a three-day week, seeing as how he'd been used to his solitude since Agnes died, and she agreed. She broke the news to the household as gently as she knew how, anticipating disappointment and even rebellion from Sheila. 'More time for babysitting,' the women chorused, without a hint of regret.

'Home maintenance has been slipping in our absence,' Gavin said. 'Time to muscle up in Stringy Bark Bay.'

Daisy simply nodded and reached to hold Rob's hand. He turned towards her, smiling widely. 'Why Daisy, you're back.'

'Yes, dear,' she replied. Sheila opened her mouth to speak and everyone held their breaths.

'We are all here for you, Daisy. All for one etcetera.' And not another word was said.

Kate returned to work at the café, but insisted Jane stay on two days a week to see to the accounts: she'd tactfully brought Marcus's spending and sleight-of-hand accounting under control and deserved to keep her job. Kate would split her time between overseeing the café, caring for Claire and building a market for Agnes's Farm House Cheese. Sheila offered to help in the café, too, but Kate caught the alarm on Jenny's face and wriggled around the idea with so much vagueness, Sheila became impatient, threw up her hands, turned on her heel and announced she'd be available if required but only with a week's notice, which, as everyone fully understood, was never going to happen.

One quiet afternoon upstairs in Ettie's old penthouse, Kate ran through a list of names from electoral rolls in the suburb where Cliffy was born. Using both Standish and Porter, she found seventy-two matches. Now, she thought, settling down with her phone, it was simply a matter of ringing them one by one and asking if any of them remembered a baby called Cliffy, and if so, whether they could be related to him in some way.

She fluked success with her first call. His name was Jim Standish and he had an older brother, Stan, and two older sisters, Maud and Mary. There'd been a baby placed in the care of a neighbour while the rest of them were old enough to go into an orphanage and then foster care after their mother died. The baby's name? Jim had taken a while to think back many decades to a time when he was still a kid aged eight. 'Charlie? Nah. Doesn't sound right. Clem? Nope.'

'Clifford?' Kate suggested.

'Yep. That's the one. Baby was called Clifford.'

Their father, she asked, did they know what became of him? 'Never saw him again,' Jim said. (Kate's research at a later date revealed he'd returned to Canada, where he'd also abandoned an earlier family who apparently forgave all and looked after him until his death.)

Jim told her he'd searched for his baby brother when he was old enough to hold a job and rent a home. He'd hit one brick wall after another. Kate explained the name change might have caused the problems. She heard what could have been a gulp and let the silence spin out for a while. When he brought his emotions under control, Jim said he'd contact his siblings to tell them the good news and organise a get-together in the near future. They were all getting old and who knew what lay ahead. Kate suggested a big bash: a surprise reunion hosted at the Briny Café, where she would ensure the presence of the baby brother they thought they'd never see again. 'By the way,' she asked, with a hint of slyness, 'do you remember what year Cliffy was born?' Jim took a minute or two to work it out. Kate guffawed. Almost a decade older than he'd ever admitted. Who'd have thought there was such a vault of vanity lying buried in his pure gold heart?

The Standish clan reunion was arranged for a date that fell two days before Ettie and Marcus departed for Paris in mid-September. Kate alerted the GeriEcstasies, who agreed that Sheila might best be left in the dark about the purpose of the get-together. Loose lips and all that . . .

౮౦

Meanwhile, in the café, Kate set up a small cheese section in a refrigerated display cabinet. 'Handmade in small quantities and only available for sale on Monday and Tuesday—the ricotta is freshly made on the day, from milk delivered straight from the dairy,' she told customers, who happily paid a premium for the freshest curds ever. There was a special price for the community, naturally. Ettie insisted. Kate gave in without argument.

'That girl is mellowing,' Ettie said.

'That girl is pregnant,' Jenny responded.

Ettie almost choked and went off for a lie down in the penthouse, from where she called Marcus with the news.

'Kate, she has told you this in her own words?'

'Not exactly.'

'Ah, Sam, he is proud and telling this to you.'

'Umm.'

'Ettie! Am I to believe this is your women's intuition alone that is giving you this information?'

'Umm.'

'Not another word. To anyone. This is understood, correct me if I am wrong?'

'A boy or a girl this time? I'm quite sure another girl. What do you think?'

'Ettie!'

In the meantime, as business grew, Kate converted the dull rear space in the café into a magnificent delicatessen where only the finest specialist products were sold, including Marcus's favourite *pâté de fois gras*, which came all the way from France in a modest can that barely hinted at the silky luxury within. The French were masters of subtle elegance, Ettie said, sounding awed. Kate was tempted to remind her of Louis XIV, whose love of gilt-laden pomp and splendour earned him the title of Sun King, but she held back. Ettie would soon see for herself.

∽

On the *Mary Kay*, business had settled back into the familiar routines of reading the tides and the weather and the less familiar requests of increasingly quixotic clients (fire-pit deliveries had quadrupled and pizza-oven orders were stratospheric). Tigger had pushed a very patient and increasingly long-suffering Longfellow aside and scratched out a private possie on the fluffy new pile of recycled cushions in the oversized dog bed Jimmy had installed in the wheelhouse (under girlfriend Becky's orders). Amazing, everyone commented, how quickly that scrappy little foundling had embraced entitlement and cushy comfort. Longfellow, everyone agreed, was a consummate gentleman and was rewarded with extra bacon by Jimmy and Sam, much to Tigger's disgust.

⌇

On a mellow evening with a hint of summer warmth in the sea air, which they guessed may well have originated in the tropics, because it was still too early to be a real taste of summer, Mike and Lizzie linked arms as they walked on the beach at low tide. Mangrove roots, they agreed, could cause grievous bodily harm, and at their age a broken hip or leg or anything was to be avoided at all costs. It was best to hold on to each for support.

'Shall we talk about us?' Mike asked.

Lizzie laughed. 'Not without the others. It would break a sacred trust.'

⌇

Cliffy finally met his long-lost family. After all the introductions were made, the five siblings took themselves to the deck and yabbered until the other guests quietly withdrew; until the kids returned from school; until the last ferry delivered the last commuters home for the night; until the sun made way for the moon.

As they filed into the darkness of the Square, Jim suggested they make a habit of getting together—there were more than six decades to catch up on.

'At the café,' Cliffy said quickly, worried about his supply of apricot jam, and the time he'd need to spend dusting and vacuuming.

The following day, the old man informed David that, as he now he had three generations of family to get to know (children and grandchildren in numbers that boggled Cliffy's mind), he'd like to withdraw from the cheesemaking venture, which he said had nothing to do with him, although naming it after Agnes was fully appreciated. He'd be happy to accept twenty per cent of the profits to avoid having to send a bill for the milk, though, if that was a suitable arrangement.

Hear, hear.

'Ten per cent!' Sheila countered, but no one listened.

⁓

With something close to a combination of shock and surprise, Ettie and Marcus found themselves checking their luggage and gratefully retiring to the Qantas lounge to recover from a tortuous drive to the airport. Sam and Mr Google would never be on the same page.

'Perhaps a taxi next time,' Marcus suggested, wiping the sweat from his brow.

He looked suave, Ettie thought, European. She cast her eyes over her outfit while Marcus fetched a glass of champagne (who knew business class could be so wonderful) and felt confident. A simple jacket over tailored trousers (with an elastic waist, important to be comfortable on a long flight). Under the jacket, she wore a soft pink cashmere sweater Marcus had brought home earlier in the week. 'It would be a tragedy, my love, to catch a chill on the plane.' Of course it would. Ettie, holding the softness against her cheek, could think of few things worse.

They clinked glasses and toasted Paris: Ettie misty-eyed, and Marcus finding instant recovery from Sam's rallycross chauffeuring in the bubbles that bolted straight to his bloodstream. In what seemed like no time, they heard their flight called and stood, gathering the bits and pieces they would take on board to make themselves comfortable. Ettie counted the bags. Counted again.

Marcus took her hand and smiled. 'You are nervous, my love?'

'Of course not,' she replied.

'It is the flying that bothers you, is it not?'

Ettie looked at him, relieved. 'Yes, Marcus. I must confess, I have no idea what holds up the plane and stops it from dropping to the ground.'

As she spoke, her phone pinged. She scrabbled in her handbag and checked the screen. 'Kate,' she said. Marcus's face fell. 'Please do not tell me at this late stage we will have to abort our mission to the city of eternal romance.'

Ettie smiled, put away the phone, counted the bags, and said, 'Let's go.'

On board, they took their seats, received another glass of champagne and, content that they were as good as on their way, Marcus leaned over and asked, 'And this message, my love, what did it say?' He paused. 'Unless, of course, it was private.'

Ettie hauled her phone from her handbag and scrolled to the message.

'Bon voyage!'

'But wait, there is something below,' Marcus said.

Ettie turned off her phone.

Marcus guffawed. 'But I have seen this message that you are trying to hide. Your women's instinct, it appears, has let you down at this time. Sam will have a young son alongside him as he grows into his old age. This is good news, my love, and worthy of celebrating.'

'But the next child, Marcus, will be a girl. I am certain.'

'I have one request,' Marcus said, trying not to laugh.

Ettie raised her eyebrows. 'Yes?'

'Promise me with every bone in your delightful body that you will never change.'

The fasten seatbelts sign came on. They settled back and minutes later, holding hands, they rose into the vast blue yonder that encircled the earth.

'Paris,' Ettie sighed.

'Paris,' echoed Marcus, raising Ettie's hand to his lips.

∾

Back at Cook's Basin, Sam figured his life-or-death drive to the airport had earned him the rest of the day off. He gathered his shattered wits, made a mental note to have the clutch in the ute replaced, and strode into the café looking for Kate. 'The sun's out and we should be, too,' he told her, swinging her chair so it faced away from the computer screen. 'There's a sweet little cove, sheltered from the wind, where the sun shines and the sand will be soft and dry under our backsides. What do you say?'

'A picnic?' Kate asked. 'Now?'

'No time like the present.'

'I guess so.'

Sam, who'd half expected her to make excuses, took off up the stairs to Ettie's penthouse before she had time to change her mind. He found his child on the verge of waking and lifted her gently from the crib. 'You are about to have your first taste of true luxury, my sweet. Nothing beats a picnic in Cook's Basin with the sea lapping, the birds singing, and the bush filled with the honeyed scent of spring. Bloody magic, that's what it is.'

Kate, who'd followed, smiled. 'I've asked Jenny to put together a basket of nibbles. Nothing fancy. Stuff left over from the lunchtime crowd.' She crossed to the fridge and collected Claire's food, placing it in a cool bag.

'Reckon we could make it an overnighter?' Sam asked, grinning.

'Pushing your luck a bit, aren't you?' she retorted, but the laughter behind her words wiped out the smidgin of insecurity that rose in him occasionally even now.

On the beach, Sam laid the blanket and set down Claire before helping Kate unpack the basket. He found a beer and held it up in query. 'You looked like you needed one,' she said, referring to his sweat-soaked earlier arrival.

After they'd cleared lunch, Sam lay back with Claire balanced on his chest. Using a leaf, he tickled her nose. The kid thought it was hilarious. Kate, lying beside him, warned she'd tire of the game soon and it would end in tears.

'Nah. This kid's got adventure written all over her.' The second after he'd tempted fate, Claire began to sob. Kate's face had *I told you so* written all over it. Sam pointed to the sky as a distraction. As luck would have it, a jet trailing a long white tail of vapour put on a show. He pointed and Claire looked up in amazement. 'Marcus and Ettie on their way to Paris,' Sam informed her, without a clue whether it was true or not. He looked over at Kate. Her eyes were closed, her breathing steady. His family, he thought, feeling a powerful wave of emotion. He scrambled to his feet, picked up Claire, and walked off to leave Kate in peace.

She met him halfway back and wordlessly placed her arms around his waist, holding on tightly, the child squirming between them. 'For a minute there, I thought I'd lost you both,' she murmured.

'Nah. You're stuck with us. Have I ever mentioned that kings never had it this good?' Kate laughed and let go, giving him a playful slap on the back.

When they finished tidying up, Kate carried Claire and Sam managed the rest as they waded out to where the tinnie was anchored in shallow water. Sam loaded the picnic gear into the boat, then held Claire while Kate used the gunnel to heave herself aboard. There was a chill in the air now, the sun lost behind the brow of the hill.

Kate held out her arms to take the baby. Sam leaped in and started the engine. 'Let's go home,' Kate said, strapping Claire into her lifejacket.

Home, thought Sam, with a feeling close to awe. The time ahead belonged to them now. In due course, he and Kate would become history and the years would be snapped up by their children and then their children and so on. The wheel turns. A ripper cliché that he wisely decided to keep to himself.

ACKNOWLEDGEMENTS

THIS BOOK WAS COMPLETED UNDER difficult circumstances. There are no words to adequately express my appreciation for the support of Richard Walsh and Annette Barlow. Their kindness, understanding and patience were extraordinary. As always, the team at Allen & Unwin, particularly Courtney Lick, was the silent strength that brought the manuscript to fruition, and the eagle eye and wise suggestions of Emma Neale made it a more cohesive (and baby behaviour accurate!) story. Gratitude to one and all.

Heartfelt thanks, too, to Meaghan Lewers for sharing her father's history, on which the family background of Cliffy is based. Meaghan's dad, Bruce Jack Harrison, was separated from his siblings as a baby, spent years in foster care where he was expected to work from dawn to dusk, but found a way to live a full and useful life without bitterness or recrimination. A hero. He also raised an awesome daughter whom I count as a friend and organic farming mentor.

Cliffy's personality, though, belongs to my Uncle Frank, aged ninety-eight (my cousin, Jayne, reckons he'll live to see George crowned) and still a force. I hope his common sense and resilience shines through in Cliffy and inspires all of us who have lived beyond the biblical three score and ten cut-off point to keep having a go.

I would also like the thank the Oncology and Radiology teams at the Northern Sydney Cancer Centre for their incredible kindness and support over many months. Without their (and Bob's!) gently persuasive arguments to give everything in the cancer arsenal a shot, this book would never have been finished.

Thanks, too, to my former flatmate in New York, Elizabeth Sobieski, and my old school friend, Ann Willcock. I could not have had a more dedicated cheer squad.